Hilary G

CW00691174

To Mutti
with all my love from

EMMA x

WEST OF WESSEX GIRL

Happy Birthday   *18th December, 2013*

A Novel by

PETER TAIT

Peter Tait

THE SUNDIAL PRESS

EMMA West of Wessex Girl
First published by The Sundial Press 2013

THE SUNDIAL PRESS
Sundial House, The Sheeplands, Sherborne, Dorset DT9 4BS
www.sundialpress.co.uk

A CIP catalogue record for this book is available from the British Library

Front cover images:
'Emma Lavinia Hardy' by British School
'Bulbarrow, Dorset' by Emma Lavinia Hardy
© Dorset Natural History and Archaeological Society

Jacket Design: Frank Kibblewhite

ISBN 978-1-908274-06-9

Printed and bound by CPI Print Group (UK) Ltd, Croydon, CR0 4YY

For Christopher, Elizabeth and Catherine

CONTENTS

PREFACE

Later in his life he would recall seeing the silhouette of her riding along the crest of Beeny Cliff. He would remember the scene that lay before him with a feeling of agitation, stripped bare of everything, but the most elemental. A bent tree, doubled up by the Westerlies; an evening sky exploding in a fiery tempest; and, set against it all, a horse and its rider. She looked magnificent, like Boadicea, standing high in the stirrups thick auburn hair billowing out behind. He watched her as she fell off the edge of his view into a furze-covered gulley, and disappeared. Yet it was frozen in his mind, this picture of the high-spirited and unsettling young woman, one that he could recall at will for the rest of his life.

Time can give a gentle wash to memory, that much he knew. It can smooth out the rough edges and make mellow the astringent, destroy the glass cage. But Tom knew that what he had seen, in that one vivid snatch, was real. Whatever else changed in time, that image would remain unshakeable. A rider on a horse, skirting a cataclysmic sky. A heart aloof and vagrant, one and the same. His West of Wessex girl. He felt the first drops of rain. What had become of them? What had happened to pry loose the grip that once held him so tightly? What had led him to betray her?

Emma Hardy had been estranged from her husband for more than a decade before her death in 1912. Labelled as 'half-cracked' and 'phenomenally plain,' disliked even by members of her own family, few mourned her passing. And yet, almost as soon as she was buried, Thomas set out to rediscover the high spirited and timeless West of Wessex girl that he had fallen in love with, more than forty years earlier.

What sequence of events, what deceptions, what unravelling led to the state of affairs that enabled her to become his muse in death, while having been his antagonist and his antithesis while she was alive?

Who was this unusual woman who, after her marriage, had satisfied neither her husband's desires, nor his ego, who publicly railed against his final novel and humiliated him at his own hearth, yet also had strangely

vii

provoked him into writing his most enduring works of fiction, and his greatest poetry?

There were strains of eccentricity that bordered upon madness in her, but there was also a love, however ethereal and unreal, that was cruelly tested and beaten down. Her husband's agnosticism, the shock of his later novels, his faithlessness, all tested her to the limit, until she withdrew into herself, appearing only as some eccentric apparition that gave folk cause to pity Thomas the more. But she felt his rejection deeply, the feigned interest and the ghastly pretence which cast their lives under the shadow of his need for others' approval. And she suffered more than just the ignominy of a lonely death in a small loft bedroom, in a house that she hated. She endured the loneliness of a life lived in parallel, of a husband shared, and the scorn of those who saw her as the biggest impediment in her famous husband's career. Therein lay the contradiction – while in life, she was misunderstood and downtrodden, in death, she became the inspiration for some of the greatest love poetry ever written.

Chapter One

WHEN I SET OUT FOR LYONNESSE

He had cursed when his employer, Crickmay, wrote to him with the request. For the past month, he had been preparing the draft of *Desperate Remedies* for his publisher. While he could not admit as much, he did not want to leave his manuscript when he was so close to completion. Apparently, the architect had unearthed yet another commission for a church restoration – one that had lain unanswered since Hicks had made an appraisal of a church two counties away, some three years ago. Now that Hick's business was Crickmay's, as was Tom, he turned to the young man. To his knowledge his assistant was single and capable of doing the work required and as Tom could furnish no contrary reason, he grudgingly agreed to go.

The irritation for Tom was two-fold: the timing was unfortunate, with the final draft so nearly finished; and the remoteness even more so, for the job was on the far coast of Cornwall, a good day's travel away. His first obstacle was however removed when Crickmay, though keen to complete the outstanding work, did not insist upon Thomas travelling at once, allowing him to engineer a delay of some three weeks, ostensibly while he organised matters. Tom was taking advantage of this brief interlude to finish off his final proof and send it to the publishers, before turning his mind back to the trip out west, and the church restoration that awaited him there.

While initially frustrated by the inconvenience of such a difficult journey, Tom soon realised that, once his manuscript was sent off, there was little to do but wait – it was better by far to fill the time by practising his trade. Further, and it was a thought that filled him with a certain mix of gloom and resignation, the one person who had held him to Weymouth six weeks ago had already gone to London. Without her, there seemed less

1

of a reason to mind the time away. Indeed, he thought, he would welcome the distraction.

The trip to St. Juliot's Church, by train and trap, took a full sixteen hours. He had set out from home at 4.00am, and it was a weary traveller that eventually knocked on the door of St. Juliot Rectory, late in the evening on the 7th of March.

Whatever else he might have anticipated, he most certainly did not expect to be greeted as he was, by a young woman, full of face and good humour, who ushered him in before calling upstairs to the lady of the house. It transpired that the Rector, for whom he was to work, was temporarily bedridden. Instead it was his hostess, Mrs Holder, and her younger sister, Emma, who first bade him welcome and fed him. Before showing him his room, they interrogated him, as if any visitor to their home was a curiosity. They asked about his journey, the trains and the weather, until the meal was ready to serve, and he was bade sit down and join them.

After supper, the two sisters retired to the parlour, inviting Thomas to join them. He was tired from the journey, but was easily persuaded to sit with his new and intriguing companions, spending much of the evening talking of music, while being entertained on the piano by both sisters. Eventually, as the candles began to dim, Mrs Holder excused herself for the night to attend to her husband. The younger sister, who had first greeted him, seemed disinclined to follow, although propriety demanded it of her. Thomas lingered for a little longer than would be usual, out of consideration for her, for she seemed desperate for the company he offered.

The next morning Thomas rose early, and after a pleasant and companionable breakfast, he set out to examine his commission. He was to draw up a plan and take down the relevant particulars of the Church of St. Juliot's, in order to substantiate the recommendations of an earlier report, which indicated significant structural repairs. His host, The Reverend Caddell Holder, was still bed-bound, his gout being particularly troublesome. Consequently, while the Vicar was looked after by the older sister, Helen, it was Emma who offered to accompany him along the short distance down to the Church.

The church building itself was in a ruinous state. Several years prior to Thomas's visit, the decision had already been taken to remove the existing tower, as well as the north aisle and transept. On first inspection, he felt such actions would be drastic, and that the ensuing damage to the pews and rood screen would be regrettable, yet he felt little inclination to pitch against them. Emma had decided to stay with him while he did his preliminary drawings and measurements. Before long she had engaged him in conversation, asking him what he was doing at each step. Not surprisingly, with the new distraction, his mind wandered until he was keen only to finish the task ahead and be done with it, before taking the chance to talk on subjects that would be far more appealing to them both.

Thomas was intrigued by the young woman, who had attached herself so easily to his side. She was a strange combination, appearing both shy and familiar at the same time, talking apace and filling in Thomas with all the politics and gossip of the parish, and much else besides. He had never had such talk directed at him, and it took some time to formulate a response. When he did find a topic that he felt confident about venturing an opinion on, he discovered that they had much in common, at least in subject matter, and the conversation soon took on an undulating rhythm, gentle and easy. By the time they were ready to return from the church, for she had stayed with him throughout while he made his preliminary drawings and measurements, he felt enchanted by the strange creature that he had unexpectedly come across, in this remote and dilapidated parish.

Once he had packed up his tools and papers and prepared to make the journey back to the Vicarage, Thomas decided instead to walk slowly about the churchyard, looking at the various headstones with graven curiosity, as was his wont.

'Do you wonder about the souls buried here, Miss Gifford, and what they might have been?'

Emma smiled, a warm, easy smile. 'Often I do. Often, I come here just so to wonder. But after a time, it makes my head ache and I walk down to the stream, and when I look back at the church, the headstones are hardly visible, and I wonder less. The dead are done, I say to myself, and have had their time, whether or not there was enough of it.' She paused. 'Do you think we spend too much time wondering?'

'I hadn't thought of wonder as a bad thing,' answered Thomas kindly, 'not at all.'

'Not a bad thing, no.' Emma paused. 'Just that there is enough wonder in the commonplace, in how people end up as they do, and where they do. Here, come, let me show you.'

Without giving Thomas a chance to answer, she reached for his hand. Half running, laughing as she did so, she pulled him down the pathway, through a gate that fell onto the dome of the meadow, leading down to the Valency river.

'There,' she said, when they had reached the bottom. 'The dead are up there still, but you can't see them. But I am here and worth the wonder, and it is of greater profit to you than focusing on dead things.'

Thomas stood transfixed, unsure how to answer.

She looked at him and laughed, a gentle, lilting laugh.

'You are a serious thing, Mr Hardy.' She reached forward towards him. 'Here, you are about to lose your drawings.'

Thomas looked down and saw a page of manuscript hanging precariously over the lip of his pocket. He took it out to fold and replace it, but something compelled him instead to reflect upon it.

'Thank you, Miss Gifford.' He paused. 'The truth is, it is not part of my brief.' He hesitated, as if weighing up the moment. 'While it is of no consequence, other than to show that I wonder too much, it is a poem I wrote some time back.'

'A poem? You write too, as well as measuring and restoring buildings? Really Mr Hardy, you should have told me, for I much prefer to be in the company of a poet to a draughtsman. Will you read it to me?'

Thomas shifted his feet awkwardly, clearly embarrassed.

'Not now. Not this one, for it is not suitable. Perhaps I could offer some Tennyson, for he is a favourite of mine. Or Wordsworth, for this is his season.'

'O will you? I adore poetry.' She looked at him, her eyes wide open. 'But I'd rather hear one of yours, Mr Hardy. And to think you hid this talent from me for a whole day!'

Thomas laughed. 'Miss Gifford, I only met you last evening. Such a disclosure should take weeks, months even. Perhaps we will read some poetry at another time, for I fear your sister will be waiting.'

With that, he turned and started to walk slowly back up the meadow, with Emma treading lightly beside him.

'That will be a promise, Mr Hardy. I have recorded it so.'

They walked back to the vicarage in silent contemplation, as if to establish some distance from the closed space they had just inhabited. When they reached the gate, Emma turned to Thomas and asked, 'and do you think you would mind if I didn't have to call you "Mr Hardy" while you are here, even though you do seem much older than me? Can I not call you Thomas, and you can call me Emma? For that seems a much friendlier thing to do.'

'Of course, Miss Gifford – Emma – that would seem eminently sensible and desirable. And I course I accede to your request.' As he said so, Thomas made a mock bow, but she could tell it was more to hide his pleasure than anything else.

That evening was one of jollity at the Vicarage. They dined exceedingly well, with the talk becoming increasingly convivial, covering an impressive array of subjects. It was a revelation for Tom to be in such erudite company, and he could not but help think about how different it was to his own home, where there was little by way of conversation, most of which was barren. After supper, they left the oval beech table, as he reclined in a comfortable armchair and Mrs Holder and Emma sang sweet duets of the West Country, long into the evening. By the time he retired, only a little shy of midnight, he did so with the words of 'Let us dance on the Sands' ringing in his head, and a sense of wonder, that had descended rather unexpectedly upon him.

With his work done, Thomas knew he could plan his return to Dorchester on the next morning, but felt strangely disinclined to do so. That Wednesday, the two sisters were intending to travel the short distance south to Tintagel and, sensing that Thomas was in no hurry to return, they asked if he would like to accompany them. As if to persuade him further, although he did not need it, they let it be known that they intended to visit Penpethy Mine on the way, to look for slates for the church roof. With that justification of professional interest in mind, he gladly agreed to accompany them, in their rather cramped basket carriage.

Just as the previous week, the weather was calm and settled. The day, as it unfolded, was memorable in each particular detail, so that in times to come he could easily embellish each image, each sentence, from the notes he had recorded in his diary. He was struck by the otherworldliness of Tintagel, the relentless pulse of the Atlantic, dark and brooding, the sharp-edged scream of the seabirds – in fact, with the whole mythology of the place. Nor was he any less taken with the company. The day spent with the two sisters had led him on to a world he could not have envisaged, just two days earlier. Mrs Holder, who had not invited him to call her otherwise, was quieter than Emma, altogether more deliberate, more measured. Her questions, likewise, were more predictable and less adventurous, never scratching beneath the skin. Nevertheless, it was she that seemed more inclined to talk than her sister.

'So Mr Hardy, what family have you?' she had started, before seeking his views on architecture, his apprenticeship, prospects, travels, reading, views on religion and architecture, London and much more besides. Emma remained quiet as she did so, perhaps in deference to her older sister, but more likely, Tom felt, because she was interested in his answers to questions she would neither have dared, nor bothered, to ask herself.

The next day, after another evening of song and laughter, it was decided that he and Emma should visit the coast. A decision taken, Tom reflected later, without his inclusion in any discussion upon the matter. Helen and Emma had decided on the trip, and he was in no way disinclined to go along with their suggestion. Indeed, he was conscious of a sense of absolution that came from being excluded from the decision making process, and being reliant on the women, he was glad to accede.

The morning was crisp and clear. While the incipient hint of sun was in evidence, it had not yet penetrated the valley along which they walked. Tom still felt the cold, trussed up with the reinforcement of a coarse woollen shirt and vest beneath his greatcoat, as they set off down the valley towards Boscastle.

Emma set out in front, leading her mare, Fanny, that that had been given to her by a previous employer at Tintagel, while Tom walked beside her. With one hand on the reins, she produced a volume of Wordsworth from under her cloak and, handing him the book, asked him to read to her, 'as he had promised.' By the time they had reached the road above the town, they were jesting, each with the other, comparing their favourite poems, and laughing at what it was that amused or entertained them.

Thomas was conscious of how staid, how urban he looked, and not at all elegant. His years in London had affected his sense of dress and manner, in ways that he felt were inappropriate in the country. His mannered visage, his colloquial restraint and measured conversation, all seemed impervious before this maid in a flowing brown robe, who, from a distance, looked to every intent like a Franciscan Monk. But her naturally pink face, made more so by the sharpness of the air and her exertions, and the golden tresses of hair, which spilt out from under her brown felt hat turned up at the side, told otherwise.

When they reached the edge of the small township, she proceeded to lead Thomas and the horse with equal firmness along the harbour's edge, to the path that led off to the north of the town. She was animated, gaily so, commenting on this and that as they walked. Suddenly, as if on an impulse prompted by some untimely word, she mounted Fanny, waved freely to him, kicked the mare's flanks and set off at a gallop across the brow of the hill. Thomas was stunned, both by the rapidity of her actions and by the oddness of it all. Unsure what was expected of him, he ascertained that the best course of action was to continue climbing on the same trajectory, across the contours of corrugated sheep tracks. He had reached the first hillock when he saw her again, her golden hair having broken free, riding high in the stirrups, and gliding across the crest of the eyebrow of Beeny Cliff.

He sat on the small mound, until she came back towards him and dismounted. 'There', she exclaimed, 'I am done for now. It is so grand riding the cliff tops.' She shook her hair vigorously and started to stuff it in, back into her rather unwieldy bonnet.

'Sometimes it feels like riding the edge of a precipice, and I have to fight the temptation to glide over it and float like an angel, but Fanny would not do for that.' Noticing the look of alarm on Thomas's face, she laughed.

'How earnest you are, Mr Hardy. How seriously you take things!' And then, after a pause, 'how little you know of me.'

With that, she next turned away, and he could allow himself to look at her a little more closely. How old was she? She seemed like a playful youth at times, and younger, much younger, than him. Yet her face and figure were well-formed and resolute. She was extraordinary, in her detachment from the ground that lay beneath her feet, and reckless in both her actions and conversation, but he could see she would never be dull. He granted her face was strong and forceful, her jaw square and set, giving her a rather stolid look, but her eyes were agile and mischievous, her wit keen, and she amused him. In truth, he did not know what to make of her.

That afternoon, he walked Emma and Helen back into Boscastle, where they took tea beside the harbour. They talked at him, around him and over him, but for Tom, the impressions of the few short days had swallowed him up completely, and he was oblivious to what questions were asked, and what answers given. Beeny Cliff had embedded itself in his writer's memory, growing into part of some enduring legend that extended from St. Juliot's and the Vicarage to Beeny Cliff, before finally resting on Emma. Emma, as he realised with a start, most of all.

The next morning Emma rose early and came alone to see Thomas off.

'Do let me know when you are safely back, Tom,' she whispered to him, as he buttoned his coat in readiness for the ride to the station at Launceston, 'and do keep writing. Perhaps you will write a poem of me one day.'

And with that, she leant across and kissed him. Tom had never been the involuntary recipient of a kiss before, and it stayed with him, the touch of her lips on his cheek and the significance of it thereof, all the way back to Upper Bockhampton. For the days to follow, when the memory became embedded and grew, so too did his sense of wonder, that such things were even possible.

Chapter Two

ON MY ERRANT PATH, UNKNOWING

By the time that Thomas arrived at the vicarage of St. Juliot, Emma had been living there for almost two years, ever since her older sister's marriage to the Reverend Caddell Holder. The wedding, which had been arranged in indecent haste lest the old man died prematurely, had taken place in St. Petroc's Church in Bodmin, near Kirland Manor House, where her parents had been tenants for several years. The ceremony was simple, without the fuss of a wedding breakfast, which the widower had deemed inappropriate for a second nuptial. At its conclusion, Emma was swept up by the newly-weds, and taken with them like chattel to the vicarage at St Juliot. The truth was, Emma felt pleased to escape her parents, for life had not been easy at home of late. The opportunity to be part of the new household, and a companion to her older sister, was one she responded to positively when it was put forward to her.

It was a role that initially, suited her very well. She and Helen enjoyed the time they could now spend together, away from the stresses of their cantankerous and unpredictable father, while Emma found her new brother-in-law surprisingly good company, despite his antiquity and various infirmities. Moreover, she found that he was a keen conversationalist and, after supper and into the evenings, the three of them would discuss literature, as well as their mutual interest in classical music. When they had finished with talking, they would call up the popular songs of the day or else sing the old Cornish ballads and ditties that they remembered from childhood. Invariably, it was Emma who sustained and extended each conversation after Helen had tired, until her exuberance drove the married couple to bed. When Emma sat alone with Caddell, while Helen saw to the household, she enjoyed quizzing him on his family's colourful history in the West Indies, where his family had been sugar plantation owners, and where he had been born. Moreover,

9

Caddell had been at Oxford and acquired a classical education, something Emma greatly admired. He was well bred, she thought, a gentleman, and she was sure it was Oxford that had made him so. That she would find such a one as civilized as him, but younger, was more than she could hope, but she hoped anyhow. Yet as much as she enjoyed the conviviality of the couple, she was grateful that her role in the household was only that of a companion, and she envied Helen not a whit for the intimate part of their life that husband and wife had pledged to share together.

Despite some occasional traces of the older sister's girlhood jealousy towards her, remnants of their childhood spats and her position as her father's favourite, there were few occasions when voices were raised, and the tranquil veneer of the household was rarely threatened. In the main, Helen was glad of her younger sister's company, being stuck in this out of the way place. For the first year at least, Emma was equally content. The house, built some twenty years before, was designed for a Victorian vicar's family which always seemed to err on the generous side; it was, therefore, commodious and gave each the space they needed to co-exist. In those early months, Emma would spend late summer afternoons reading on the veranda, facing a rolling garden that fell away to the south of the house, until the dusk drove her inside. As the nights darkened she continued in the same pattern, using the adjacent conservatory as her retreat, where she would read or paint until called in to supper.

It was not long, however, before the isolation began to gnaw at her. She had watched her sister who, by marrying a much older man, had fallen headlong into middle age. She was conscious that she herself was also aging – and without the sniff of a husband, waiting in the wings. Inevitably, the fate of her sister preyed upon her: poor Helen who felt compelled to marry a man some thirty five years older, in order to escape her job as a governess and the drudgery of looking after her parents.

'Don't be surprised when you meet the vicar. You will see there's an age gap – more like that between a father and daughter,' Emma had whispered to Thomas when they had been alone that evening, in case he made some inadvertent comment upon meeting Caddell the following morning. She didn't doubt that Helen was fond of her husband, although being fond of someone and being in love with them, were she had already surmised, quite different things.

Although both sisters were bound in similar ways to this remote part of Cornwall, their routines and their obligations were as different as could be. While Helen was charged with running the household and tending to her ailing husband, Emma could play the part of the footloose younger sister, free to roam the countryside on her mare. Yet Helen possessed something that still evaded Emma, the security afforded by marriage. It was little wonder that the younger sister could never entirely feel complacent with her lot, knowing that she was now thirty, the same age Helen had been, when she had felt compelled to marry. The trap into which the older sister had fallen was a lesson that was not lost on her. She might pretend to be carefree, riding the cliffs with abandon, being seen by the townsfolk in Boscastle as a blithe spirit, yet the imminence of her thirtieth birthday disturbed her, for it posed questions she could not easily avoid. What of her future, she would wonder, living in this out of the way place? What was there in Boscastle for her?

She tried to make herself useful about the vicarage and was especially prominent when the very occasional guest came to stay, perhaps a visiting preacher, or the dentist from Plymouth on his rural rounds. She took enjoyment from going to visit the scattering of parishioners, the more distant the better, even though she found it was Methodism or worse, the old popular religions, rather than the Anglican Church, that occupied the minds of the more primitive inhabitants. She enjoyed the musical evenings at home, when the three of them would join in singing or playing their respective instruments, as well as singing and playing the harmonium in church. Such times, she thought, were reminiscent of their childhood, when father and mother would lead the five children in the singing of rounds, popular at the time, father with his violin and mother on the pianoforte. Yet despite the music making and the time she had set aside to pursue her painting, the truth was that, apart from assisting Helen with her household chores, there was precious little for Emma to do. She knew intuitively that she felt more at home in the rectory than in Bodmin, especially after the unsettled time following her mother and father's move from Plymouth. It was as if being in a house of the Church gave her some sanctity, some link with her previous family, connecting her to the saintliness of her mother and her uncle's calling into the Church. But now she was bored, anticipating and fearing the barrenness of the years stretching ahead. Godliness was all very well, she thought, but it was not enough to secure her a husband. Once that was achieved, she pledged she would be devout again, but she prayed for a little leniency in the meanwhile.

Prior to Helen's marriage, Emma had done little with her life, and certainly no more than could be expected of someone considered as genteel as she. After the family left Plymouth, however, and their financial circumstances deteriorated, she reluctantly followed Helen as governess for a local family. Imitating her sister, she had only stayed for six months. Helen had gone on to become a companion for an old lady, Miss Robartes, a few miles south at Tintagel, until, accompanying the old lady in a dogcart, she fell out and was knocked unconscious, leaving her bedridden for several weeks. Thankfully, Emma was able to take over for a second time, looking after the old lady while nursing her sister back to health. It was during this time of enforced convalescence that the Reverend Caddell Holder came to visit the old lady as part of his visits to the sick and infirm of the Parish and first met Helen, before making his audacious yet welcome offer of marriage.

The consequence of the running to and fro whilst looking after others, was the damage to her own health although there were compensations. When she had recovered and returned to the old lady, with whom she stayed until after the wedding, she was given a mare by way of appreciation. Emma named her 'Fanny' after an old aunt. She had been taught the art of riding side saddle by her father, and when she, her sister and Caddell moved to the vicarage at St. Juliot after the wedding, the mare became her dearest companion.

During the first months in their new home, Helen remained housebound and waited at her husband's beck and call. Emma, meanwhile, rode out to the furthest boundaries of the parish, along the coastal tracks north from the township towards Pentargon Bay, along the ridge of Beeny Cliff, and occasionally, even venturing as far north as Rusey Beach. She cut a fine figure riding as she did, her cheeks invariably flushed with colour, roughed by the wind and sharp sea air. If she had hoped to draw attention to herself by doing so, then she had succeeded.

Twice in the past two years, she had been aware of a member of the opposite sex looking at her, whether strangely, or admiringly, or both. Caddell and Helen both found it amusing to try and find a suitable suitor for Emma, although most suggestions were laughed off, as they would have expected them to be. When the son of a local farmer, who she had met when the trio first arrived at the vicarage, indicated his interest in her, she was initially dismissive. He was a decent enough man, although he was several years younger, and so reserved that she wondered how he would ever pluck up the courage to talk with her. But eventually he did, and Emma was charmed by his honesty and devotion to his livelihood, knowing his livestock by name, and talking endearingly of the land he and his family had farmed for several generations. He was not for her however, that she knew, although it did not stop her making play with him when the opportunity allowed.

She also met another young man, still younger again, but one who held her in great admiration. William Serjeant was the son of a nearby curate and was an aesthete, gentle and beguiling. He was also a consumptive. Emma was enthralled by the effect she had upon him, but ensured she allowed him no more contact than she felt was good for him. When he died, two years after she had met Thomas, she found herself more upset than she would have thought it proper to be, as if this young consumptive could have ever been anything more to her, than an admirer born of desperation for a young woman to sit beside him, while his life ebbed away.

Occasionally, Emma would visit her parents at their home near Bodmin. They were seldom happy occasions – she regularly found herself sandwiched between hushed conversations about her mother's pious religion, and further revelations of her father's continued bouts of drinking. The latter only served to despoil the memory she was trying to cement of him in her mind, as an educated and benign gentleman, and not the rambling and dishevelled creature he too often presented on her arrival. Emma was saddened to see her father in such a dissolute condition, as it evoked memories of the bouts of inebriation she had witnessed when she was a small child. But those had been contained; now, the realisation that their family circumstances were in a dire state, exacerbated by the death of his beloved mother, had sent him over the edge and had ended up scattering the family, ending their time of tranquillity. Moreover, bereavement and his weakness for excessive drinking had seen her father readmitted to the Cornwall Lunatic Asylum at Bodmin, where, unknown to Emma, he had spent some time the previous year for intemperance. Their presence now, in Kirland House, only a few short miles from the asylum where his dissolute character was well known, was something she was eager to keep from Thomas.

Her father's fall from grace was a matter of great personal shame for Emma. Inevitably, she preferred to remember their time in Plymouth, and the first two decades of her life. Safely closeted under the umbrella of her charming and attractive grandmother, her father was not only able to give up his practice as a lawyer, living instead as a man of leisure, but the whole household, by then numbering seven, was well provided for. They lived in a fine Regency home near the centre, from where they could walk down to the Hove and take part in the social life of the town. As a man of leisure, their father would declaim and read to them, taking a great interest in their arts and pastimes. In the evenings, however, he would disappear for hours at a time, often returning to the house in a state of inebriation, which would awaken the household. Her mother, on her part, would take great pains to teach her and her sister the importance of being genteel and refined, to prepare them for a life of delicacy and finesse. They both took dancing and music lessons, and attended a dame school where they learned French and where a love of reading was encouraged. Despite her father's bouts of drinking, she revelled in the fact that they were of a better class of people, and were shown respect by townsfolk when they were about. It was a time of great security and happiness, despite its fraying edges, and Emma would always look back with fondness on her years in the provincial town and all that it afforded her, when contrasted with the meagre life on offer at Boscastle.

Plymouth in the middle of the century was by no means a place for a woman to be out unaccompanied, for there were sailors aplenty and trains of convicts awaiting deportation, as well as a number of ruffians and 'low-life's' drawn to the town, through the opportunity to turn mischief into money. As a result, Emma was forbidden to walk into town without a chaperone.

Once, when she was sixteen, she had disobeyed her father's edict and had slipped out of the house to go to the quayside to see off a ship destined for Australia with its boatload of convicts, only to watch in horror as of one of the convicts turned on a guard and murdered him, there, on the ship's deck, before the shocked crowd of bystanders. It was a sight that affected her deeply. When she returned home, weeping in shame and fear, she confessed to her father what she had seen. She was placed under a curfew that remained until she was deemed old enough to look after herself – something that did not happen for the remainder of her time in Plymouth. Only now, at St. Juliot's, where there was little opportunity for her impetuosity to lead her awry, was she finally afforded a measure of independence, while she pined for something out of the ordinary to happen to her, for some romantic gesture to fall from the skies.

By the beginning of 1870, Emma was finding life at St. Juliot tedious. She had wondered if her sister might start a family, or if the old man was even capable. She could hear that they tried often enough, much to her distaste. And so the news that an architect was coming to stay aroused in her no little interest, although no great expectation either. If only he would be a tall, dark stranger and sweep her off her feet, all would be well, but she knew such a thing to be highly improbable.

When Thomas arrived at the door late that evening in March, she had already fantasised about him as her deliverer, although she knew such wildly romantic dreams would inevitably be dashed at the first glimpse of a physical presence. Yet while his appearance was not as she had hoped, Emma was intrigued to meet one who was as knowledgeable and well read as herself, even though she realised after a little conversation, that he was neither as refined or well-bred. Indeed, the only intemperate moment of the whole visit was when she engaged him in talk about her background, by way of explaining why it was proper and respectable for her to live as a companion with her sister and her husband.

'For you see, Thomas,' she paused, before asking, 'are you sure you are happy for me to call you Thomas, still?' She carried straight on as if her question had been rhetorical. 'I was never trained to be employed, for that is not our way, but for a vocation. My family prepared me to be a wife, like others of my ilk, to nurture all those talents and refinements a man looks for in a woman.'

'That is a prevalent view of a certain class, Emma, I dare say, if it can be afforded.'

'It is not a matter of affording, Thomas, it is a matter of one's birth right, what one should do. A lady should not take work unless she desires to do so and even then, she needs be cautious.'

Thomas shifted uncomfortably, thinking of his sisters and his cousin, all training to be teachers.

'But do you not want to be someone, Emma, to do something with your life?' he countered.

'It will be enough that I am recognised for my accomplishments, and for the credit a genteel upbringing will bring to another,' she responded. 'For if I was to do regular work, even if not of a menial nature, what would make me distinct from those who have to work for a living?'

She looked up at Thomas, wondering if she had said too much, if, in the hope of impressing him, she had overreached herself.

But Thomas said nothing, although he was much quieter than before, altogether subdued and more reflective. It was as if he was starting to feel a sense of shame, of position and standing in the light of her eyes. While he had wanted to tell her of his family, he quickly decided that if he had any hopes of her, he would have to wait until a more propitious time.

Chapter Three

WITH MAGIC IN MY EYES

After his return from Cornwall, Tom found it difficult to settle at work or home. To his chagrin, he felt frustrated by the blandness of his parents' conversation. Having little in common with his younger brother and sister, he would confide to his older sister, Mary, and even then only to say that he was feeling a little queer and ill-disposed, for no evident reason. Staying at Higher Bockhampton may have served its purpose when he had sought some quiet to finish his manuscript, but now he could not help but see the cottage as cramped and dingy, his own room particularly so, and he felt hemmed in by its modest dimensions. The Rectory at St. Juliot was not grand, not by any measure, but it wasn't mean and pinched, and its furnishings and company exuded a modicum of refinement that elicited a richer conversation, from those within its confines. Yet the idea that this was somehow superior to the company his family afforded him appalled him, and he quickly dismissed it.

When he reflected on the week just passed, he did not know how to measure the truth of it all. In the end, he decided it would be better not to try, but instead, to manage and harvest the impressions garnered. He had no sense of whether Emma was real, or had merely been some wayward spirit visited upon him. Conversely, he realised the little she knew of him could only be gleaned from words said, for she had not known him in any other context. For all he knew, she may have seen his words as a contrivance. He worried that she might think less of him, were she to know him better. But he could not forget her; nor did he have any inclination to do so. She was strange and quixotic, so vibrant and magical that he was prepared to let her swim about his head, unable to place her under any category, bar the inexplicable.

Within a few weeks, Thomas had begun to find provincial life and the tedium of his work at Weymouth almost unbearable. Three days after his return, he received notice from the publisher, Macmillan, on whom he had pinned his hopes, that they were not prepared to publish his novel in its current form. Dismayed, he sent it off by return mail to Tinsley, who had published *The Poor Man and the Lady*. They agreed to publish a revised manuscript, on the receipt of an advance of £75 from the author. It was not the homecoming he had wanted, nor the endorsement of himself as an author that he greedily sought, but he accepted the charge as necessary in order to see the book in print, although he felt ashamed and angry in having agreed to it.

This setback, along with the suffocating closeness of his family, impelled him to re-consider the decision to move back to Dorset. Even his subsequent move to Weymouth did not have the desired effect, and the town seemed tight-lipped and close, compared to the unregulated freedom of Cornwall. In an unguarded moment, he made the mistake of mentioning Emma to his mother. She had harangued him once more about the perils of matrimony, the devilry of women trying to trap young men, and reminded him, as she had always done, of his obligations to his siblings and her wish for them not to marry, but to take care of their own. He could not stay to fight her, for he knew how relentlessly she could turn a single battle into a campaign, waged with persistent ferocity. Better to run, he resolved, than stay put. And so, after a few short weeks of tedium, he decided to throw in his job with Crickmay and head to London.

His decision to move was coloured with the additional frisson of knowing that Phena, the indelicate subject of the poem that Emma had spied protruding from his jacket pocket, was teaching in the City. While they had come to an agreement that, between them, there would be no agreement, that she would demand nothing of him, she still held a ring of his and carried more than a little of his affection. She was also used to him, to his follies and his laxity and not averse to his company. She would, he reasoned, give him the entertainment and the comfort he required.

But when he called upon her, he found her distracted by the fate that had befallen her older sister, who had fallen pregnant during service. Maggie (and he remembered with a start that he had once thought of her as 'his Maggie') was soon to be the mother of twins. She had been dismissed from the household in anticipation of the event, although she was fortunate, as Phena noted pointedly, that her beau was standing by her. The scandal had had a salutary effect on Phena and while she was happy to accompany Tom to the theatre, she would no longer allow the dilly-dallying he wished for, and had taken part in so readily, in the past.

Whilst in London, Thomas took on work for another seasoned architect, a Mr Brandon in Clement's Inn, yet the weariness he had experienced in his home county soon extended to his profession. Indeed, he was starting to feel his whole foray into architecture was a mistake, or, at the very least, an impediment to his desire to write. Adding to that was the indifference of Phena, for whom he apparently now offered 'too little, too late', and he resolved in a matter of weeks to return to Dorchester. Before he left, however, he received a letter from Emma, prompted no doubt by his own card to the Reverend and Mrs Holder thanking them for their hospitality. Soon they were in a regular correspondence and, with her encouragement, Thomas began to hint at the possibility of a return visit. In fact the opportunity soon arose, not through Emma, but an invitation from the vicar and his wife for Thomas to visit them again in August. Without hesitation, he accepted.

Preparing for the journey to St. Juliot, Thomas experienced a rather startling and acute pang of nervousness. In spite of the correspondence that had flowed between the two, this visit to St. Juliot was an altogether different proposition. There was no cover of work now to hide behind, no other reason for being invited to stay at the Vicarage, apart from the purpose, unspoken but actual, of making Emma's better acquaintance, leading, perhaps, to some future commitment. The invitation may have been at her behest, but the fact that it was come with the compliance of her brother-in-law and sister, was not lost on him. He thought briefly about what expectations this might entail, about the meaning of such an arrangement, but for the moment, he didn't care, for the mounting sense of anticipation overrode all else. Before leaving, he re-read her letters, articulate and engaging, brimming with life and gaiety, a reflection of the memory he carried of her. In exchange, his own letters, he recalled with some embarrassment, were rather paltry, full of reserve and propriety. 'And here's me, presuming to be a writer,' thought Tom, 'but unable to let my guard down, even in the matter of words.'

The journey from London was made on a warm mid-summer day.

Much of the countryside was in drought and by the time he reached Launceston, he was hot and weary. The trap was waiting for him. Alongside it was Emma, who had taken the trouble to be there, to accompany him on the last leg of the journey.

For Thomas, seeing Emma waiting for him brought about an immediate renaissance of place. The brown cloak of his abiding memory had been dispensed with, and now, she stood in a light blue dress, her golden curls crisp and tight, her hands nervously clasped in front of her. When she had first seen him at the train window, her demeanour had changed in an instant – her eyes lit up and she flushed deeply. Before having time to choose an appropriate greeting, however, the moment was pricked by the spectacle of Tom, inappropriately dressed for such a hot summer's day, tumbling comically out of the train with a suitcase and a valise, and landing at her feet.

'You are a one, Tom Hardy,' she exclaimed laughing, before taking his valise and kissing him firmly on the cheek. 'Fancy coming as you have, done up to the nines. But it is good to see you, nevertheless.' She looked directly at him, unabashed. 'It has been a while and I've forgotten bits of you, I venture, but I trust you are all here now.'

With that, she strode off the platform, Tom following as well as he was able, before loading his bags and themselves into the waiting trap, and beginning the circuitous journey to St. Juliot.

The welcome at the Vicarage was warm and accommodating. While the Reverend and Mrs Holder had no doubt been persuaded by Emma to extend the generous invitation to their house guest, no sign of coercion affected the warmth of their welcome. Nevertheless, it was evident from the outset that Thomas was to be Emma's responsibility, and that she would be charged with entertaining her guest and planning his itinerary each day. The question of propriety, of course, would be addressed on their outings, by the presence of Helen and occasionally, by her husband too, as they set about exploring the Cornish coast from Trebarwith Strand in the south, to Bude in the north.

Interspersed amongst these outings, Tom and Emma contrived to spend more time together, without the consort of family. Thomas had turned thirty since their last meeting and while he would not deign to guess at Emma's age (and she was most reluctant to even hint at it), he felt it appropriate that they should seek a little more time to themselves to become better acquainted.

For a start, they walked until Emma's foot became painful, for she had a slight lameness that affected her gait, then he walked while she rode lazily beside him on her mare. They explored the immediate hinterland before following the Valency down to the harbour's mouth two miles west, a walk they took almost daily. As the days passed though, they were inclined to stay closer to home, where they could talk, away from the eyes and ears of the parishioners from the local hamlets.

On one occasion, when they were alone, Thomas steered the conversation towards Emma's family.

'Don't your parents live near here?' he asked.

They were in a shady glade beside the stream which had been much diminished by the drought, lying on a worn tartan rug Emma's sister had loaned to them. They chose a spot where the waters ran and eddied, surrounded by the remnants of the picnic they had just enjoyed.

'Not so near, but not too distant either,' answered Emma. She hesitated before continuing. 'They are near Bodmin, some twenty miles south of Boscastle,' and then adding, by way of justification, 'although it is not a straightforward trip.'

She picked up a stick and threw it into the stream, watching it dance and scurry as it pirouetted in the urgent corridor of water.

'And you, do you see them often? You have not mentioned them to me.'

Emma paused before responding, choosing her words carefully.

'I see them often enough. We are not so close that we know each other's goings on.' Emma paused. She knew she was being deliberately evasive, and sighed. Already she could read where Thomas was headed.

'It might seem opportune, given that you are here for a good period of time, as guests of our family, to call on them. But it would not do, Tom.'

She lowered her head and took a tress of her hair in her hand, before unravelling and winding it around her index finger.

'They are just awkward, Tom, and protective of me. That is why. Maybe one day we will have cause to meet them.'

Having been drawn into saying more than she would have been inclined to do, she blushed deeply.

'But the reason is not because of you, Tom, for they know nothing of

21

you. If they did, I am sure they would not mind so, for no-one could not like you, Tom Hardy.'

With that, she reached out her hand, and firmly pulled Tom down upon her, where they lay until the sun's shadows fell across them, and Providence told them it was time to make their reluctant way back to the Vicarage.

The next day they travelled to the Strangles to the north, in the company of Helen and Caddell. The climb down to the beach was not easy for Caddell, who was in his seventies and sedentary by disposition; nor was it without difficulty for Emma, whose limp made the descent challenging for her. Once there, they laid out a rug on the sandy beach where they enjoyed a picnic before Caddell, already somnolent, fell asleep as Helen read besides him. Rather than staying and attempting to keep up a considerate silence, Emma and Thomas decided to walk northwards along the water's edge, before climbing over the rocks into Little Strand, another bay, smaller and inaccessible. Once over the rocks, they walked slowly along the rim of the deserted beach, Emma's hand firmly clasped in his.

They were an unusual pair, he, dapper and modest of bearing; she, extravagant in word and gesture, with long ringlets framing her face, and yet strangely shy with it. Despite their differences, or perhaps because of them, they had intuitively started to see each other as two halves of one whole. Rather irrationally, the beginning of a third decade had startled Thomas: he was no longer young, he told himself and his appearance reflected this. His beard was fashionably full, yet his hair was already receding and starting to leave his pate quite bare. So, too, he felt were his hopes of escape from a profession he had little stomach for. The disappointment of the rejection of *Desperate Remedies* had alarmed him, leaving him nervous about the diminishing opportunities of making writing his career. Having shared his worries so frankly with Emma, he fell silent, embarrassed for having done so prematurely. She had not seen him so sanguine, so downcast before, and set about encouraging him.

'Hush, Tom, you do yourself down most unjustly. You must keep trying.' She grasped his hand tightly.

'I'll help. I'll read your manuscripts for you. I'll be your amanuensis. You must give me your writing and I'll tell you how fine it is, for that will be the truth of the matter.' And with that, she laughed in an effort to resuscitate the moment, and pull him back to a kinder place.

'I'm sorry Emma. I am poor company sometimes, I fear.' But she would not hear of it.

'You are a dreamer, Tom Hardy, and want to better yourself. That is not something you should apologise for, for I like it so.'

He stopped, emptied his shoes of sand, and kissed her lightly on the forehead.

'You are good for me, Em.'

She smiled. 'I know – and you for me. We must hold onto that when our families and friends despair of us.'

As the days passed in each other's company, Tom could not remember such a joyful time. Helen and Caddell tired of being part of their daily outings, and the couple were permitted to enjoy more and more time alone. They had taken to seeking out quiet secluded places, where they were able to discover the depth of their affections and interest, one in the other. Thomas, in particular, was conscious, of how these lengthy absences must have seemed to those left behind, those whose brief, it seemed, was only to wonder and conjecture on such matters. They made every effort on their returns from these outings to disguise the intimacy they had enjoyed, but their movement, their unwittingly smug expressions and the sensuality of their movements would surely have given them away.

Nevertheless, it was a shock one evening when Caddell took him to one side and asked directly his intentions towards Emma.

'We have only known each other a short time,' Tom answered, 'but she is dear to me, that I can say.'

Caddell continued to look intently at him.

'I am pleased to hear it, Thomas. For while it may have been only a short time, it is clear you have grown very familiar. Is that how it is?'

Thomas looked at the older man. His cleric's collar was too large for a neck that had once been plump and full. How had he not noticed this before? And how puce he looked. The question the man posed smelt of Church, tainted with a righteousness he had not witnessed from his host before, but which should not have surprised him, being a cleric. He felt his face colouring as he answered.

'I will not deny we have been close.'

'"Close" is a rather quaint way of describing what Helen has told me passed between the two of you'.

Thomas started. What had Emma told her sister? What level of intimacy did she enjoy, with this rather closed and earnest woman?

'The matter of our relationship is our business, sir. We are not children, and need not be spoken to in this way.'

'Not children, it is true, Mr Hardy, for children are but innocents in this world. But you are a guest in my house, I remind you, and I would ask that you treat my hospitality appropriately. And if honour is involved, you will be honourable.'

Thomas stayed his answer long enough for the pause to become uncomfortable.

'You can rest assured, Reverend Holder, that I would not know how to be otherwise.' And with that, he left the room, feeling angry and unsettled, and returned to the kitchen where he found Helen and Emma talking merrily. They looked up at him briefly, Emma querulously so, and asked him to join them, but he had not the inclination nor the energy to do so, and with one last plaintive look at Emma, excused himself for the night.

The following day, having left the Vicarage early, they followed the Valency upstream. As soon as they were out of earshot of the house, he turned on Emma.

'What was the meaning of what Caddell said to me?' he asked, after he had recounted their previous night's conversation to her.

Emma seemed unruffled.

'He is playing the cleric, that's all. He is a good man and fair-minded too, my brother-in-law. I would think nothing of it.'

Thomas was not so easily dissuaded.

'I cannot just dismiss it. He said that you had told Helen about us – in a way that was compromising to us both.'

'It was just sisters' talking, Tom. She worries about me and doesn't want to see me hurt. I had not told her so much.'

'Enough, though I venture, to feed the old man's prejudice,' he replied.

Emma paused and brushed some leaves from her coat. 'I would guess Helen has put him up to it.'

'Helen?' Why?'

'Because she wants me to be happy.'

For several moments neither said anything. Emma suddenly stopped and turned to him.

'Tom, if you do feel for me as you have led me to believe, then it matters not. If I have misconstrued your meaning, then I will and must apologise for thinking it otherwise. You must tell me which way it is.'

Thomas fell silent, but for the first time during his time with Emma, he felt a sense of unease, not because he didn't feel complicit in the journey they had started upon, but because the very idea of any expectation placed upon them made him shudder. He had desperately wanted them to be unsullied by judgements, ill-made or otherwise, for he sought for them a purity, a recognition which would bode no interference or compromise. He wanted his time here to remain apart from the life in Dorset, to keep both compartmentalised, she and his recent past.

Leaving St. Juliot a few days later, having enjoyed the most memorable, the most enjoyable holiday of his life, Thomas dismissed the episode as one of no matter, although it stayed within him, shelved and invisible. Instead, he reflected upon the time he had enjoyed in her company, and how he had even been persuaded to subjugate his deep misgivings on religion, attending Church to hear her playing the harmonium. Over the previous days, their interest had deepened, each in each, and he had listened, fascinated by all that she said and her manner of saying so. He had talked about his writing with her as openly as he had with anyone, and she had responded with undiluted encouragement. Moreover, she had offered to assist him by undertaking research and reading the final proof of *Desperate Remedies*, ensuring that the erstwhile bond between them grew, taking on another, more practical function. They had been soaked in a rainstorm at Beeny Cliff, had explored the coves and inlets of the local coastline and, most importantly, each other. And now they were to be parted, with no timetable, no plan of a future together so long as Tom's prospects remained so delicate. Once more, it was left to their letters and imaginations to keep the idyll alive.

Chapter Four

THE LOST PRIZE

A s far as Thomas recalled, he had never seen his mother so angry. He was only eight years old at the time, yet even now he could vividly remember how she stormed into the manor house, grabbed him by the arm and dragged him out the front door. His teacher, Mrs Martin, beseeched her to stay, to have tea and to talk the matter over. But Jemima would have none of it.

"Ee has bewitched thee, Thomas, cradling 'ee like some infant in her lap.' She spat out the words as she dragged Thomas towards the dogcart, ready to take him from the grand house at Kingston Maurward, and back to their cottage, two miles away.

'But mother, she is very kind and nice and loving to me,' at which point her hand smacked him firmly on his legs, more to shake the young boy out of his infatuation, and back to his senses, than to cause any physical pain.

'She is a wicked woman, Thomas, for you are too young to understand the workings of a woman's mind, especially a childless one such as she. She might live in a grand house and think she can do what she wills, but she cannot. I will not have you going back there.'

Arriving back at the cottage, Thomas remembered his father's consternation, and his displeasure at his wife for making such a scene with the squire's family – and his most important client.

'This will have consequences for us, Jemima,' he told her, 'mark you.'

'That it might,' she conceded, 'but I have pledged to look after our son and protect him from the depravities of the world. And that I'll do.'

Despite his parents' concerns, Thomas was not too young to understand. He thought of Julia Augusta, as Mrs Martin had insisted he call her. He remembered her kindness, her gentle fondling and stroking of his hair and arms, and resolved that he would love her in secret and one day, he would visit her when he was grown up and his mother was dead and they could be together again.

The time at St. Juliot had awakened many such memories in Thomas. Having reached the venerable age of thirty years, he found him thinking often of his early memories and what this new fresh-faced visitation, his confident and refined Emma, would make of his past life. Emma was so exotic, so far removed from his native habitat, that he considered whether or not he should make a full disclosure to her, accept her inevitable rebuke for leading her on, and return to the station his mother had prepared for him. Furthermore, she was the first real lady that he had met since Julia Augusta and he found the memories of the latter transferred to the former, in a way he didn't fully understand.

Despite his desires, it was not possible to be so honest with Emma, for she had got under his skin and he was reluctant to unsettle her. She knew little of his parents and siblings, and he had been careful to disclose nothing that would injure him in her eyes. He had not mentioned that his father was a mere builder, albeit a successful one. Neither did he reveal that his mother, while well read and ambitious, was of humble origins and still spoke the dialect. There were no clerics, no lawyers, no learned gentlemen and gentle womenfolk in his family, however far back or sideways one travelled. What right did he have to keep this from her?

He closed his eyes and remembered the time not long before his visit, when he and Phena had last been together. She had called on her Uncle and Aunt at Higher Bockhampton and he had offered to walk her home, through the woods to Puddletown, as had become their wont. He remembered leading her eagerly by the hand, laughing as he did so, while she responded to his indelicate whispers with her own flirtatious banter.

"Tom Hardy. You are a one. And family too. For shame."

She tightened her grip on his hand and pulled herself closer to him, dropping her head coyly onto his shoulder. He turned his head, his blue eyes merry and smiled at her.

'Kin we might be, but that only means we are both from good stock, my girl. But we are not so much kin as not to dally a while.'

He had led her away from the path and into a small, secluded spot they had stopped at before. She had recognised the deviation, but had not tried to counter it though the thought passed her mind whether he had taken others here before her? He was intimately familiar with the area. Ever since he was a boy, he had walked these ancient pathways between Bockhampton and Puddletown. It seemed to her that he knew each shady glade, each little copse, and their likely use.

Leading her by the hand across the carpet of fallen leaves and dead wood, they stopped at a hollow between two chestnut trees one Spanish, the other Sweet. Hidden by a stand of birches, they stood amongst a tangled filling of rhododendron and gorse off the main path. The bracken had been flattened at some time past, and a fine understory of whortleberry, bell heather and bedstraw had been subdued. After carefully emptying his pockets, Tom laid his old tweed jacket evenly on the ground, extending its sleeves, before placing both hands on her shoulders and guiding her downwards with a lingering kiss.

Facing each other, on their knees, she was aware of the inevitability of them ending here. She knew the incipient dangers she had invited by agreeing; indeed, she conceded, she had willed them into being. Tremulous, she held his face away from her, conscious her slight tremors were becoming as palpable as his heightened breathing. In a birch tree a little way off, she heard a song thrush signal its presence. Could it see them, she thought, and would it approve of their actions?

Tom leaned forward and kissed her, but she broke away with a smile designed to tease.

'So tell me Tom Hardy, that you like me more than Martha? Tell me the truth now.'

Thomas sat up and looked at her, a smile on his lips. He patted the ground down beside him before answering,

'Martha is a fine girl, but she isn't a patch on you.'

'And do you mean by that, Tom Hardy, that she wouldn't do for you what I do?'

He reached across and placed his palm against her cheek. She had a strong face, and her dark eyes engaged his without wavering.

'I had no inclination for her, when there was one so desirable as you lying in wait.'

'Really, Tom Hardy, you talk a fine line of words.' She reached behind her and undid her hair from its customary bun, allowing it to fall around her. Her eyebrows, dark and regular, arched as she smiled once more, this time, with rapacity.

As Thomas unbuttoned his waistcoat, she rocked back, first onto her elbows, then, confident of the bed beneath her, onto the small of her back.

'Let's be seeing you then, Tom, but heaven help us both if your mother should find out that we are knowing each other in the ways that we are.'

Thomas was shocked at the intensity of the reoccurring memory. He was happy then, was he not? And was not Phena a fine girl, intelligent and loving, who he could settle down with? She would lead him a merry dance, but what fun they would have. But as he reminded himself with more than a little bitterness, Phena had gone, first from his life and then to London. She left with nary a look back, but a smile and a laugh as if their lovemaking had only been a part of some journey, some ritual they had partaken of in growing up, a time predetermined as finite. While he had always presumed they were betrothed, especially now, she had no such understanding. When he forced the issue, it became clear, and she had cast off the ring he had given to her with a careless laugh. It was such a light-hearted gesture that he was confounded as to what to say, and so said nothing, yet the moment had affected him deeply.

But it was not just Phena. There was Eliza who he had treated so shamelessly and exchanged for her flirtatious younger sister. She dallied with him and then cast him aside, having broken her sister's heart. And Louise, to whom he had pledged himself in exchange for her favours, and then spent some considerable time extricating himself from his obligations by behaving so abominably that she wanted none of him. There were Martha and Emma too, Phena's sisters, with whom he had also dallied, in the way of cousins, before settling on Phena. He had behaved as was expected of a young man attempting to sow his wild oats, but these attempts were often unsuccessful, leaving him frustrated, embarrassed and angry at himself for being so urgent. Phena, though, was different, and the fact that she had cast him to one side, especially now of all times, only made her the more desirable.

And what then of Emma? For Thomas, the time at St. Juliot seemed unreal, a cloud of imaginings and sensations. He did not know what to make of them. He was taken by the gentle refinement of the vicarage, which was in stark contrast to his own family home. He was in awe of the unusual and mannered Emma, who seemingly belonged to a different world. But he could not place the host of other emotions he felt towards her. He only knew that she was different from all the rest, and that she had bewitched him.

After the early episode with Mrs Martin, Jemima had watched him closely, lecturing him often on the distractions of womenfolk, and his obligations to his own family. She had sent him to school in Dorchester, necessitating a much longer walk, passing the schoolhouse Mrs Martin had set up at Kingston Maurward. She was proud of how quickly he learned, for she had set her store by him as the cleverer of her two boys. She would talk long hours with him of family and folklore, and would feed his imagination with disturbing tales, so that even from a young age, he was inclined to the dark and lurid.

When he was sixteen, Thomas heard of a hanging that was to be held in the town. There had been a good deal of talk and excitement amongst the townsfolk, as if the day's event was to be a glorious spectacle and Thomas, in league with a number of his friends, was quickly caught up in it. News of the hanging had spread beyond the County and the townsfolk and inn-keepers expected a healthy number of people to come from outlying towns and villages to observe the event.

For Tom, the hanging meant having to rise early from his bed in Bockhampton, in order to get to the Dorchester County Gaol in time.

'Why do you want to see this thing?' his mother pestered. 'Some sad woman who had been pushed beyond the limits of her endurance'.

But in spite of the misty rain, Tom was not to be deterred, and set off as dawn broke in order to get the very best view. The extraordinary interest was on two accounts. First, because it was a local woman who was to be hanged, and an attractive woman at that; and second, for being the result of a crime of passion, which was always likely to arouse strong emotions, especially amongst the womenfolk.

Martha Brown had been sentenced for killing her second husband, a man some twenty years younger than her. Finding him in bed with another woman, she had remonstrated with him, until he proceeded to take a whip to her. Her retaliation had been to strike him on the skull with an axe, killing him outright. Her fate was to be death by hanging.

A large scaffold had been erected outside the County Gaol, allowing

30

enough space for the large crowd of three to four thousand people, to gather. Tom positioned himself somewhere near the front, from where he watched the ceremony of pinioning and the administration of the last rites. The crowd then fell silent as she walked the last nineteen steps to the gallows, accompanied by the hangman who placed a white cap over her face. Having left her to release the bolt that would open the trapdoor, he realised he had not bound her dress to her and returned to do so, adding to the growing suspense amongst the eager onlookers.

Tom was besides himself with nervous excitement as Martha fell with a jolt, not many feet in front of him. He watched her death throes, the dying body jerking about violently, until eventually all life was extinguished. After the crowd had dispersed, he stayed for the full hour that her body was required to hang, until she was removed inside the gaol and he started his long walk home.

Later, much, much later, he could still recall what a fine figure Martha had been, against a sky washed by misty rain. He recalled how the tight black silk gown had set off her shape as she wheeled half-round and back. He could still recall how they had put a cloth over her face and, as it got wet, her features came through it like a death mask. But it was with some shame and consternation that Tom remembered that it was the image of the slender Martha swinging loosely, her wet dress pressing against her, and the intense sensation of excitement he felt that disturbed him the most, and made him wonder at himself and his own amoral feelings.

How was it that the appearance of Emma made him recall these thoughts? The memories that had lain dormant within him over the past fourteen years were stirred by her arrival, but he knew not why. Contrarily, they had also pulled him down into a spiral of guilt and self-recrimination about his unspoken past in which, however hard he tried to purge himself from, still remained, and for some brief seconds he saw himself as others would see him, were his soul visible. For several days he had awoken, terror-struck, with the image of the body swaying gently before him. He had been wracked with guilt, not for having been there, but for the sensations it had set off in him, and the vividness of his recollection. How to tell Emma that it was possible for a writer to see and feel things, to write about them, without identifying with them or being sullied by them? And by extension, how could he tell her about his family, his past, his most intense feelings, when he could not admit them to himself, for fear of what they would reveal? In the end, he resolved that he could not, indeed, should not tell her of his previous life, for fear of upsetting her finer sensibilities. Instead he ventured that if she were to come to him, she would have to find out for herself, for he had not the courage to divest himself of the most extreme thoughts and inclinations that regularly troubled him. Such imaginings were for his own conscience, not for a life shared with another; they were part of his writer's trough from which he would feed He comforted himself that such secrets resided in all people, just as dark and disturbing. His were of no great matter, therefore, for he had no way of knowing if his imaginings were more extreme than those of others. What he did know, and in this he saw the departure of Phena as an omen, was that he had gone as far as he was able to in one extremity of his life, and now he wanted to pursue his writing. In order to do so, he reasoned, Emma would be the ideal companion for him. Despite all his doubts and misgivings, and the stirrings of his most recent infatuation, he had decided that he wanted to pursue this rather alluring woman, who had given him the confidence to write, and had stirred the poetry within him.

Chapter Five

A LOW-BORN CHURL

On his return to Dorchester, Tom found himself confounded by the events of the past month. While he had tried to view her life in relation to his, he had unlocked his own demons, and was more conscious than ever that he and Emma had grown so close, so intimate in their short time together, that the sudden rupture had been excruciatingly painful. On the night before his departure from St. Juliot, he gave his manuscript of *Desperate Remedies* to Emma to copy, with careful instructions as to what licence he would allow, requesting her to make any pertinent comments (he was loathe to say edit) as she saw fit. It was as dear a love token as he could ever have offered. But it was not the only keepsake he left behind; he had also gifted her some intimation of himself, some unspoken words of communion. While they were necessarily vague, he knew it spoke of a commitment, however nebulous, that each had made to the other, tacitly, without the need for further explanation.

Yet within the matter of a few days apart, Tom's thoughts of Emma became less corporeal, taking on a dreamlike persona that he could shift and place as he wished, by a waterfall or cliff top or in a space that only they inhabited. When he shared this idea with Emma, of a love that was mutable and staged, that was both loving and poetical, she rebuked him. 'The very thought,' she said. It showed the smallness of men, she went on to tell him, to think about love as mock theatre, staged whispers and conceits instead of recognising the contractual obligations which were not remote from the world, but at its practical heart. Thomas was bemused, as if love was grown by distance, not diminished, but kept his peace.

Afterwards, they wrote. Or at least, she wrote and he responded, always, he felt, inadequately, never being able to put into his letters anything that was not painstakingly constructed and guarded. 'Feelings,' he would think angrily to himself, 'feelings! Why can I not write them in a letter when I can conjure them up for a story? Why can I not be more demonstrative, more transparent of emotion? Why can I not tell her?' But he could not.

Even when she laid her heart bare, his remained fettered.

'Dear Tom,' she had written to him, 'what a distance you seem from me – would it that it was not so. I am writing this letter to you in that little crushed glade beside the Valency immediately below the church, where we spent that last afternoon. Do you remember it, Tom? You must, for it was the most perfect day. Please do tell me that you do.

Last night I had a presentiment that you never existed, that I had dreamt of you, and made you up and imagined the abiding gentleness of your touch. When I woke up, I determined to write to you immediately to tell you that you must exist, must always exist, for me, for me. If you wish it, Tom, I will be your scribe and your companion for I am as one with you, although I would not presume to ever be your muse. Let me help you become who you must, for I believe in you, Tom, with all my heart.'

Tom's response was characteristically muted, responding to Emma's overtures, but offering none of his own.

'Dear Em, Your letter is so typically kind and generous. I can reassure you that I do exist, although most probably not as you remember. You make me sound finer than is the truth, but I am disinclined to disabuse you of feeling so, if it is to my betterment.

It has been quiet in the office. I have been working on the drawings, for Crickmay is pressing me for them, but I fear I was not as attentive as I should have been and may need to check some measurements. It is unfortunate that the last renovations despoiled the church and that such alterations made are not easily undone. Meanwhile, I am waiting for Tinsley to write for he has had the manuscript for some two months now. What is he doing with it, I pray? What I would give to abandon my work to be an author, instead of having to juggle everything so, and to write as I would wish. I have even asked him what sort of stories I should write, for I could temper my writing accordingly, but I have heard nothing so do nothing.

I often think of our walks along the harbour, upon Beeny Cliff, around St. Juliot and of the kindness of your sister and brother-in-law in making me so welcome. Lyonnese is indeed a magical place and I am sorely tempted to appropriate it for my next book. You were kind indeed for sharing it with me.

Yours affectionately,

Tom.'

But Thomas had other things to occupy him. Now he was back in Dorset, the time and thought given to his distant romance ebbed away, as its charms were swamped by other needs, more pressing and primal. He thought often of Phena, and his last walk with her, not as a rival to Emma, but as a parallel existence which he could still enjoy. He had decided against going back to Crickmay although his employer had come to value the work of his architect's clerk and had ample commissions for him. Instead, he set to his writing once again, a new manuscript which, this time, he had decided would be a rural idyll of a more pastoral nature, un-complicated and altogether less contentious than his previous work.

As for Emma, the letters continued to come regularly. She used words well and was endlessly encouraging of his writing. He, in turn, valued the comments she made neatly in the margins of each page as she copied out the manuscript of *Desperate Remedies* for him. It was a task he knew to be exacting and laborious, but which she tackled with a lover's appetite. Sometimes the only comment left was simply one of approval or appro-bation, a mere phrase or two, but it was stirring to have her critically reading his words, to share in his precious creation, though at times, he wondered if she understood the emotions that lay behind it all.

By contrast, a letter came one morning in mid-June that was neither expected nor welcome. He half-recognised the writing, and it was, he dis-covered on opening it, from Emma's sister, Helen. Towards the end of his visit, she had been strangely off-hand with Thomas, and her letter now explained why. She wished to inform him, she wrote in her tidy, elongated hand, that, admittedly only for a matter of days, there had been a strong suspicion that Emma was pregnant. While she – they – now knew this was no longer the case, the realisation that such a thing could even have been possible reinforced her opinion, and, implicitly that of the Rector too, should he have been made aware, that he should do the right thing by her sister. She urged Thomas to make a commitment to Emma, and set out a plan by which he could provide for her in the future.

Thomas was shocked and angry. His first thought was to ask why Emma had placed him under an obligation to her family, when the matter had already been discussed between them. What could be advanced by this letter, written after the event, other than to make himself feel forced into an action she would certainly know he could neither afford or entertain. Why?

Emma was apologetic when he regaled her with the letter's contents, both for not telling him of the pregnancy scare and, more so, of her weakness in telling Helen.

'I needed some support, Tom, for I had no-one else to turn to,' was the extent of her explanation and apology. She reassured him that Caddell did not know, for she had made her sister swear she would not tell him. Disclosing such information to him would make future visits nigh on impossible, whereas Helen was more amenable. She would see that, should love unexpectedly triumph over advancement and background, he could still make a suitable match for her. Yet by this rider, her letter was undone in Tom's eyes, and more so, by Helen's assertion that she did not want to ruin either of their reputations – especially that of dear Emma, the genteel daughter of a solicitor. Nevertheless, the content was laced with sufficient truth, to trouble him more than a little.

The ambiguity of his position was not lost on Tom. Emma loved him, he was sure, and he, in turn, loved her, not just the physicality of flesh, but in the visage he had of her which, in his mind, was at least as real. How could he doubt her, when she alone had encouraged him to give up his career to write, when none of his family would venture the same support? She must know that to do so, would prolong any courtship, for he had no means to support her. That realization alone raised her considerably in his mind. For love should be selfless, he thought, like this, although the possible expectation of reciprocity, in the present or future, never crossed his mind.

By early December, Tom had received the newly scribed copy back from Emma and with little pause, sent the complete manuscript on to Tinsley. She had done an excellent draft, and her amendments and editorial suggestions were sensible and precise. He was impressed. The receipt of a letter from Tinsley confirming its arrival was a balm to him, and he felt reassured enough to spend his Christmas at Higher Bockhampton with his family, and their usual gamut of festivities. Meanwhile, he continued to work on the manuscript for *Under the Greenwood Tree*, though his mind was often distracted, by Emma, by the distance between them, and lately, by Phena, who had returned from London, and whose presence had un-expectedly begun to play on him once more.

In January, Thomas travelled to London. The city, for five years his home, now felt remote and unwieldy. He was conscious of how, in a little over two years, his horizons had diminished. His thoughts were now as inclined to lie in the west as in the city, although he resolved to guard, in matters of the heart, against the dangers of parochialism.

Visiting the publisher, he paid Tinsley's deposit, churlishly laying down his contribution in crisp new banknotes, as if it was the publisher's fault that his book had not been deemed more suitable for the marketplace. He had planned to stay on in London, but Phena, who was the reason for planning to do so, was teaching all day and had only the occasional evening left over for him.

Twice they met up for dinner, but the evening did not go as Thomas had imagined. They talked as cheerfully and indiscreetly as ever, of family, of the folk at home, of London life, but no more. When Thomas tried to steer the conversation towards the more intimate, the amorous, she only laughed at him.

'Time's have changed Tom, and this is not Dorset, thank God.'

'But we have not changed, surely,'

'Of course we have, silly,' she answered. 'We changed when we got away from family and saw there were other things to engage us. We've both grown up, Tom, as we should. Family was fine when that was all we had, but now we have other choices.' She paused, having noticed the pained look on Thomas's face.

'What has happened has happened, and is behind us. But we'll still be friends, Tom, always friends. I'm grateful to you for caring for me.'

Her lukewarm response towards him, as well the lack of time she gave Thomas to convince her otherwise, only served to unsettle and confuse him further. He was fond of her, fond of the warmth and succour she had once given him, but she was right to suspect the transitory motive of his suite. With little encouragement from her, and nothing to persuade him otherwise to remain in a damp and bleak London, he resolved to return to Dorset.

For the next few months, the weather lay across the country in a grey, un-remitting shroud and he used its cloak as a reason to remain secluded in his room and write. The manuscript he had been working on was progressing smoothly and he felt that, all being well, he would be ready to offer it up for publication by the summer. He had also started another, shorter manuscript which he worked on when the mood took him, for it foreshadowed Emma and was as revealing and intimate as his letters failed to be. During this time, he seldom ventured away from Higher Bockhampton, apart from walks taken in Thorncombe Wood usually in the company of his sister, Mary. He still received letters from Emma, and replying to each in turn, was forever adding to their spool, and yet he could not, but help seeing the various strands of his life running in parallel. Unsure of what either of them felt, he resolved not to allow the edges to blur or the ink to run. It was this ambiva-lent dichotomy of feeling that led him, on Valentine's Day, to send a card each, in the nature of casting dies, to Emma and Phena.

Throughout early spring, Thomas was impatiently biding his time, waiting for the appearance of *Desperate Remedies,* eventually published in late March. When he received the first copy, he clutched it to his chest, as proud as any new father could be. Initially, he was not even depressed by the mixed reviews the book received. Nor did he feel compromised by having had to invest in the cost of its publication. This was to be his vin-dication and, he felt, it would prove itself a worthy book when set against other modern writing, whether subsidised or not. All it required was time. Another truth, however, was less palatable: the investment had left him significantly short of money, and he was forced to look once more for more basic sustenance to allow him to write. So it was that he was enticed back to his draughtsman's work, and before long, was asked to oversee the ren-ovation work on the church at St. Juliot, which was now ready to begin.

Having told Emma that he was to travel to St Juliot in late May, he was prepared to accommodate himself in a local hostelry. But he was surprised, and relieved, considering Helen's letter of six months ago, to receive a generous note, inviting him to avail himself of their hospitality once again. Thankfully, he noted it was not accompanied by any reference to their previous correspondence.

Emma met him at the station as she had done previously, and seemed little changed from the intervening nine months. She wore another blue dress, having taken Tom's compliments to heart about how well blue suited her, and had coloured her wardrobe accordingly. They were tentative in the first offerings of conversation, but soon both grew bold, and by the end of the evening, their words and affections had recovered an old momentum. They delved increasingly deeper into each other's character and habits, gently probing the other for an opinion or a thought, one that the other would recognise and engage with.

Emma could talk about anything it seemed, exploring the physical and cerebral domains they had staked out for each other through the course of their letters, before coming to rest upon matters of a more spiritual nature, something Emma delighted in ragging Tom with.

'Your faith seems so pliable, Tom. How can you work in churches and not feel the spirit within?' she would ask, while he would stumble over his reply, telling her of his readings of the testaments and his wish to believe, had there been only the evidence to allow it. But she would not desist when faced by his discomfort.

'What evidence do you need, Tom? What spiritual proofs could convince you?' Then, if by way of easing his plight, she would stop, but usually with a closing comment he wore as a slight.

'You are always so literal, Tom. Not everything can be put into words, you know.'

Once she had been confident enough to ask him 'How can you still be content to spend so much time with your family, when you have exceeded them?' He was acerbic in his reply. Later, though he regretted his bitterness, he could not disguise his anger at the folly contained in such a question, and the inference within. Yet their days were as close as they had previously been and he felt himself drawn back to her, resenting the time apart and wondering, for the first time, what she had been occupying her time with, when he had not been there.

By the end of his visit, he discovered he was only more confused, more bemused, more perplexed by her than ever. He knew he had enjoyed her company, but was equally baffled by her. She tried to encourage him into giving up his architectural work and had extolled the quality of his writing and story telling, but he could not take her confidence and wear it as he would a shirt, for it did not quite fit him yet. For a brief moment, as he left the station he looked back hungrily, determined not to take his eyes away until her airy blue form had disappeared from sight. Then, just before she passed from his view, he saw her turn away impatiently from his gaze, busy to get on, and realised that the pain of their parting affected him far more than her. This, compounded by finding his recently published novel remaindered on the platform at Exeter, and the anxiety that had compounded over the long trip trapped with his negative thoughts, resulted in reaching Dorchester in low spirits indeed.

Returning to Weymouth and Crickmay's brought a welcome sense of routine back to his life. After the initial thrill of being published, he had soon grown irritated by the criticism his book had received, and poured his energy into his new manuscript. By early August, he was ready to send it off to Macmillan, in spite of their previous lukewarm response.

In October, the restoration work at St. Juliot's necessitated another visit. Once again, Crickmay, acutely aware of the attraction that resided there, called upon Thomas to monitor and report back on progress. Emma was on hand to meet him once again, and while their trip back to the Vicarage was less animated than before, she was clearly still pleased to see him. Their recent letters had reached an impasse of late, neither wanting to say or give too much to the other. Nor had they talked of what lay ahead of them, although it was evident that Helen wanted things to progress to a tidy conclusion. She and Caddell had always appeared exceedingly tolerant of their frequent house guest, but increasingly, Tom sensed it was to achieve an end. Perhaps, having Emma lodging with them for some years now, they had grown concerned about how long the arrangement may continue, and when they could regain their space and privacy. With those concerns aside however, he felt beholden to their relationship, which had grown somewhat sporadically after the delicious summer they had enjoyed the previous year. Now it faced a resistance against being bullied into some sort of arrangement that both of them were uncomfortable with.

Two days later, they found themselves in the little purl of the valley where they had previously picnicked. They sat on a flat overhanging ledge, side by side, deep in thought as they listened to the stream gurgling over the table of solid rock, slipping away beneath the foliage and overhanging branches. It was cooler, for the season had begun to turn, with the carry of dead leaves, curled and lifeless, pulled to the water's edge where they gathered in shoals.

'It is over nineteen months now, Em.' Thomas spoke quietly, without looking up at her.

'The seventh of March.' She ran her hands one across the other, as if in supplication. How short her fingers were, he thought, how regular her nails.

'You looked so surprised, Tom, when I opened the door to you that night.'

'That I was. I had expected some old cleric, not you.' He reached across, took one of her hands and drew it to his lips.

'What is to become of us? I am compelled to write, but I cannot provide for you by writing. I am at a loss why you still urge me to do so.'

'I do it, Tom Hardy, for I know you would never be happy not writing.'

'Then you are alone in that, I venture.' He picked up a stone and lobbed it into the small pool of water, immediately regretting having disturbed its mirrored surface.

'But what of us, Em? It will not help us.'

'We can still plan for us, if that is what you want. But you must be sure it is what you want.' She paused. 'But I don't want to come between you and your writing. I never want you to see me as an impediment. You must trust more, be sure of yourself, and be sure of us.'

'How? How can I be sure? How can I think so? And even if I did know your heart's mission and mine, how could I know that your family would ever countenance it?'

She reached across and ran her hand down his arm, teasingly, before reaching his hand and coiling his fingers in hers.

'They may not, but if you felt the time propitious for doing so, you should not be afraid to ask.' She let his hand go and sat up.

'They only want to know that you would care for me. They want to know that the refinements of home life they had given me would be reflected in what we sought for ourselves. It would be quite usual for them to think that.'

Thomas sat silent for a time, his eyes fixed on the cascading water.

'I despair of us when you talk like you do at times, you and Helen both. What does it mean, this refinement you speak of? What is it to us?'

'It is for you to appreciate where I have come from, Tom, that's all, for you would ask a lot of me to jeopardise my upbringing, in order to marry you.'

Thomas looked at her.

'I did not think I was asking anything of you.' He paused for several pregnant seconds aware his words could be taken as those of a recidivist. 'In fact, at times it seems I am hardly a suitable one for you,' he continued eventually, his words heavy with irony.

'O but you are, Tom, you are. I am just anticipating what my father might say to us, and what argument we must prepare to repel.'

For the remainder of the year, Thomas was kept busy with commissions. While he remained curious as to what happened to *Desperate Remedies*, being naturally protective of his first-born, savouring in particular, some of the belated reviews that were more generous towards it, he knew that his next book would have to succeed, in order to be able to pursue a serious career as a writer.

He was met however, with frustration, at Macmillan's intransigence with *Under the Greenwood Tree*, and Tom once again turned to Tinsley. In April Tinsley agreed to buy the book's copyright, an act Thomas later regretted, after it was enthusiastically received upon its publication in June. The fruits of its immediate success were quick to follow, and soon after, Tinsley requested another story to serialize for Tinsley's Magazine. Tom took very little time before offering another manuscript, as yet unfinished, which he entitled *A Pair of Blue Eyes*, and his heart was buoyed by the turn in his fortunes.

Encouraged by this success and the first significant earnings from his burgeoning career, Tom and Emma agreed that the occasion was ripe for the couple to present themselves before her parents, who lived at Kirland House near Bodmin.

They travelled down together from St. Juliot, full of optimism. Emma had arranged for them to stay with an old family friend, Sir William Serjeant at St Benet's, before calling on her parents the following morning. She had told Thomas little of the host family, other than that she had once stayed there whilst convalescing after nursing her sister. The family, she assured him, had good intentions and would support them in their venture, though contradictorily, this only served to fill Thomas with unease. Nevertheless, their evening was joyously expectant, and the conversations with their hosts so reassuring that when they set off the next morning, it was with an inflated confidence which would only serve to exacerbate all that was to follow.

The visit proved to be a galling experience. After a few moments of pleasantries that seemed cordial enough, despite Emma's mother doing little more than nodding at the couple, Thomas made the request to speak to Emma's father, Charles Gifford, 'in private'. He was duly ushered into his host's study and was but a little way into presenting his credentials, when the older man launched a bitter attack at him.

'I would beseech you to stop there, Mr Hardy. This purpose of this visit was not unexpected, for I have known of your existence, and it was never welcome. You have been presumptuous in coming here thinking that you could marry into my family – a family of considerable standing, a professional family, a family with connections in the church and law. Even if you wrote books that were not unsavoury, which I gather is the case, you are little more than a tradesman, a hack, a low-born churl who is unworthy to presume you have the right to ask for my daughter's hand.'

There was no space for rebuttal, no hint that Thomas would be allowed to speak at all. When he tried at one point to interject into the stream of invective, he was talked down as the older man sallied onwards, his words bruising and contemptuous. The ferocity of the attack, its unexpectedness and sheer persistence, gave him little option other than to take his leave, with the tail ends of her father's words, and finally Emma, flushed and horrified by the exchange, trailing in his wake.

'We do not need his permission, Thomas, we do not!' she cried, half-stumbling, as she attempted to keep up with his striding pace down the pathway. 'He is wrong in this and we will prove him so.'

Thomas said nothing until he had slammed the gate to the house behind him, when, at last, he turned to her, his face ashen.

'Be that as it may, but for families not to sanctify a union bodes ill for any man.'

'Don't say that, Thomas, don't,' she urged.

He turned on her, grasping her firmly by the shoulders, fixing his eyes with hers.

'Then tell me Em, what am I to make of it? The man was more than unreasonable. He seemed unbalanced, like someone possessed.'

Remembering himself, he relaxed his grip and let his arms fall limply to his side.

'I fear he was under the influence too, Em, for he stank of it.'

Emma lowered her head.

'You must tell me, Emma, what I should already have known of your family. For this is not what I expected, not in the least.'

Emma turned away for several seconds, as if gathering the resolve to answer his question, before turning back and looking straight at him.

'I will tell you all I know Tom, for of course you must, although it is not much. One hope's that such intemperance is peculiar to the person afflicted, but it is in my father, I confess. There. It is of no great matter, but I should have told you, nevertheless.'

Thomas stared at her, not sure what to make of the ambiguity in her answer. Her eyes began to redden as tears welled, and he could feel himself soften.

'There, there, Em, it is of no matter. It is you and I that plan to marry, not our families,' he reassured her. 'They are of no consequence.'

With that, he took her hand and led her down the path, away from the house. She could see Thomas was upset, and while the hurt was his own, she felt equally diminished by her father's exchange. They wended their way back to Lavinlet along the Saints' Way, arm in arm. No words passed between them, only the spirits of both, crucified by the sentence that her father had passed upon the couple.

Chapter Six

MR AND MRS HARDY

It was a subdued pair of erstwhile lovers who made their way back to St. Juliot's after the savage attack by Emma's father, unsure of the welcome they would receive. As it transpired, on hearing of the unpleasant confrontation, Caddell was sympathetic to their plight, and quickly made it clear that they did not hold with the sentiments of Mr Gifford in any shape or form.

Indeed, as a public show of support, Caddell invited Thomas to read a lesson in the partially refurbished Church the following Sunday. Helen, meanwhile, was quietly solicitous to them both, and although she excused their father's reaction as a result of the stress he suffered following his own personal circumstances, she seemed to Thomas to be less sympathetic towards him, and decidedly less comfortable with his presence there, than she had previously been.

For Emma, the entire visit had been galling. The humiliation of Tom by her father had embarrassed her deeply, and she was both ashamed of him having let her down so deeply, and wary now, that Tom would suspect the lurking instability in father, since his irrational outburst. She had heard that her father had been re-admitted to the Asylum the previous year after suffering from hallucinations and delusions, but her mother had recently written to her, assuring he was well again, when he was patently not. Yet it was Thomas who was most subdued. Despite the constancy and gentle encouragement she offered him for her father's behaviour, she could not explain it without betraying her father's state of mind, and the threat of contagion lurking in the Gifford blood.

When they parted in the middle of September, both were quiet and downcast. Emma knew the falsehood that lay beneath her father's aggressive words, and yet said nothing to appease her suitor. Tom, meanwhile, saw that growing literary reputation amounted to nothing in the face of the social gulf that Emma's family had so crudely identified, one which, it appeared, no measure of literary success would diminish, in their eyes.

With the publication of *Under the Greenwood Tree*, and the serialisation of *A Pair of Blue Eyes*, Thomas had at last acquired the confidence to strike out on his own as a writer. His final act had been to turn down the offer of architectural work in London, not long after his return to Dorset and to stow away his bag of surveying tools. It was a risk, he knew, yet before long, his decision was vindicated, with an invitation to contribute to the Cornhill Magazine, from Lesley Stephen. The offer presented Thomas with the recognition he had long sought, and he was quick to accept the commission. He wrote back to Stephen making the tentative offer of a book he had been working on, tentatively called *Far from the Madding Crowd*, in spite of the inevitable pressure the growing number of commissions would place upon him.

He and Emma continued to correspond. He found his letter writing benefitted when he imagined himself penning a scene in a novel, albeit one of rare unbridled affection. His 'bon mots', his promises of affection to her grew more tender and loving for each month apart, and she treasured his letters as promissory notes for the future they had planned together. 'Dear Emma' had become 'Dearest Em' and the restraining walls that had guarded his words were breeched, releasing a wash of emotion.

To make herself indispensible to him, to support him in his work and, in so doing, to demonstrate her love for him, was her calling, Emma felt. Thomas would respond in kind, and their exchange of correspondence built up a precious keepsake – one which they could look back again in time, whenever that time might be.

Thomas continued to work frenetically on the draft of his new novel for the ensuing months, until breaking off his labours to return to St. Juliot for Christmas and New Year, with Emma and the Holders. On Christmas Eve, he and Emma walked out to the lookout on the southern mouth of Boscastle Harbour, overlooking Meachard Rock. The walk was difficult, especially for Emma, while they were buffeted by icy winds as they skirted the Eastern Blackapits, grateful that they had wrapped themselves up like mummies.

They said little to each other on the outward leg, for their attention was focused upon safely navigating the difficult terrain. While they sat on the leeward at the lookout, they reflected on the past few months, their mutual silence only occasionally interrupted by a few sparse words. They had both been bruised by their altercation with Emma's father, and had aroused different feelings in each, both guilt and anger, but also a quiet satisfaction that at last Tom was able to sustain himself by his writing. Tom was rightly inclined to see the success as his, yet he was not blind to the part Emma had played in encouraging and supporting him, when others had not. It was Emma who had stood by him and extolled him to 'write, Tom, write.' He resolved he would acknowledge her help, he decided, by a foreword in some future book, some generous attribution, for she deserved such an acknowledgement.

Returning to Higher Bockhampton, Thomas immersed himself in his writing and was relieved when he completed the manuscript for *A Pair of Blue Eyes* before the end of the winter. Each day, he set some time aside to write to Emma, and was quietly expectant as the mailman came to the house. He was acutely aware of the irritation his mother felt with the arrival of each letter at the cottage, placing it before him, usually with a curt aside or weary sigh, but her pettiness did not deter him from his correspondence. His mother would have to accept that he was of an age to make his own decisions about matters of the heart, despite the solemnity of the covenant he once had with his mother, and the campaign of passive resistance she waged towards the invisible Emma.

What Thomas could not have surmised, however, was Emma's determination to reach beyond this impasse in their relationship. In order to win over his parents, she instigated a meeting, in an attempt to convince them that she would be an asset to their eldest son.

In early April, Tom decided to travel to London to talk over the final proofs of his manuscript of *Under The Greenwood Tree* with his publishers, the Tinsley brothers. It was the opportunity that Emma had been waiting for, and without a word to Thomas, she resolved to travel to Bockhampton and do what Thomas had shied away from doing himself, which was to introduce herself to his family.

The journey to Higher Bockhampton was long and complicated. She had resolved to travel first to Dorchester, and from there, to send a card requesting permission to visit the following day. While irritated by the effrontery of the woman and deeply resenting the impending visit, Jemima curtly acceding to the request. She would not be accused of rudeness, of lacking manners, of anything that might present an opportunity of charging her with being ill-mannered or, worse, ill-bred. Jemima was waiing at the door of the cottage the next day, when Emma turned up at the allotted time.

'Mrs Hardy,' she said when the older woman opened the door, holding out her hand as she did so. 'I'm Emma Gifford.'

Jemima looked at her down the length of her nose and sniffed, 'that I had presumed.' She stood and looked at the young lady sternly. 'Thou best come in then, Miss Gifford, since 'twas so important to come all this way for the purpose.' She stood aside and ushered Emma past before adding dismissively, ''ee must take us as 'ee find us for we are not so grand here.'

Ignoring the older lady's acerbic tone, Emma went into the room, determined not to be thwarted by the delicacy of her visit, or the momentary discomfort she might experience. Having so carefully engineered this moment, she was left standing there before moving over to the window seat and sitting herself down. Mrs Hardy busied herself with the teacups she had laid out neatly for them, before retiring to the kitchen, where she lingered for an inordinate time. Emma waited silently, until the lack of activity encouraged her to look about her at her surroundings.

The interior of the cottage, what little she could see from the window seat, was sparsely furnished. A single sketch, unframed, hung on the wall – Emma guessed it was one of Tom's. The cushions were badly faded, the colour drained from them by years of sun, and the cold stone floors were sloped and irregular. It was, she felt, altogether less refined, less commodious than she had been led to expect by her conversations with Tom. Looking beyond the immediate garden, the land was harsh, wilder and less orderly than she had imagined, creating the impression of a greater remoteness than was real. For a time, she was unnerved by the cottage, by the family it housed, and implicitly, by the contradiction that was Thomas.

Eventually, Mrs Hardy returned with a teapot and quietly poured the two cups, before addressing her.

'Well, Miss Gifford. What brings 'ee here if not to lay claim for my boy's success?'

'That is not so, Mrs Hardy. But you will know we have been corresponding for some time now and that Tom has asked my father for my hand.'

Jemima started. Thomas had not mentioned this development. In fact, he had avoided speaking of Emma as much as possible, not wanting to feed his mother's prejudices.

'And the father of thee? Am I to assume he'd agreed to this?' Emma shifted uneasily in the seat in which she had been placed.

'Well no, he did not. But he was only wanting to establish that Tom could look after me.'

Jemima stared at the young lady.

'So thou hast travelled this distance to tell me that in the eyes of your father, my Tom is not good enough for 'ee?'

Emma's started to feel even more uncomfortable. This was not going as she had intended. The woman was going to be difficult, that much was evident.

'No, Mrs Hardy, that is not what he meant.'

'Well then spit it out girl. Do you think me dunch or somewhat? What t'was it he meant?'

'Only that he wanted Tom to be able to support me, that's all.'

Jemima sniffed again, only more loudly.

'And thee would be an expensive one to keep, I'd venture,' she said. She stared at Emma, unnerving the younger woman. 'Being not from these parts 'ee would not fit in well here. What's more,' she started, looking the younger woman up and down, 'I fancy thee might find us less than 'ee imagined. No doubt you wouldn't be here if 'ee weren't so needy yourself as to depend on Tom's writings.'

Emma's resolve to maintain a manner of decorum was starting to waver.

'Mrs Hardy, my purpose in coming here was to introduce myself to you, to request that you see me as one Tom has chosen as a close and dear friend.'

Jemima glared at her. 'What nonsense 'ee talks! He has chosen others before thee and younger ones too I would venture.' Emma started to rise in her chair, puce with anger, but before she could say anything, Mrs Hardy rose too, higher and quicker and spoke over her.

'I think thou might say the visit is over, Miss Gifford. See, Thomas is of like mind and doesn't agree with marriage. He has his family here to help him – and for him to help, in turn. He might have chosen thee as 'ee might say, or thee might have chosen him, but be careful if thee thinks he'll always be thine, for you will see he is fickle too.'

With that, it was evident that any hopes for a productive meeting were over. Emma was ushered to the door only to be met by someone she assumed was Tom's father, who removed his cap, smiled benignly at her as he passed, and walked into the house past Jemima, without a word being spoken.

When Tom heard of the visit he was aghast. 'What madness persuaded you to call on my parents, like this, without me knowing of it?'

Emma was as shaken by the intensity of his consternation, as she had been by the hostility and unpleasantness of the confrontation with his mother. 'It was time, Thomas, it was time she met me and I was right to call.' She looked at him, accusingly. 'There was no point waiting for you to organise for such a thing to happen. What choice did I have, Tom? You have shown no desire to have me visit, as if you are ashamed of my company.'

'Of course not, Emma. It is just that was no way to meet my mother for the first time. She doesn't like things happening that are not in the natural order of things.'

'There is no natural order with you, Tom, or her, I'd venture. Moreover, if I'd waited for you, there would have been no first time, or second or third. That much is evident.'

'That is unfair. There would have been a time. . .'

'I think not. She was lying in wait for me and had time enough to prepare herself.'

'It sounds as if you felt the sharp end of her tongue, Emma. She is not one for exercising reason in matters where the emotions are stirred.'

Emma hesitated. 'I would say she was unreasonable, not wanting to listen to me. But I suspect it was the shock of me calling on her when she had clearly been kept in the dark about how close we had grown. It seems that someone had not bothered to tell her.' She glared at Tom. 'It is not so important for the future. I don't doubt she will come round when she sees how happy we are together.'

'You should know, Emma, that my mother is not one for turning, although she is not as unreasonable as you seem to think her.' He paused before adding by way of closure, 'You should not have gone.'

Despite his protestations, Emma was right in suspecting that Tom was in no hurry for her and his mother to make an acquaintance. She had made a grave error in judgement by calling, he felt, and had made his imminent time at home rather more difficult. What Emma could not appreciate, and what Tom found so difficult to communicate was that his mother was not likely to ever approve of Emma or, for that matter, of anyone else, nor even countenance the suggestion of marriage for her dearest and oldest boy.

While outwardly defending her actions to Tom, Emma had silently reproached herself for making the visit. They faced the unfortunate position that two parents now, one of each set, had lined up against them. But there was also another feeling that ran through her as a consequence of the visit, one which she could not vanquish; it was the feeling of isolation, of rural poverty, of how different the Hardy family was from hers. The dwelling, which had originally been a two-up, two-down cob and thatch cottage, now appended, was set on the edge of the heath, surrounded by untidy woodland and was as rustic as the father she had glimpsed briefly at the door. And yet, it was his mother that had cast the longest shadow. While short in stature, with dark hair parted strictly down the middle of her large head, her strong features and dark weather-beaten face housed the distinctive sharp eyes and even mouth of her son. Yet there was a malevolent feeling exuding from the older woman, some dark, brooding spirit that unsettled Emma. She was thankful that, in his inheritance, Tom had been spared a good deal more than his mother's pronounced Roman nose, for, as Emma reflected, he was as modern and civil as she was coarse and feudal. But she also remembered that Thomas was her son and the ties of blood were close, fuelled as they were by the vapours of the same heath. So overpowering was Jemima's bearing, that Emma had confessed she had no wish to meet her again under such circumstances, and never without Tom by her side to shield her from the prejudices of his vindictive and overbearing mother.

For the next few months, Thomas flitted between Dorchester and London, and, when visiting his childhood friend, Horace Moule, further afield to Cambridge. During these long weeks apart, their courtship was again confined to a trade of letters, imbuing each word, each phrase, with an extra turn of meaning that transcended the literal. It was a nervous time for Emma for whatever else she had gleaned of Thomas, his propensity for being turned by a pretty face had not escaped her.

In June, they met again, this time in Bath, where Emma had gone to stay with an elderly spinster friend of her family. After a few days spent on her own exploring the Roman remains of the city, Tom joined her, having first sent part of his manuscript to Stephen, the publisher.

Each night, Emma was signed in and out by her aged chaperone, who was punctilious in carrying out her charge. During the days they wandered, both within the Georgian town and further afield, going as far as Tintern Abbey, where Thomas responded to her persistent request to read Wordsworth to her. Solitude and time together, they found, was not easy to find, and they talked, as ever, of promulgating their clandestine engagement, though Thomas felt far less urgency than Emma to do so. He was not sure why he felt so little enthusiasm. Away from her natural habitat in the West Country, Emma seemed altogether more ordinary, and he found himself glancing at her more than once, wondering what it was that had drawn him to her, for he could see more clearly than previously that she was no beauty. Such a notion, he knew, was cruel and disloyal, and he rebuked himself for thinking so, but it would not undo the thought.

With writing now his sole source of livelihood, Thomas returned home to continue working on his draft of *Far from the Madding Crowd*. He was shaken by the suicide of his dear friend Horace, so soon after their previous meeting in Cambridge, and had felt strangely distanced from his dead friend's family, when they gathered at the grave outside the small parish church at Fordington for the committal. He had admired Horace's scholarship and wit, but it niggled at him now, at the closure, that they had never talked as equals, and this early death would prevent this from ever happening. Someone he had so wanted to impress was gone. But there were others, he was sure, who he could yet impress and he determined to do so.

Before Christmas, he travelled once again to St. Juliot to see Emma, but the circumstances of the visit were far from comfortable. There had been a discussion before his arrival, and while the subject was unknown to him, the mood in the Vicarage was prickly and uncomfortable. It took some time to pry the cause out of Emma, and even then she would only say that her sister, her very own dear sister, was telling her she could not live there year on year, as if she was part of their marriage. She had now formally asked for her intentions.

She looked at Hardy and spoke sharply at him.

'What could I say, Tom Hardy, other than it is your intentions that determine such things, not mine.' She glared at him. 'And while they might think I should know your intentions, in truth, I do not.'

Her emphases were clear and pointed. Thomas could only respond by reaching out a soothing hand, which she declined to acknowledge.

'I know, my dear, that I have been too busy, and have not been as attentive to you as I should.' He looked at her, but she averted his gaze. His hand still lay passively on hers as if resting on a stone, cold and inanimate. More. He needed to say more.

'We will marry this year, if you would like it so.'

'Is this your idea of setting a date for a wedding, Mr Hardy? If so, it is a clumsy one and does not reflect well on the recipient.'

'We will – forget the other words – we will marry. I promise.'

Emma waited for a respectful length of time, before answering him.

'Then so be it. It is time for some metamorphosis, Tom, time to present ourselves to those who know, but one part of the whole, to show that your magic is ours, that we are as Browning and Barrett, indivisible in your work and your imagination.'

Tom started. He had never thought of them like this. How could he? It was pure folly to intertwine all aspects of lives thus. Was this what his mother had always warned him of, such thoughts as these? What was Emma thinking of with her colourful imagination? Darkly, he thought, not altogether unkindly, whether this is what riding on the cliff tops alone in inclement weather had done for her.

He left soon after, for he had pledged to have Christmas at home. Before he left, he agreed to marry in the summer, once the arrangements could be made. The vexed question of their families was allowed to lie there, unspoken, though in his eagerness, Tom spoke of travelling to the continent with the idea of beginning a new family.

Emma soon followed, not to Dorchester, for she would never countenance that again, even if the world would. Instead she headed out to the Sergeants in Lavinlet, and once her welcome there was exhausted, to her brother, Henry, in London, in turn. Helen's irritation had spilt over when she questioned Emma after Tom had gone, and words were said which rendered the subsequent breach, in Emma's mind, irreparable.

Thomas, meanwhile, had returned to Dorset and was thrust into a test of his resolve when he attended a local wedding to find Tryphena sitting across the table from him. 'How youthful she looks', he thought, 'how dark and pretty, and beguiling,' and all his resolutions were undone as he spent the evening trying to woo her. Nor was it she alone who distracted him, for he found himself reminiscing about Cassie Pole, with whom he had once flirted with shamelessly, Liza Nicholls, another serious subject of affection, and several others, local girls mainly. More recently he had enjoyed more sophisticated company in the City, through his connections with Stephen and Tinsley. Even his illustrator, Helen Paterson, whom he met but once, fell to being the subject of his fantasies. His imagination was that of a precocious and overexcited youth, he told himself, and he knew that each visitation, each silhouette, meant nothing beside Emma, who was an educated woman, armed with ideas and bearing and a varied and extensive general knowledge. He could not resist comparing each to Emma, though often, it would seem, it was not always in his beloved's favour.

Emma was almost 34 years old when she and Thomas married although he thought her younger. It was an age that for some women may have signalled the turning of the seasons, and Thomas thought her much changed from the young lady riding along the edge of Beeny Cliff, four years previously. He wondered, as he waited, just how well he knew her. Which Emma was real, this rather bland and unprepossessing woman now standing beside him, who he hardly recognised, or some woman he had had spent four years creating in his imagination, some ideal he could no longer conjure up? Perhaps all men thought like this at such moments?

Emma's brother, Henry, with whom she had been staying in London, attended the service at St Peter's Church in Paddington, and the ceremony was conducted by Emma's uncle, Canon Edwin Gifford. From Thomas's family, there was no one. While the sky was soft and luminous, the church, by contrast, was grey, dank and cold, and the Kentish Ragstone disease that was tearing at the structure of the building, seemed to afflict them too. Emma glanced at Thomas as the vows were spoken, but he was implacable, grave beyond measure, intent only on seeing the matter through. It was hardly a propitious start for the newly married couple.

Chapter Seven

SHE CHANGED ME

The full realisation of what marriage would mean became evident to Thomas, as soon as he picked up the pen to the sign the registry. Three years before, Thomas recalled when he had been at St. Juliot when the census had been taken, and as he and Emma filled in their forms together he had distinctly noted, with a lover's natural curiosity, that she had entered her age as being 25 years. And yet here, in the sanctified body of the Church, Emma entered her birth date as 24th November 1840, making her a mere six months younger than he.

Immediately after the ceremony, the discrepancy having preyed on his mind throughout, Thomas asked her in a whisper the year of her birth. She replied, 'why, as you have seen it written. What an odd question to ask at your wedding.'

The proceedings allowed for no further conversation however. They sat down to a wedding breakfast with Emma's uncle and her brother, before taking a hansom cab to the Palace Hotel where they were to spend their wedding night. The realisation that something may not have been as he had supposed it to be, had begun to eat away at Thomas and he was restless and on edge, once they were alone. Later that evening in their hotel, the two of them sat perched upon the edge of the bed, neither seemingly inclined for the usual wedding night meanderings. They remained so for several minutes, silent and fully clothed, as if the significance of the day had exhausted them.

Tom knew that he had to have the conversation that was welling up inside him, although he was unsure how to begin without upsetting his new bride. Eventually, in a soft, ingratiating voice, he turned to her to ask. 'Emma, three years ago, you filled in a census form stating your age as 25 years. I was there – do you not remember? How do explain the date you have now put onto our marriage certificate?'

Emma seemed nonplussed by his question.

'You must know Tom, that women are too often judged by their age, and not by who they are. It is not that extraordinary,' she insisted. 'Who knows if we would be here, if you had thought me six years older than you did then.'

'But a census form is an official document, Emma, for goodness' sake, not something to be trifled with for the sake of vanity.'

'It is not a vanity. It is what was needed to be done. Can you say, hand on heart, we would have been here if you had known? You, with your eye for younger women!'

'That is unfair Emma, and no way to talk on our wedding night. It is crude to talk in such a manner.'

'Then realise I did it for you, Tom.'

'But six years, Emma. Six years. What do I know of those six years?'

Emma stared at him, her complexion reddening.

'What indeed, Tom, do you know about anything?' She continued stubbornly. 'You have always preferred to answer questions than to ask them. That is the way of men. When did you ever ask me my age? Each birthday, did you ever wonder to ask me?'

'Ask you?' Thomas was baffled and infuriated. 'Why should I ever have asked you, when I had seen it written with my own eyes?'

Her response gave him no ease. 'Because you should have shown more of an interest in me, and not trusted something I would write on some form or other. You should have been curious, you who profess to know women. Besides,' she paused momentarily, 'you should be pleased that I look six years younger than I am.'

But her reply did not satisfy Tom. He simply did not agree with her. She didn't look younger, she had never looked younger, but simply acted as if she were. And he felt stung, as if he had been the unwitting dupe of a conspiracy. He wondered what other duplicities she had committed without him knowing.

After a brief sojourn in Brighton, their trip to Rouen and Paris was a strangely muted affair. Emma found the city picturesque, but seemed as interested in what the Parisians thought of her, as she was in the city. The shops, the markets, the Seine and its brightly adorned river boats charmed her, and she would set out early each day walking along the extensive boulevards, before returning several hours later. She dressed extravagantly, with considerable colour and finery, as she imagined Parisians to do, and was pleased to see heads turn as she passed. She realised, however, that Tom was less enthusiastic about the extravagance of her appearance, although even when she wondered aloud about whether or not a particularly flamboyant hat made her more picturesque, she could not sense her own incongruity, amongst the 'pygmy-like' Parisians she saw working in the streets.

Emma visited the Church of Notre Dame alone, lighting a candle for her and Thomas. She walked endlessly throughout the heart of the City, while Thomas went off, in order, as he told his new bride, to gather some material for his next story. It was as a newly married couple, however, that they visited the Cimetière du Pere-Lachaise. They stood by the tomb or more accurately, as Thomas pointed out, the monument to Abelard and Heloise, each thinking private thoughts on the lovers' fates. Emma wanted to see Chopin's tomb and that of Gericault, for she had earlier seen his painting 'The Raft of the Medusa', in the Louvre, standing ceremonially beside each, as if thinking of some circumstance relating to their interment. Yet Thomas realised with a sudden start that in fact he had no idea of what she may have really thought. Nor, he acknowledged truthfully, was he interested enough in her thoughts at this moment to warrant the question.

The city remained stiflingly hot throughout their stay. Having exhausted the most popular sights, Emma was more than a little nonplussed by being taken on their last day, to *la morgue*. As they travelled there by carriage, the streets grew so ripe with the stench, of horses, of rotting food, of the perspiring throngs, that it was some relief to enter the cool morgue. To Emma's horror though, she was confronted by an array of dead bodies aligned neatly on marble slabs.

'Tom, why have you brought me here?' she hissed as they entered a room. Several corpses were laid out before them, naked.

'It is to help give authenticity with my writing,' Thomas answered, unconvincingly. 'It would be unusual if I didn't write on the dead sometimes, and accuracy is so important.' He looked at Emma and saw she was quite pale.

'I am sorry to have shocked you, Emma. I hadn't thought it would be so graphic,' he apologised.

They stood looking down upon the naked body of an elderly man. His pockmarked and scarred corpse gave every indication of a destitute life.

'It is not offensive, Tom. Just repulsive, that's all.' She peered closer at the body. 'To think we will all end up like this, stripped of our clothes and dignity.' She shuddered. 'What a strange thing for a husband to show his new bride. It is as if you wanted me to see intimidations of my own mortality. I fear being haunted by it all, Tom, I do.'

Tom shuffled awkwardly. 'It was not thoughtful of me to bring you here my dear.' He led her outside, steering her towards a teashop where they enjoyed their remaining hours in Paris.

London, on their return, was grey and damp, and Emma took time to adjust to the transformation that was about to become her married life. She had been without a set domicile for the past nine months, but wherever she had been, it had been with family, her family. More importantly, she had felt comfortable and secure; now she was to set up home in the City, away from their natural habitat of the west of England with a man she only partially knew. She feared the effect that geography would have upon them.

They spent several days looking for somewhere suitable to live, before finding a house in Surbiton. With enough countryside about it, Emma could happily raise the possibility of sending for her beloved mare, Fanny, that she had reluctantly left with her sister. Thomas was adamant that this was not the time, and insisted she wait until they were more settled. Perhaps, he suggested, when they returned to the West Country. Instead, he exhorted Emma to enjoy the life of the City, to visit the galleries and the great museums, and to learn to be a wife who would care for and support him, as his own mother had done for his father. But while her visit to Higher Bockhampton should have warned her that she would be expected to cope alone and look after her new husband, this was not the life Emma had imagined for herself.

The very idea of washing and cooking for Thomas she felt to be completely abhorrent. Her resistance to the idea eventually forced Thomas to re-think his expectations, and he employed an elderly servant, who Emma immediately busied herself organising about, to the great irritation of both

Thomas and the servant. It was clear to Thomas, that the servant knew far more about domestic life than Emma. Likewise, the servant resented this 'foreign' woman with an accent, presuming she didn't know her duties.

Despite this, and other teething problems common to any couple in the early throes of marriage, she and Thomas began to establish some sense of routine to their lives, which suited them both. It represented a tenuous accord on which to build their marriage.

Tom had soon caught up with the contacts he had previously made in the city and was about to add another important name to his list. One day, while lunching at the Savile Club, he met another West Country man, whose company he quickly warmed to. Edmund Gosse had recently published a collection of poetry, and was talking with a number of literary friends beside a blazing fire. He spotted Thomas and came over to him, his hand fully outstretched.

'Mr Hardy, sir.' Thomas looked up from his newspaper, before standing and squaring up to the stranger, taking the man's somewhat flaccid hand as he did so.

'Edmund Gosse, at your service,' at which the man gave a slight bow, which could have been interpreted as gently mocking, were it not for the solemnity of the voice behind the introduction. 'I am an admirer of your writing, Mr Hardy, and wanted to take this opportunity to say so in person.'

Thomas looked at the man suspiciously, but having sat down again, her motioned for Mr Gosse to take the seat beside him. They conversed easily, especially after finding that both companions were fellow West Country men. After an hour, the two men had formed a fledgling friendship, given weight by their mutual determination to see each other again. Edmund had just married and both men saw that in each other's wives there was an opportunity for a wider friendship, and a means of appeasing their own conscience for going about their own business, especially one which might seem rather less strenuous at private luncheons and clubs. Instead they could feel safe, in the knowledge that their wives would also have companions of their own to entertain. Whether the two women might welcome such a contrivance or even have anything in common, did not occur to either man, both seeing the natural extension of their own friendship to the wives as a natural thing, and a gift to both.

Emma and Thomas spent Christmas alone in London, save for a visit from Emma's brother, Walter. Early in the New Year, they moved nearer to Westbourne Grove, in the heart of the city. The weather was cold, the sky army blanket grey and more than a little depressing, challenging their flagging spirits. The mutual accommodation demanded by marriage which would, over time, create a shared identity, seemed some way off. Neither Thomas nor Emma found compromise easy, and as they discovered more about the other, the frustrations that had seeped into their consciousness served only to build walls, not break them.

'This is not the life I'd have thought we'd be leading, Thomas,' she would say to him accusingly, at times adding, 'and not one a lady should have to accept. You chose to marry up, Thomas, and we should raise our standards accordingly.' Thomas could only mutter something about learning to live within their means and that she should be patient with him, while urging her to send a letter of invitation to meet with Nellie.

'What, and let her know how we live, Thomas?'

'One doesn't have to do that Em. You can meet in the city at one of the tea shops near the Museum.'

But Emma was not to be persuaded. 'Not yet, Tom,' she would answer, 'it is too soon for that. Besides, I am not at all sure I like London, or that I would want to make friends here, whom I would have to then abandon. Sometimes it is better not to make the effort in the first instance, than to let someone down later. Besides, you have only just met this man, and I am sure Mrs Gosse – your Nellie – has more interesting people than me to spend her time with, despite what you two might suppose.'

'I just want you to have friends here, Emma,' he resigned. 'Give it some thought, when you feel more settled. It is no good being solitary, with me out all day.'

'But I do have a friend Tom. You, you are my friend. That is why we married, surely. And I am your partner in your work also, ready to help like I did before, would you let me.'

Thomas shivered, involuntarily. Had he not thought what marriage meant before entering into it? Did he not realise the permanence of it, the restrictions it would inevitably bring to his life, the caveats and conditions implicit in becoming a husband? Did he not see that things would now have to be considered, shared, discussed and that he might not always like the outcome? Did he not see that he would have to share his emotions, his thoughts, his time, and most of all, his time? He almost choked as he answered himself. No, he did not.

They had not long settled into their new domicile with their rather meagre possessions scattered about them, before Thomas felt the need to attempt to seek to reconcile himself with his family, who had been aggrieved by the surreptitious nature of his marriage. He had not seen his parents or his brother and sisters since his wedding to Emma, and before picking up his pen once more, he resolved to make the trip as soon as the weather improved.

With preparations duly made, they took the train to Dorchester, staying at the King's Arms Hotel. They were uncertain of the welcome they might receive at Bockhampton. Tom was confident of winning around his father and his siblings, but wary of his mother's truculence. Still, he knew, or hoped rather, that she would come round. He could only trust that, now the event was passed, she would accept what had transpired with good grace.

Having settled into their room, soon after seven, Tom and Emma made their way to the dining room. They had not long settled at their table when three young ladies entered the dining room, and seeing Tom, came bustling over to him.

'Tom,' exclaimed the first of their number, 'what brings you back here?'

There was an awkward pause. It was immediately evident to Emma that the visitation at their table discomforted her husband. He had no option but to stand up and introduce Emma as his new bride.

News of their marriage, apart from a brief note that had gone largely unnoticed in the Dorset County Chronicle, had not passed readily around the district, even amongst family. Jemima had resolved it was of no matter to local folk, and had not even told her sister, so the information given to the young ladies was greeted with surprise and excitement. Emma, however, could not fail to notice that the dark, coquettish girl, who had been first to approach the table, blushed and fell silent at the news, before quickly recovering herself and offering her congratulations to them both. Even as she did so, Emma, with the keen observation of the newly-wed, noted that her eyes rested on Tom longer than they ought. She resolved to find out more of this young woman.

'And who were they?' asked Emma after they had moved over to occupy a table across the dining hall.

' Two of them are cousins of mine, ' said Thomas hurriedly, 'so just family.' He stopped as if considering how much he needed to say. 'We knew them as children.'

'And the one called Phena, was she one of the cousins, or was she perhaps not family?'

Tom coloured at hearing Phena's name, but was relieved by having an answer he could give her quite honestly.

'No, she is a cousin, although she is much younger than me. She was a friend of Kate, I think, and of the same age, near about.'

'And Kate, how old is Kate?'

'You test a man with such questions! Twenty-three, or twenty-four, or thereabouts.'

'Not much younger than the woman you supposed me to be, then.'

'A little.' Tom was disconcerted by her questions, and wished she would stop.

'And cousins, country cousins, can be familiar, so I hear.' She paused, before concluding to Tom's relief, 'Although in this instance, I agree, you are a little old for her.'

And with that she laughed out aloud, dissipating the tension that had been mounting, question by question. Nearby diners paused to turn and stare at her. But it had discomforted Tom, of that she had no doubt, and while she felt it prudent to draw the conversation to a close, Thomas doubted whether that would be the end of the matter.

The next day they set out for the cottage at Bockhampton by hackney cab, where they were to join the family for lunch. Mr and Mrs Hardy were there to greet them, and they were soon joined by Tom's younger sister Kate, and his brother Henry. While the conversation was amiable enough, with Kate asking many questions of them both, Mrs Hardy was watchful and said nothing. Thomas Senior was likewise subdued, but, Emma deduced, accurately enough, this was only his normal state of being. No wonder, she thought, being married to Jemima.

After lunch, Thomas proposed a walk in Thorncombe Woods, a suggestion readily taken up by Kate and Henry. Emma, however, felt her lameness would hold the others up, and decided not to join the three siblings. Instead, she offered to stay and keep his parents company. It was a decision that made Thomas feel uncomfortable, for he feared what could transpire by leaving the two strong willed women together, but there was little to be done about that, other than to shorten their route, and reduce the time they would be left alone.

Jemima ushered Emma back into the house as the siblings departed, and sat her in the sitting room while she busied herself clearing away the lunch. Emma looked desperately for something to read, anything to amuse her, but in the end resigned herself to sitting in uncomfortable silence, aside from the noises of domesticity emanating from the next room. After what seemed a considerable period of time, however, Jemima reappeared at the door.

'Perhaps you would like to get outdoors and sit in the garden, Miss Gifford, rather than stay trussed up in here, which I venture is not as much space as you are used to.'

Emma was determined not to be drawn by any such thinly veiled comments.

'Thank you, Mrs Hardy,' she countered. 'I think that a good idea,' and gathering herself up, made her way to the door, conscious that Jemima was following her out. She sat herself down in the small garden seat, only yards from the cottage, but, looking out towards the forest and heath, it felt as if a much greater shift had occurred.

'So, you managed, Miss Gifford, to press the case for marriage.' Ee know I think it folly?'

Emma answered, choosing her words carefully.

'Then I hope we will prove you wrong.'

'That I doubt, Miss Gifford.'

Emma looked at her adversary, before asking as calmly as she could.

'Why do you persist in calling me Miss Gifford, when you know we are now married?'

'Because there be only one Mrs Hardy, and that be me. It is not a name we share in the house.'

Silence. Emma bit her tongue and sat there, knowing better than to react to the old woman.

'Best you know I've been Mrs Hardy for nigh on forty years, and I don't see a reason to share my good name with an upstart such as 'ee.'

She was angry – they were both angry – but Emma could not allow herself to be drawn into further acrimony. She had something she needed to ask, the reason for her contrivance – and so she chose to ignore the insult.

'Mrs Hardy, may I ask you about Tom's cousins.'

Jemima fixed on her, with grey beady eyes.

'What cousins do you speak of, Miss Gifford? We are country folk and have more than enough to choose from, should thee wish.'

'We met one of them at dinner last evening. She was called Tryphena Sparks.'

Jemima said nothing for a moment.

'Phena. You met our Phena. How strange.'

'Strange?'

'Strange that it was her that ye met on the first night since your wedding, she who could have been you.'

'I do not understand.'

''Tis best you don't, Miss Gifford, 'tis best you don't. Let us just say she and Tom were very comfortable friends, for being cousins.'

Emma stared at her, trying to measure the mischief in the mother's eyes, but before she could ask another question, they heard the sound of the gate opening, and the walkers coming up the path. Mrs Hardy scurried off to put the kettle on the hob before they returned to town.

Emma was shaken by what she had been told, although she knew how biased her mother-in-law's views of her were. How much truth lay in it? Some, no doubt. And what to do with it?

She would wait. She resolved to do nothing. She would not charge Thomas for an explanation when she had only half-truths. Besides, she knew, he would deny anything his mother told her, and she did not want them to be caught in a place between truth and falsehood. But, nevertheless, she became more watchful and less trusting, as if waiting for the time when such misalliances might rise up again, and she would need to speak out.

Their time in London was brief, only long enough for Tom to gather material he needed for his next book, to which he had given the working title of *The Hand of Ethelberta*. In the early summer, they moved back to Swanage on the Dorset coast. They had intended to spend a few days enjoying the fashionable seaside resort of Bournemouth, but it rained continuously. By the time they reached Swanage, their spirits were well and truly dampened, while they took their lodgings in a small cottage above the town.

They had been married less than nine months, yet for some reason neither could quite understand, their life together had not been the harmonious union both had expected. Just why they had grown quite so distrustful and suspicious of the other's emotions, Emma could not comprehend. Perhaps, it was the adjustment still lacking in their relationship, for two to become one, that lay at the heart of it. She had helped him as she could early on by editing, researching, discussing, and at those moments, they worked with one accord, but then he would force a distance between them, and put his work out of her reach. It was a slight that ate away at her.

She wrote too. It was not as he wrote, but she had stories of her own and excellent powers of observation, and she felt that the manuscript she wrote whilst in Swanage merited Tom's encouragement. But when she placed it before him expectantly, hoping for some comment, some small gobbets of praise, none were forthcoming.

There were further signs that they could not be happy together. Tom was an exacting taskmaster, and his growing reputation did not make him an easier husband. Tom's impatience with her was exacerbated when they travelled, as his own, carefully drawn up itinerary paid scant attention to either her, or to them as a couple, always attempting to do more than was sensible or possible.

The couple moved on once again, from Swanage to Yeovil, for a matter of weeks before, almost immediately, setting up a house in Sturminster Newton, overlooking the River Stour. After so many changes of address, Emma hoped it would be the start of a more settled period in their lives, a time to put down roots. But for Thomas, impatient and singular of purpose, and grappling with insecurity, he saw, in both himself and Emma, two souls wrestling to understand the charge needed to set their lives right.

Chapter Eight

THE LATICE-GLEAM

Emma and Tom had rented Rivercliff Villa, with the serious intention of settling down for an indeterminate period of time. Having established themselves, Emma proceeded to furnish the household from scratch, on the back of the excellent sales of *Under the Greenwood Tree*, watched on by her nervous husband. At last, she had her own domain, distant enough from London and Bockhampton. It was a place where should look ahead to the future with greater optimism, and she felt confident they could grow their marriage here.

The villa offered generous space, with the lush and luminescent mead, full of kingcups and buttercups, stretching down below from the house towards the river. Moorhens moved along the banks, while swallows darted overhead, criss-crossing the cornea. Though the house was tacked onto the edge of a country town, it faced westwards and away, towards the river and the open pastures beyond. On a summer's evening, Emma could sit on the lawn outside the villa and watch the sun's transit some hundred miles or more to the west, as it dropped inexorably into an imaginary sea, where she had once ridden the western cliffs. She visualized it, embellishing and romanticising it, though she knew it was only an imaginary landscape, its horizon ever-shifting. Place was always better perceived at a distance and Cornwall's redeeming feature, it's *only* redeeming feature was where she had met Tom. Any other affinity to the land, the clear translucent air, the vicarage where she had lived for several years, the wild Atlantic waters, was incidental, a by-product of this attachment. There was nothing else that really mattered, and certainly not this framed landscape.

Occasionally, in the early days, she and Tom rowed on the river and strolled about the small market town, exploring each shop and side street, searching out the curiosities, both human and inanimate. Later, they were taken under the wing of the local gentry, the Dashwoods, who imparted to them a degree of self-importance that was not really appropriate in this rural backwater, but which they wore proudly nevertheless.

Once they were settled in their surroundings, Tom set up a study for himself and set to work writing. He began the manuscript of *The Return of the Native* while Emma busied herself about him. Tom's proprietary approach to his writing had increased in proportion to his growing sales, and he had less inclination to ask for her help although she continued to read his daily output, offering her advice where she saw fit. Emma was left, for much of each day, at something of a loose end. With the extra time on her hands, Emma resolved to resume her riding, and looked to the possibility of reclaiming her old mare, but on enquiry she found it had become very lame and subsequently been put down. The news, imparted to her by her estranged sister, disturbed her deeply.

Undeterred, she tried to hire a horse, but meeting with little success and with no encouragement from Tom, she eventually gave up. Instead she wrote. She sketched. She dreamt. Yet the detachment from her husband, her sudden irrelevance to his work, left her discontented. The assistance she had given to the earlier proofs had been so considerable, that she had expected rather more than a mere acknowledgement, (and even that was not forthcoming), but some sort of declamation from Thomas. Her contribution placed her as his literary equal, she felt. After all, without her encouragement, he would still be a draughtsman, scared to commit to his writing, as he was, she reflected wistfully, scared to commit to her now.

He worked late into the night. When he came to bed, he was tired; but still, she wondered about his physical needs, which had abated at the very time when they had been granted the privacy to enjoy the companionship so essential between man and wife. Occasionally, there were dim glimmers of the previous physical attraction, but the attention was short-lived and sporadic, and she blamed his lack of passion for their failure to produce children of their own.

Her brothers visited them there, but his family, though considerably nearer, failed to make the effort. They were ones for keeping themselves to themselves, Emma thought, although she wondered if his mother had not poisoned Kate and Henry against her, for she would not expect any less of the old woman.

When they did set out to visit Higher Bockhampton after several months of living in Sturminister Newton, Emma could not help but feel a certain trepidation. This time the visit was cordial and Emma felt relieved to have escaped with not much more than a scalding word from Jemima, though she was not spared of the occasional malevolent stare. She felt both of Tom's younger siblings were well-disposed towards her and they had promised they would write and come to visit them in their riverside villa.

Between her and Tom, little changed. He settled into a routine of writing, starting early each morning, and became oblivious to those around him, and particularly Emma. She had resorted to seeking his attention in ways that he found irritating and even pathetic, but he humoured her outwardly without ever responding to the mood within. Emma's square, almost masculine face had kept its same naïve quizzical look, one that he had found charming at their first meeting, but now her lameness was becoming more accentuated, her form stouter, her face more plain and she seemed, as he looked at her now, greatly changed. At times, when she was not aware of it, he would look at her through damp, misty eyes, and see a young woman in a thin blue dress, drawing him in; on other occasions, he would see an eminently sensible companion, someone who would make sure his life was ordered and whom he could trust to support him. Seldom though, did he see Emma, in his dull soul-swoon, just as she was, lonely and desperate, isolated by a husband who had seemingly forgotten her.

Once his manuscript was finished and sent to his publishers, Thomas hankered for a change. They had enjoyed their time at Sturminster Newton, so Thomas would tell her, as if she needed to be so convinced, but it had not altered them. The sojourn, for that was how their time in the villa had seemed to Emma, had passed without progression, neither untangling the marital cord nor advancing her well-being. It was simply time lost and a subjugation of what she had to offer her husband and that was a great pity. But Thomas knew no such feelings and was already looking beyond Dorset once again. London, his friends told him, was where he should be. There would invitations now, and doors would be open to them. Plenty of rich and respectable people would be ready to fete him. Emma was sceptical.

'This is just Edmund, isn't it, Edmund telling you about life in the City and how exciting it is for him? But we've tried London and found it wanting, Tom. We are not city types, you and I.'

'Nor do we need to be. We can be interlopers and just enjoy what it has to offer us.'

'And what is that, Tom, that we don't have here?'

Tom sighed.

'It is to be with like-minded people, and to enjoy some of the company of my readers.' He paused. 'Surely you would not begrudge me this, Emma?'

And she conceded, she would not, but she worried about the insecurities of her husband and his constant need for approbation. If only he could see that she was enough for him, that they were well-suited together, then they could settle here. But he could not, or would not, see what was obvious to her.

Once they had stored their excess furniture and given a final farewell to the Dashwoods, with whom Emma had developed a keen rapport, Tom and Emma moved to their new London residence in Upper Tooting. His friends were right. Once settled into their new residence, a rather unprepossessing end of terrace house, it was apparent that Tom's literary success had had a dramatic impact upon their social standing in London, opening doors to the newly discovered author and his wife.

Within a few days he had returned to the Savile club, and, encouraged by his friendship with Edmund Gosse, revisited his old haunts and friendships from previous stays in London. He was busy editing the final proofs of *The Return of the Native* while starting to think of his new subject, which he resolved would be set during the Napoleonic Wars.

By the summer, Thomas's daily pattern had been established, writing in the morning, going to his club for lunch and then to the British Museum to research his new book. For Emma, however, there was less to look forward to. With Tom's long absences from the house, a creeping loneliness began to take hold, eating away at her ebbing confidence. They were invited out occasionally and she made arrangements with Nellie Gosse to lunch with her, finding her unexpectedly good company, but the daily absences garnered a cumulative weight that weighed down upon her and left her feeling numb and neglected.

As the summer passed, the cold air gathering in the northern skies had started to descend upon London. With it, fuelled by tens of thousands of fires, the fog also returned and hung oppressively upon their neighbourhood, leaving Emma more often than not, bound to the confines of the house. *The Return of the Native* had been published in November and Tom continued to make his daily trips to the museum, often visiting various publishers or literary friends, while Emma stayed in their damp and draughty house and struggled to keep herself warm. Occasionally she would accost Tom, 'was this worth giving up the villa for?'

Her leading questions, for they were always similar in meaning, were inevitably rhetorical.

'It is for me, Em, if I mean to go on with my writing. I have publishing houses, editors, other writers all within a stone's throw and they are interested in me. It is so important to live in the City. You know, I feel that I can do so much more here.'

'It is for you certainly, Thomas, and I have supported you throughout your writing although, heaven knows, I get precious little support for mine.' She continued, her accusatory rhetoric gathering momentum. 'But you are not writing, Tom, not like you should be, you are busy at playing being a writer and there is a gulf between the two roles, if you would but see it.'

Tom coloured at the suggestion, but he knew she was right. His writing had dwindled to a trickle. He was rather embarrassed to find how much he enjoyed being feted, playing the part of a humble writer at soirees and luncheons, even if his humility was just another cloak he would don as occasion demanded.

Christmas, likewise, was a cold and miserable affair. While they had been invited to spend part of the day with Mrs Proctor, an elderly lady who had befriended them both, and then on to dine with the Stephens, for Emma it was a solitary period, even when the two were bound together by proximity, shivering, in the same bed.

In February, Tom responded to a call from home to visit his father who had been ailing for several weeks. He made the journey alone through the bitter weather that was afflicting the south of England. His absence for more than two weeks left Emma in the house without any companionship and only a thin layer of ice growing upon the inside of the windows to remind her of their apparent penury. This was not what Thomas had promised. Even a visit from her brother, Walter did little to lift her spirits. Not for the first time in their marriage Emma felt abandoned, both by her husband's indifference and by her own parents, who seemed to make little effort to keep in touch with her. While she could never forgive her father for his cruel words to Thomas when he had asked for her hand, she was starting to understand his concerns about whether Thomas's world would be fit for her, and whether he would properly keep her as he had promised.

Her one small pleasure was the correspondence that she had begun with Tom's younger sister Kate, from her visit while in Sturminster Newton. Yet by the summer of 1879, it was through this burgeoning friendship, her first with any of the Hardys, that she was taken back rather unexpectedly to an incident that had taken place on her first visit to Dorchester.

Kate would intersperse her letters with the occasional snippet of family news, assuming, rightly, that Emma would share this with Tom. It was one such piece that caught her eye. 'Do tell Tom that Phena has had a baby girl whom she has called Nessie. I am sure he would like to send the mother and baby a card.'

Emma read it several times, looking for any inference or allusion, anything other than the bland meaning of the words as they appeared on the page. She knew it was trivial to bother with it, but could not resist in telling Tom in such a way as to discomfort him, before relaying his visible embarrassment to Kate.

'Tom seemed rather nonplussed by the news,' she wrote and then, summoning up her courage, she added speculatively with more than a little mischievousness, 'I assume it is because of what went on between them that caused him to look thus.'

Kate's reply was not entirely unexpected, but it shook Emma all the same.

'I didn't mean to embarrass Tom, for as you know, while she and Tom were betrothed, that was all before he had met you and come to his senses. It was all childish stuff really for she was so young and family too, but you would know that for mother told me you had met Phena and knew about her.'

Jemima. She could see the mother's venal words dripping onto the paper through the pen of her daughter. For all her suspicions, for all his denials, the revelations still stung, but not so much as what was written in the next paragraph.

'He was upset for a while when she gave his ring back. I wouldn't have done that, but Phena wanted to. My view is when men give a ring and then change their minds, they deserve to lose it. It was a lovely ring, a really delicate gold band. I'd have kept it, for I would not have had so many scruples as she.'

And as she read the last few sentences, Emma was conscious that her right hand now grasped her own ring finger. Slipping off the wedding ring Tom had given her not eighteen months before, she looked at it carefully before laying it quietly on the sideboard, staring at it with detachment, as if she had seen it for the first time.

When Tom proposed that they should visit Dorchester, the memory of the letter was still raw. While no words had been spoken on the subject, Tom sensed a new hostility, which he could only attribute to Emma's aversion to meeting his mother again. Consequently, he proposed that he went first alone, to Bockhampton, to see his parents before she joined him for a seaside holiday. Emma, with the memory of the letter still resonating, agreed, suggesting that they try Bournemouth again, where they she might feel the salve of time alone. Instead Tom chose to go to Weymouth, unaware of the antagonism that would provoke.

Tom had met her at the station, very much at ease after his time at the busy family home. He led her to the hotel, talking ebulliently, despite the rain which seemed to followed them whenever they ventured to the seaside. Emma was quiet and subdued, the shadows of the town falling across her. She had felt from the moment Weymouth was first proposed that this was not her holiday, but his, his place, his time, and his past that she imagined constantly revealing itself.

After they had supped and retired to their room, Emma could no longer contain herself.

'So, tell me, Tom Hardy, who else you have wooed in Weymouth?' Tom was initially disarmed by the question and answered lightly,

'No-one, of course, my dear. This is our town – it could become one of our special places.'

She stared at him.

'And Phena?'

Tom shivered. This was something new. The tone of voice held a sharp warning. What did she know of Phena?

'Phena?'

'Phena.'

'I met her here a few times. We are cousins, Emma, we met, we walked and talked. She was little more than a child . . . '

'But old enough for you to propose to and goodness knows what else before that. And probably here too, if the truth be known, in this very town you have brought me to, maybe in this very hotel.'

And with that she vigorously pulled the ring from her finger and held it tightly in her hand.

'You have lied to me, Tom Hardy.' With that, she threw the ring at him. 'You have lied to me. And you can keep that too for I'll not have another's cast-off. If you want to stay married to me you'll buy anew.'

Tom was conscious that her raised voice would be heard through the thin walls.

'Emma, Emma, for propriety's sake, be quiet,' he urged. 'This was all before I met you. It was not necessary to relate it to you.'

'Then you should have said nothing other than an untruth when I asked you of her. I'd have respected a silence more than a deceit. But to pass on a ring meant for another is unforgiveable.'

Tom looked at her, aghast, not sure how to slow her stream of invective. His attempts to soothe her were futile. 'Emma, hush, I am sorry if I have hurt you. But it was in the past.'

'What past Tom? What is the past with you, Tom? Even now if I was to forget this – this slur, do you think I don't see you looking at women, at the theatre, when we are out to supper? Do you think me blind and foolish? It is trust, Tom, trust that makes a marriage, and at this moment, I have precious little in you.'

Tom lowered his head. He reached out for Emma's hand, but she shook it away. 'Just go to bed Tom, and leave me alone.'

'Emma, the ring . . .'

She interrupted him curtly, waving her forefinger. 'Do not say anything else, Tom, nothing else, for you will only make matters worse.'

And with that, Tom fell silent.

In the morning, Tom got up early after a restless night. Emma had gone, and he set out for a walk along the promenade in order to find her. Before long, he saw Emma heading towards him and when she neared, she slowed and quietly reached out and took him by the hand.

She looked at him with an air of resignation.

'Let us forget the matter,' she said, and he nodded quietly by way of assent.

He took her hand and leaned forward to kiss her, but she would not countenance him to do so and drew away. She had made her peace and had put the matter to one side, but would give no indication of whether the matter was closed or merely dormant, for she did not know her own thoughts in the matter. It was all Tom wanted to hear, but he would have to wait.

The weather brightened a little for the following days and Emma's mood brightened alongside them. She expected Tom to buy a ring for her the next day, but he said he would do so when they returned to London, for that would be prudent and sensible for the choice she may have. Instead, he implored her that she must wear a ring for respectability's sake, and so she reluctantly restored the damaged item to her finger.

On their fourth day, Tom's mother and father joined them along with his younger brother Henry and sister, Kate. She talked guardedly to Kate, unsure of her part, if any, in the disagreement she had had with Tom. She discerned that Kate had no idea that what she had written in her letters could have caused such distress. Moreover, faced with the family, she was reluctant to let any of the family see any trace of disagreement between her and Tom that they could seize upon, and so they presented as a compatible and contented couple. Even Jemima seemed to be civil to her, though Emma deduced by her comments that Tom had told her of the conversation between them. It had, if anything, greatly amused her.

Returning to London, Tom settled back into his writing. Sometimes, they had the distraction of visitors to tea, usually writers, publishers or academics, and Emma revelled in her role as hostess, invariably speaking proudly of Tom's writing, often to his embarrassment. She busied herself with her Kensington stitch work, and entertained herself with shopping trips into the City as well as the galleries and museum. More often than not, she was left increasingly to enjoy her own company. The theatre was treated with caution as a breeding ground for immorality, and when she and Tom did attend a play, she was always watchful of those about her.

Tom made several visits to Dorset alone to pace out the topography of his next novel 'The Trumpet Major', which he had been busy researching at the British Museum. Since Weymouth, he had tried to be more attentive, more solicitous to Emma and while the need to buy a new ring had apparently been forgotten, he endeavoured to think of her needs. He knew he lacked awareness of others, as was his nature, unless circumstances impelled him to be so. Yet now he found himself more often than not feeling protective of her, when eyebrows were raised in her company. At times she spoke inopportunely, it was true, and he was conscious that she was not as elegant or well-informed as the women who regularly enter-tained them, but she meant well and he would instinctively defend her. She was his wife and surely she could also see that while he was not as attentive as he should be, his intentions were good. At times, he could conjure up Emma, as through a lantern slide, just as he had known her at St. Juliot, but such moments were fleeting and the reality thereafter much too real, for such an elusive image to be sustained.

Thomas made regular trips to Dorset to see his parents, spending more time with his younger brother, Henry. He spoke to him often of moving closer to the family home at Higher Bockhampton and looking for some suitable land on which to build, conversations he deliberately kept hidden from Emma. He had often discussed the idea of moving back closer to Dorchester and while Emma was not adverse to the idea of living somewhere in Dorset, she appealed to Tom to seek their own space, and to ensure they were not in the vicinity of his family, for she feared that could suffocate them. Tom gave her the chance to speak, but he had already made up his mind to follow his own inclinations, confident in the knowledge that, given time, she would eventually come round to see this as a good thing. He could persuade Emma that he needed to reside in the heart of the geography he had created. What he could not admit though, least of all to himself, was that he was acceding to a request from his for-midable mother, to come home.

Tom had finished 'The Trumpet Major' by the early summer and by way of celebration, he and Emma travelled to Normandy. He had earned his success by dint of hard work and her unstinting encouragement. For once, they holidayed with a greater peace than they had ever known since they had married. Sailing back from Boulogne, the realization began to settle upon Thomas that he was now someone who was looked up to, who people wanted to read and listen to, and he was determined to revel in the attention. Emma would just have to put up with it.

Chapter Nine

THE ROAD TO MAX GATE

After their time abroad, Emma and Tom returned to Tooting where Tom resumed his rhythm of writing. With the manuscript for 'The Trumpet Major' safely delivered to his publisher, he had started work on a new novel, 'A Laodicean', which he had subtitled rather enigmatically 'A Story of Today.' To emphasise the modernity of his plot, Tom planned that his main characters would be a photographer and an architect, and had resolved that the plot would feature examples of contemporary technology, set against the traditional doctrines of faith. When he told Emma of his intended subject matter, she was sceptical.

'Why try to write on subjects with which you are not familiar?' she asked him.

'Why, in order to make myself familiar,' Tom replied. 'One does not want to be typecast as a writer of a world that is dying, but one that is modern and vital. Besides,' – and he paused before continuing – 'I am not giving up anything, just adding to what I have achieved already. A belief in science is the future, Emma, not an irrational faith, and I should be writing about it. It is not superfluous, as you can see from your reading, for science is at the heart of the book and is the conduit for the romance around which lives turn and stories are woven.'

Emma's concern lay with more than the risk to his reputation as a writer of rural stories. Her real issue was less with the sudden change of direction that Thomas had taken in order to become 'more modern', but rather, with the title he had chosen for his book, and all that it implied within.

'Why have you called your main character "a Laodicean?"' she had asked him, 'it is a provocative title.'

'Because that is who my heroine will be,' he had answered. 'She will be a woman dogged with self-doubt and uncertainty, when I have fleshed her character out. She will be someone not prepared to take things at face value, without questioning them, especially matters of faith.'

'Someone like you, Tom?' she offered.

He paused. 'Perhaps.'

'Then she is not a heroine,' she answered, 'for to be half-hearted, especially in matters of faith, disqualifies oneself from ever being so.'

As had become increasingly common in discussions between them, Emma won the last word, irking Thomas more than he ever could acknowledge. He reflected that her inclination to pontificate and to take the moral high ground, was an unpleasant trait in her character, one that had become ever more pronounced over recent years.

Despite her reservations about its dubious themes, Emma soon found herself inadvertently taking a greater role in the writing of Tom's latest novel, than in any he had written since *Desperate Remedies,* one which she had helped him with intimately, and so early on in their courtship. Her reasons were hardly propitious. Soon after the publication of *The Trumpet Major,* Thomas's health, already a source of some discomfort, suddenly deteriorated. A doctor diagnosed internal bleeding caused by calculus in the bladder and ordered an immediate period of rest, alarming both Thomas, ever morbid, and Emma, suddenly forced to extend her role from his caretaker to his full-time secretary and scribe.

His concern was, as always for his writing, and his obligations to provide the text of a new novel to Harpers, an American publisher he had recently met and with whom he had placed himself under obligation. While Emma, for her part, was concerned for Tom's health, she felt the illness was not without solace. Removed from the immediate circle he had gathered around him, she became a necessity, as he was dependent entirely upon her.

'Tom,' she had reassured him at the outset, upon the doctor's orders of complete bed rest, 'you must not worry so. We will do things as we once did, together. I will write for you and we will make sure all is in readiness for your publishers.'

And Tom would look at her appreciatively, his dark greenish-black eyes lighting a little, and for a fleeting moment, he would imagine the gentle rhythms of St. Juliot washing through them both, as they had once before.

Amongst her other responsibilities, of looking after Thomas's physical needs and requirements which varied depending upon Thomas's state of mind, and trying to lighten his mental state, which wavered between depression and morbidity, Emma picked up her pen and paper, and sat beside Tom as he began dictating his story. It came in coherent paragraphs, delivered sentence by sentence, and, as often as not, after lengthy discussion with Emma.

'Why do you make Paula quite so unlikeable, Tom?'

'She is not. She is just modern – and wealthy. Such a woman would naturally vacillate about her faith.'

'Then I don't like her, and I suspect nor will others. Can you not brighten her up a little, make some slight judgement on her wavering morality?' And as always, they would fall into a discussion about morals, leading into the bog of their own religious quandaries, before silence reigned again and she would carry on, as if nothing had interrupted them.

'That last sentence, Thomas, before we started up, what was it again? Something about lukewarmth not being something she can avoid, as if it is part of her being.' She would add, unhelpfully, 'At times, Tom you are in danger of suspending credibility. But I will write it as you want.'

Despite their differences, inevitable and usually beneficial as they were, they worked well together once again. Tom's discomfort had made him more reliant on her, but it had also subdued him, making him, in Emma's view, as he had once been, gentle and self-effacing. She had always felt that London and his success had undone him, inclined him to be rather bumptious and ambitious. He had pushed her to the periphery, and while she dared not say so, she felt his illness was a blessing, reviving their marriage that had grown increasingly stale and stagnant.

Christmas, nevertheless, when it came was cold and miserable. For Tom the merriment of the season only accentuated his own incapacity. They had remained in Tooting and worked when Tom felt sufficiently well to do so, but the cold sat heavily upon them.

Few visitors called upon them. Edmund came, staying some time talking with Thomas, and then, in a rather laboured way that characterised their relationship, with Emma. Tom was gratified he had come, and said so frequently to Emma, who could only sigh and remind him that his other London acquaintances appeared to have vanished completely.

Progress with his writing had been painfully slow, but sufficient at least for Tom to meet his monthly commitments to his publisher, the only measure of well-being he allowed himself. It was not until April that he had recovered sufficiently to venture outdoors, and was well enough to complete 'A Laodician' in his own hand. But the illness had drained him and for that, he blamed London. Once he had gathered a little strength of body and resolve, his own physical frailties and the separation from his family helped him make up his mind to move once more, nearer to home. As Emma saw it, 'home', as defined by Thomas, was Higher Bockhampton, with all the dangers the hamlet presented to their marriage. While she felt just as keen to leave London for the countryside, Emma could anticipate the pull of family upon him, and the machinations of Jemima, whose presence was always lurking in the background.

As soon as Tom had recovered, they made the move back to Dorset, settling first in the small market town of Wimborne Minster, away from the influence of Higher Bockhampton, which helped to ease Emma's initial fears. With the manuscript for 'A Laodician' now with his publisher, Thomas was already planning his next novel, but his own recovery had slowed him down, and he had left the practicalities of moving house to his wife. It was not a task that Emma approached with any relish, as the seventh move in their short marriage, presuming rightly that this would be yet another temporary residence, until Thomas had decided where they would finally build a house, as he now seemed inclined to do. Nor did she risk hoping that he might consider her feelings at the thought of living in his parents' shadow, for he invariably dismissed her fears as groundless, whenever the matter was raised. Consequently, she suspected, his choices had almost certainly been discussed with Henry and his parents, but never with her. It was more likely that he would tell her only once a decision had been reached, and she would have to accept it, as she had done so much else. She had been used to feeling excluded, by both her own family and his, and now it was her own husband who gave no credence to her thoughts and opinions, nor showed any consideration about what she felt of where they might live.

The house Tom chose for a comfortable brick villa, with a luxuriant and well-stocked garden, and at the back of the grounds, some old stables, which led Emma to reflect wistfully on the mare she had left behind at St. Juliot some nine years before. It was as far away from Dorchester as they had been when they had taken their earlier villa on the Stour, some distance to the north at Sturminster Newton, yet somehow she felt the omnipresence of Higher Bockhampton more keenly. Tom's preoccupation with moving back nearer to his family home was always likely to take them into the heart of his Wessex, and while Emma admitted to herself, it took him further away from the temptations of London, Dorchester had distractions of its own. His visits to the cottage at Higher Bockhampton grew increasingly regular though Emma's were rare; but, she noted, with a mixture of relief and irritation, the visits were never reciprocated.

Emma had long fretted about Tom's abandonment of the Christian faith. She was appalled in early 1882, when he told her he was travelling to London to attend Charles Darwin's funeral and did not hesitate to say so. 'This man has done great damage to the church with his preposterous theories,' she exclaimed, 'he should not be honoured in this way.'

'What nonsense, Emma. He has only torn away the veil of ignorance and replaced it with scientific proof.'

'Proof? Proof of what, Thomas?'

'Proof that we evolved, Emma,' he continued, with thinning patience, ' and that the world is much older than your uncle would have you believe. The strong do survive, Emma, by changing and adapting. Even in my books, I think it is so.'

'But your characters don't fit in with this new way of thinking.'

'Some do Em, some, for others exercise free will.'

He looked at her patiently.

'This is why he is to be buried in Westminster Abbey, Emma, because he is a great man. He may have been agnostic, but never an atheist. The world has accepted him, as has the Church, except for the more strident and bigoted.'

Emma stared at him and turned red.

'You are guilty, Tom, of a great wrong. Go to the funeral if you must, but you walk in the face of God by doing so.'

Emma was left with little contact with her own family. It had been over ten years since she had last been in Cornwall, and Thomas had no inclination for them to return to the place of their courting. John Gifford's disdain of Thomas still stung and while Helen wrote to them very occasionally, her parents even less so, she still felt the pull of her family, and the life she had left behind. The death of Caddell, so slightly reported by her sister earlier in the year, had affected her keenly, for she remembered how kind her brother-in-law had been towards her and Tom, especially when compared to his own judgemental family. Looking back, through the intervening trickle of prejudice and condescension, she could see it was Caddell, rather than her own sister, who had supported their betrothal when her father would not, and that Helen had fallen into step with her father, turning on the happiness that she and Thomas had enjoyed at St. Juliot. Emma had tried to understand Helen's recidivism, attributing it to her sister's own foreshortened marriage. Having given up her own youth to an older man and the jealousy it aroused at her sister's happiness was understandable. But worse was that Emma had hidden so much from Tom about her family's own failings, and yet they continued to sneer at him. Helen, dear Helen, with whom she had lived at St. Juliot for so long, was the most disappointing of all, her letters cold and patronising, with no allusion towards her husband.

It was, therefore, a rare moment of exultation when Emma heard the news that her Uncle Edwin, the only family member, apart from her brother Walter, who had kept contact with her since he had officiated at their wedding, was to marry the daughter of Bishop Jeune of Peterborough. Emma quickly apprised Thomas of the prestige that such a connection would bring, but such an intimation was dismissed by Tom as being ridiculous, just as the Church itself, he viewed, was ridiculous.

But though neither he nor Emma could realise it at the time, what was to impact upon Tom was another connected marriage that happened soon thereafter, between the Bishop's son and Mrs Stanley, one of the most celebrated of London hostesses who had been widowed some years earlier, and who, as Mrs Mary Jeune, would soon set the London seasons alight with a ready stream of luncheons and crushes at her home in Wimpole Street, for the shakers and movers of London society.

The publication of *A Laodician* met with mixed reviews which initially dispirited Thomas, although he attributed it to his illness and to Emma's help which he felt had affected had his spontaneity of thought. It was an unkind judgement, made more so by Thomas's decision to share it with Emma, who bore his criticism stoically. Having drawn closer together through the duration of his illness, Emma could feel him drifting away again with each disparaging comment, each lurch taking him towards his old life, in which she was nothing more than an observer. Thomas was always disinclined to share any of his success with Emma, but in this case he was not averse to, attributing the limited success of the novel to their close collaboration, the closest they had been since they had married.

'It was clumsy, working as we did, Em,' he told her. 'I'm grateful for you being my scribe when I could not write, and by that I mean no criticism of you at all, but it was not easy to write in such a contrived way.'

'You mean no criticism, Tom!' Emma was indignant. 'Why, how could you criticise me for the nonsense that comes out of your head! It might be, as you say, that there is more of you in this book than in any other, but maybe; perhaps, it may be too much of you, for such a thing is possible. What's more, there is a lot of contentious rubbish too. If you had listened to me, it could have saved you and me both much embarrassment.'

Emma's criticism was given weight by the poor reviews the book received, that focused more on Thomas's treatment of faith and the Church than on the author's alter ego. But while she felt vindicated in her own eyes by the concurrence, Emma was angry that Tom had ignored her, and worse, had treated his readers with contempt by soiling his story with his irreligious and irrelevant meanderings.

'So this is the influence your Mr Darwin has had, is it? Shame on you, Thomas, shame!' It was a statement to which Tom, knowing the vacillations of his wife, declined to answer.

Tom's response to his critics was inevitably to become less communicative. Instead he withdrew further into his writing. She realised it was how he coped with any criticism, and while he could be brazen with her, Emma knew him to be easily scarred by those reviewers who were inclined to see him still as an outsider, a writer of rural tales or, worst of all, in his eyes, as someone lacking the benefit of a university education.

The writing of his newest manuscript 'Two on a Tower', occupied much of the spring and summer of 1882. By now, their life had settled back to a quiet routine, and while Emma was not desperately unhappy with her lot, she felt isolated and unfulfilled. She wrote, she kept house for her husband, but her own life had little of account. They had no children and the time, she felt, had almost certainly passed them by, for which she blamed herself. She was isolated from Cornwall and her family, and from the small coterie of friends and family they had in London, including her two brothers. The fact that they were also geographically closer to his parents and extended family unsettled her, and while the distance from Wimborne Minster and Dorchester provided some protection, Tom spoke increasingly often of the need to return nearer to the place where he grew up, from where he drew his greatest inspiration. The improvement in Tom's health was commensurate with them speaking less and less, and she was conscious of the time he spent with Henry and his family. The isolation gnawed away at her, for the more Thomas sought to keep his family close to him, the more Emma was separated from hers.

Tom had said little to Emma about his new book during the preceding months, having relied on Stephens for editorial advice. It was a shock when 'Two on a Tower' was published in October, and met with public outcry. After the baptismal vacillations of Paula Power, Emma was now fully aware of the danger of Tom's agnosticism creeping into his writings, but she was not prepared for the extent that he would compromise them both, in order to shock his readers in his new book. To have a younger man, of an inferior class, falling in love with an older woman and a member of the aristocracy at that, crossed a number of boundaries that gave great affront to Emma, as well as, she suspected, many of his reading public. When she reproached him, Tom acted surprised that his writing could provoke such a response.

'Why,' he remonstrated with Emma, 'it is a natural progression from *A Laodician*. It deals with aspects of life that may be much changed on a decade or so ago, but it is modern, Emma, and as good a work as I have written.'

'I disagree, Tom. It is a disagreeable book, scurrilous and lacking in morality and you should be ashamed of yourself. What would your mother say if she could read it?'

Her statement gave Tom pause for thought, and he reflected, gratefully, that such a scenario would not happen, for while he was comfortable upsetting the literary world, he would not want to upset his mother.

By the following summer, Tom had made up his mind: they would move closer to Dorchester, to Bockhampton, to Stinsford, to Puddletown; the places that lay at the heart of his inspiration.

Accordingly, Tom had decided that they would forgo their lease in

Wimborne and move into Dorchester itself, a decision that saddened Emma, who had enjoyed their brief life in the small market town. In the meantime, assisted by Henry, Tom had found a plot of land on the eastern outskirts of Dorchester, owned by the Duchy of Cornwall, and had prepared to design the plans for a house that his brother could build for them.

'A home, Emma, this will a home for us at last,' he enthused to Emma, 'somewhere where we can put down roots and grow old together!'

But she could only respond, sullenly, 'But why here Tom, in the shadow of your family? It is not *our* place, as you call it, it is just yours. It is wrong to live in the same place you are brought up, especially if you have exceeded your relations as you have,' she added, pointedly – 'it doesn't reflect well on us.' She looked at him beseechingly. 'We will never be happy here, that I will tell you. It will never be just us anymore.'

'Nonsense, Emma,' he insisted, 'just give it time.'

'It is not a matter of time,' Emma retorted. 'It is a matter of geography, and the proximity to those who don't approve of me.'

'You must not be so paranoid, Emma. My mother is an old lady. You should be a little more tolerant of her.'

'Tolerant! Do you know what you are saying, Tom?' She sputtered in helpless fury. 'Why, your mother is not one to . . .'

'That is enough Emma.' Thomas's voice was firm, insistent. 'You will make an effort. For me, Emma. You must.'

As Emma had feared, their time at Shire Hall foreshadowed what was still to come. Now within reach of the Hardy clan, Emma found them visiting the family home at Bockhampton at regular intervals. She had never found Tom's father in any way disagreeable, but he was as remote from her and the world as anyone could be, and try as she might, she found him so reserved and taciturn that she could never engage him in conversation. She noticed that when he was with his father, Thomas hardly spoke more than the occasional sentence to the older man. It was not rudeness, but simply the fact that there was little in common between them as Tom had grown up. Both men seemed to be quite content resting in the silence that they laid down, each before the other.

Amongst Tom's siblings, Mary's job as Headmistress of Bell Street National School in Dorchester meant that she was at home less often.

Emma saw her occasionally, but only in the town, and while she was always cordial, she felt more reserved with Mary, than the younger two siblings. Kate was Tom's confidant, his childhood friend. She was also closer to her parents, and sometimes that would run against her when matters of family were involved.

Yet it was Henry with whom Tom spent the most time, talking of the plans for the ghastly house, that she felt was planned only to entomb her. In the summer of 1884, after Emma and Thomas had spent several weeks in London for the season, they returned to Dorchester, both feeling out of sorts and weary of each other's company. Tom and Henry went off together on holiday to the Channel Islands, leaving Emma at home in Dorchester, preferring her own solitary company to the ignominy of suggesting to her family in Cornwall that she might visit, even without her lowly husband.

After they settled back in Dorset, Tom and Emma had few friends and even fewer visitors. Edmund Gosse called upon them whilst at Shire Hall Place. While Emma had never been comfortable in his presence, she ended up talking garrulously across the table at supper, which only served to overwhelm him and embarrass her husband. The next day, they visited William Barnes at the nearby parish at Winterborne Came, and again, Emma felt, as she was so often made to feel, her presence was an embarrassment to her quietly spoken husband, who tried to deflect her comments whenever he was able. It was cruel that, amongst all else, Tom had made her feel so uncertain in company, had drained her confidence to such an extent, that she had forgotten how to be herself.

While waiting for the building of Max Gate, Tom settled once again into his routines. However selfish his daily life appeared to Emma, she could say nought to alter them, even though she sorely wished he would do so, if only to acknowledge her presence. When, early in 1885, she was taken ill, Thomas declined to stay with her. She insisted that he left her alone, while he visited Lord and Lady Portsmouth in north Devon. In one of his letters home, he remarked that Lady Portsmouth had charged the young ladies, who as he pointedly told Emma, were very interested and attentive, to take especial care of him. It was a portent of things to come, particularly as they prepared to move into Max Gate.

Chapter Ten

THE NEW KINGDOM

The piece of land that Thomas had leased for their home was almost a mile away from Dorchester. The terrain was bare and desolate, exposed to the weather, and the site would remain so until the protective ring of pine and beech trees Tom had planted started to grow sufficiently, to offer some protection. He now spent much of his time with Henry as the house was being built, in mounting excitement. Emma visited the site only very occasionally and, by contrast, watched the proceedings with a sense of foreboding. The discovery of three skeletons during the digging of the well, reinforced her view that the move was not a propitious one.

'It is not a good place to be building, Tom, out here all exposed to the elements. Does not the fact that it was chosen as a site to bury the dead tell you that? I don't like it. I sense the house will be full of the dark, Tom, whether you will it so or not.'

Thomas would try to reassure her, but Emma was disinclined to alter her view of the house – as a metaphor for all else in their lives. Yet the real darkness she feared, as she told herself, was not in gloomy rooms and corridors, but the spectre of darkness brought on by the impending shadows of Jemima and her kin, shadows that stayed with her constantly, even in daylight, when others were banished.

'Why so close to Bockhampton?' she would ask, but she knew there would be no coherent reply. She would change tack and ask another question of him, and yet another.

'What kind of name is 'Max Gate', Tom?' she had asked him on one occasion and when he answered, she persisted in questioning him: 'Is it really necessary to name our home after a toll keeper? What status is there in that, Tom, especially when you have altered his name for your convenience?' She had suggested a number of Cornish names that would be more apt for the house, and would offer a reminder of their romantic beginnings in Lyonnese. Thomas however would not be dissuaded.

'It is a fair name,' he countered, 'and marks the history of the last gate-keeper who was here. It marks this place on the map for future generations. It is a responsible thing to do.' Seeing she was not convinced he continued, 'do you not see, Emma, that we are building on the history of what has gone before us? We cannot presume to arrive as if nothing had preceded us, for it is the accumulation of lives that makes a place resonate. There was a livelihood here once, and it is proper to acknowledge it.'

And our lives, Emma thought bitterly, are they always to be lived in the shadows of others, in your dreary Wessex landscapes, populated by the meanderings of your pen?

She would question what little space he had allowed for them so often and so forcibly that by the time the house was completed, even Thomas had started to doubt whether building this red brick house, topped by its solitary turret, had been a wise decision. He was already thinking of ways to extend and improve it. It looked grand, he felt, despite the objections, and yet, he conceded to himself, probably too much so, and far too ostentatious for a house that could boast only two bedrooms and two reception rooms.

Emma had seen the house as an end to their wanderings. But it was also an end to her hopes for them as a couple, alone and together. There would be no prospect now of living further west where she might have felt at ease amongst her own, or of living away from the shadow of Jemima, for this is where Tom had determined to put down his roots. And it was with a sudden wave of sadness that she realised that Tom's intentions: a home, just for the two of them and whatever menagerie they might otherwise gather. The thought of them ever having a family of their own had silently passed them by, wished away by that woman, who would always haunt her from the edges.

Tom had been writing *The Mayor of Casterbridge* prior to their move. Now they had settled finally, he was soon back at work in his new study, which looked out over the fledgling kitchen garden. Emma turned her attention to the one and a half acres of the property they had acquired. It was afforded protection on two sides by a long running brick wall, six foot in height, but the ground was unwelcoming and it would take some time to break it in. Nevertheless, she thought, she would have her garden now, and an orchard too, linked by a lawn. She would seek to make Max Gate a home for them both, a cultivated home, with a presence and status that would be recognised by friends and visitors. Yet she feared that however luxuriant and productive the garden might become, however welcoming the house, she would not easily take root here, that her soul and mind would atrophy. Max Gate was just something she would have to endure, in the hope that it might eventually grow on her.

After eleven years of marriage, Thomas and Emma had reached an impasse. Thomas had made a success of his writing and saw Max Gate, his 'cottage', as a marking of his achievement. They had lived an itinerant life and the opportunity, finally, to settle down to a routine, was one that filled him with a sense of satisfaction. But it was London, London he needed to win over. Despite his achievements, he craved something more, and that was the acceptance from those whose opinion he perceived to matter to most.

He was 45 years old, when they left Max Gate for London for the new season, leaving the half-built house behind them. Thomas had the appearance of a scholar, with his intense probing eyes set within a pale, wan countenance, but he had grown vain. While he still held to his Elizabethan beard as an appropriate attouchement, his slightly bent nose, lack of stature and receding hair caused him to worry about his appearance and to choose his clothes carefully. But as he grew more punctilious about his own dress, Emma's tastes, though always flamboyant, had regressed, and her appearance looked, to his eye at least, but likely to others, as dowdy, frumpish and plain.

On the publication of *The Mayor of Casterbridge*, one of Thomas's first actions had been to send a copy to Mrs Jeune. Not long before, at Thomas's behest, Emma had written to Mrs Jeune through her Uncle's connection, and had received a courteous note in response, inviting them to call. Thomas had recently become aware of Mrs Jeune's burgeoning reputation amongst the haute monde through Edmund, who had frequently attended her dinners. He had, therefore, started to look forward to the London season with greater relish, than he had ever felt for some years. Emma soon deduced that her family connection had been the catalyst for his unseasonal optimism, and while she felt concerned he would overreach himself by being too familiar, assuming equal status to their host and hostess – which they most decidedly, she affirmed inwardly, were not – she was pleased to have provided such an important new link for her ambitious husband. Perhaps, now, he would see value in her, as he once had presumed to do?

The gift of Tom's new novel had the desired effect in moving matters speedily along. Within a few days of their arrival in London an invitation arrived to dine at the home of Mr and Mrs Jeune, an invitation which Thomas accepted with alacrity. Emma often pondered on the change in Thomas since they had decided to live away from London, with his newfound eagerness for the season. She recalled his visit to the Duke and Duchess of Portsmouth in Devon the previous year, and she could dismiss his own observations to her about the appeal he seemed to hold for young ladies as mere boasting, yet she was also becoming aware of the preening peacock in him.

Before leaving for the soiree with Mr and Mrs Jeune she had questioned Tom. 'What is the attraction of the people you will meet this evening, Tom? For the most part, they will be your highers and betters, and I know how you resent being told so. Besides' – and she paused as if constructing her next sentence with particular care – 'while they might appear to befriend you now that you are in favour, it is just your words they are after, not your company.'

As if not knowing how this sentiment would rile him, and before he could answer, Emma persisted, 'at least, Tom, you have married into a better family, something that I have provided that for you. But don't think for an instant, Tom, that you can ever be the equal of those who will be our company this evening, for it will only upset you.'

Despite Emma's misgivings, the evening passed remarkably well. Mrs Jeune had greeted them at the door, addressing them effusively and Emma's earlier words of caution quickly dissipated.

Taking them by a hand each, Mrs Jeune, started to lead them into the drawing room before pausing and turning her attention to Emma, asking about her family in due order, her parents and then her siblings. But even as she did so, Thomas sensed that it was he that she most wanted to talk with, and as the evening passed, it was indeed Mrs Jeune and her close circle of friends that appropriated him, and left him feeling nourished by their attentions by the evening's end.

Emma, who had been left to her own devices during the evening, was less impressed with his demeanour. 'You were like a country peasant cavorting with Lords and Ladies this evening, Thomas. It was not very dignified of you.'

'Nonsense, Emma,' he answered. He was glowing from the triumph of the night, and nothing, not even Emma in her most deprecating tones, was going to undo that.

'They find me interesting, and told me so. They've read all my books, you know.' He looked at Emma, and his voice softened.

'Why is it so hard for you to be charitable towards me, Emma? Have you insufficient empathy not to feel excited, that we are so received?'

'Empathy? It is a strange word for you to use, Tom Hardy, for I did not think you knew of such a thing.'

She left Tom in his study to pen a few words of appreciation, before the evening wore off and, as he wrote, he quickly dispersed the small dark cloud she had floated across his evening's levity, leading him to reflect upon the very considerable impression he had made upon the assembled company.

Emma conceded in her diary that evening that the meeting had gone exceedingly well, in spite of Thomas's posturing. Mr and Mrs Jeune were exceptionally welcoming and hospitable, even extending an invitation for them to stay when next in London. Emma was quietly pleased at the generosity of her family opening their arms to Thomas, without considering that it could be Thomas, the writer, not the family connection, that could be the greatest attraction to the Jeunes. Surely, she thought, Tom could have no pretensions of 'belonging' on his own account, for while the Jeunes appeared to show a genuine interest in Thomas's writing, he should not be so foolish to think that he would ever be properly accepted as an equal, not without her by his side. She would warn him. For Tom, however, it was a door back into London society, and one he was determined to enter. Having renounced living in London, for reasons of his health, the appeal of spending the season in The City, with the comfort of his permanent domicile in Dorset, held great appeal for Thomas. His literary success had given him the confidence to put his own humble beginnings behind him, and he started to savour the company of a new group of aristocratic and literary friends he found around him. Under any circumstances, he was not about to let Emma put him in his place.

While the season had run its course, at first only Emma returned to Max Gate, though she was fearful of being in the house alone. Tom had said he needed to do some research and meet up with his publishers, but, Emma suspected, not without reason, that he was reluctant to give up the social life he so enjoyed. Preferably, she felt, without her there beside him, to chastise and rebuke at each evening's end.

Thomas returned from London several days later. Soon after, they had their first London visitor at Max Gate in the person of Edmund Gosse, who Thomas had persuaded to come and visit them in their new abode.

While there, Thomas had organised a day trip to Bridport. Although the atmosphere at Max Gate was rather fraught with Emma out of sorts, this outing provided the two men with an opportunity to talk about matters other than their literary pursuits. They had alighted from their wagon near Abbotsbury and were proceeding on a walk towards Chesil Beach, when Edmund had asked, 'So, you are happy with Porta Maxima, Thomas?'

Thomas smiled. He has used the Latin translation in the scrawled invitation he had sent to Edmund, and was touched that the gesture had registered with his guest.

'On the whole, yes I am.' He paused to remove a stone that had become caught in his boot. 'I would have done a few things differently in retrospect, but it will serve us fine.'

'And Emma? Does she like living in her own home after all your traipsing around?'

Thomas paused, considering his answer, before replying. 'I think she will feel so. She needs time, does Emma, to come round to new ideas and new places, but it will happen soon, I venture.'

They walked on another twenty, thirty yards in silence, before he added, 'she feels herself very alone here, Edmund, despite all I do. I know she has been looking forward to having you to stay, and is sorry Nellie and the children could not come too, but she doesn't attract friends like I had hoped. Of course,' he added, 'not having children has not helped her sense of fulfilment.'

Edmund started. 'I am sorry for that, Thomas, for that would have altered her, altered you both. Nevertheless, she has been an excellent hostess, Thomas, and I'm grateful to her for making me so welcome even if I am not always sure how to talk to her.'

'Talk to her?'

Edmund swallowed hard. But he had started down a line of conversation and could not easily now back out.

'She seemed a little put out when I asked her about her family and seemed disinclined to answer. So I moved on to mention Nellie and the children, but she seemed oblivious to anything I said. I do hope I haven't upset her.'

He waited for the other man to respond, to lead the conversation in another direction, but Thomas just walked on, head bowed, hands deep in his coat pockets.

'Perhaps it is my tedious London talk that has spoilt me as company,' he laughed awkwardly, 'for I could not fault Emma's hospitality.'

Thomas slowed to a stop and looked at Edmund. 'No, you are right in your observations. There is an . . . an oddness about her that disturbs me also.' Another pause came, this time, too long to avoid a rising sense of unease. 'Do you know how she challenges me, Edmund, about all manner of things? It has got so that I don't feel she supports me anymore. She has fallen out with my family, has no discourse with her own, and just seems so dogmatic, so difficult about everything. I feel I hardly know her sometimes.'

Edmund looked at his companion. Thomas was normally so discreet, so private, that he considered there had been some deep turmoil to make him speak so out of character. His reply, when it came was composed, gentle and tactful.

'I venture she could say the same of you, Thomas. It was just that I had never heard any mention of her family, which is why I asked her of them. I thought it a natural line of enquiry for a gentleman to make. I see now that to do so was a mistake. That must be hard on her, Thomas, to be so removed from her home, and to only have the company of the Hardys.' He laughed nervously, eliciting the smudge of a smile from his host.

'What's more, I'm sure you're a difficult one to live with. We writers are all the same, as Nellie tells me frequently. She says that is the lot of a writer's wife, and so in that regard, we may not be so different, you and me. Perhaps we need to be more solicitous, that's all.'

'That may be so, Edmund, and I am sure Nellie means it in good humour for she is still supportive of you. Not so Emma. She has no respect for what I write and is quite disposed to work against me if she believes herself to be in the right.'

At this, the matter was allowed to drop and the conversation turned to the geology of the Fleet and of Chesil Beach, yet Edmund, having unexpectedly been taken into his friend's confidence, was troubled by the unhappiness he had found lurking there.

Soon after Edmund's visit, as Emma had feared, Tom was once again in thrall to the family yoke. In London, in Sturminster Newton, in Wimborne Minster, they had been left to fend for themselves, but now, Thomas had started to visit the old cottage again regularly, drawn back towards his mother's bewitching orbit.

Jemima. Emma could not fully understand the relationship that existed between mother and son. That she had raised and protected him, had encouraged him in his education, she could understand, for such was the compulsion of motherhood. But there was something else, something deep-rooted and primal about their relationship. He was too bound to her, too solicitous, even for a doting son. However much it concerned her, it was not something she could broach with Tom.

She had tried once.

It had been a simple question about the new book Tom was working on.

'Why,' she had asked, 'have you set it around your mother's village, Tom? Do you not think that people there might be upset if you write of them and their lot?'

'Why should they be upset? My mother is helping me to understand the hardships and conditions they had to endure. It is nothing to be embarrassed of, although folk elsewhere should be embarrassed that it befell them to exist so' – and then, quite unnecessarily, he added, – 'not that you and your folk would have ever had to undergo the sort of hardships she went through.'

'That is not fair, Tom. We made our own way as a family and it wasn't all plain sailing. We worked for what we got.'

'And my mother didn't? By God, Emma, you have no idea of the life she has had, how she worked and educated herself, raised us all, and fought for what she thought was best for us!'

'That is what mothers do, Tom. And don't forget, if you are listing all her virtues, she can be narrow-minded and bigoted too. She thought you should not get married, or have you forgotten that too?'

Tom turned puce and raised his voice in an uncharacteristic outburst.

'Don't you dare presume to pass judgement on my mother. She is someone you should learn from, not belittle. And perhaps. . .' He paused, as if to wonder if his words were not precipitous, before blundering on nevertheless. ' . . . just perhaps she was right about the marriage too.'

Emma had stood up and walked quickly out of the room before he could say anything more. She did not want him to see the tears welling up in her eyes, or the contortions of her face, although she suspected he had not even the imagination to know the harm such thoughtless words could do.

Despite such desperate moments however, life at Max Gate had settled into a steady, if soulless routine. Thomas continued working on *The Woodlanders*, with Emma providing considerable assistance, writing much of the manuscript in her own hand. She could not help but think the prominence of religion in the book, and the criticisms of marriage which were so galling seemed to be, in some way, directed at her. Yet she was relieved to be engaged in helping Thomas once more, and sharing in his writing.

In spite of her personal misgivings of living on the edge of Dorchester, Emma's had resolved not to allow herself to be subordinated to Thomas, but to counter his indifference by developing her own talents. In the absence of a companion, she had therefore decided to revive her own interests from her days in Cornwall, most notably watercolour painting and, when the season allowed, collecting wild flowers. She kept her diary religiously up to date, and enjoyed walking in the nearby woods as well as pursuing her own writing, but the limitations imposed on her life and its daily routines saddened her. Even the arrival of her young niece, Lillian, for the summer, only provided a temporary fillip, and both she and Tom decided that as much as they enjoyed having a child about the house, neither was particularly tolerant of the prolonged intrusion. It was adult company Emma craved, more specifically, the attentions of her indifferent husband.

As always, Thomas would set himself to work early in the mornings. Though he often continued to write throughout the day, oblivious to all else, having grown secure in the expectation that the world, and especially Emma, would shape their lives as necessary, in order to fit in with his.

With the manuscript finally completed, Thomas resolved to make a pilgrimage of his own, in honour of one of his own literary heroes, the poet Shelley. While Emma would not have been surprised to have been left behind at Max Gate, he had resolved to take Emma for a visit to Italy, in part at least, to atone for the scant attention he had been paying her over recent months. The couple visited Venice and enjoyed the town's art and architecture, yet, to Emma's disappointment, Tom would regularly go off on his own. In addition, more often than not, Tom alone would attend the soirees organised by local literati in his honour, which he felt would be of no interest to her. In Florence, they enjoyed a snatch of time together again, although once more, Tom left her alone, to view the frescos of Simone Martini and the Lorenzetti brothers in Siena by himself. He reasoned that the stairs would be too difficult for her. But by the time they reached Rome, Emma was determined to be a constant companion to Tom, and would share the sights of the city with him, but her ambition was met by an unusual reticence on his part to make any meaningful conversation at all, something that deeply saddened her.

At night he would often walk by himself, and while they visited the Forum and the Coliseum together, the warmth they she had so looked forward to reigniting was absent. The Trevi fountain, the Spanish steps, places that should be steeped in romance according to Emma's feverish imagination, elicited little more than a tourist's comment from Tom, oblivious to the distress his disinterest was causing Emma. When he did stop at Keats's grave to pick a small posy of violets, she thought for a brief moment that he meant to present them to her as a keepsake, but instead, he folded them carefully inside his notebook before sending them back to Edmund in England. He was, Tom informed her, a fellow admirer of the great poet.

Only one extraordinary event happened, on their last night in the City. They had purchased a small painting to hang in the drawing room at Max Gate, and were making their way back to their hotel when Tom was set upon by three men, only to be rescued by Emma's shouts and flailing arms, as she rushed at them from the other side of the road. It was a fright for both of them and they were shaken by the incident, but he was quick to praise Emma's pluck and courage, in acting so boldly.

'I was frightened for you, Tom,' she told him that evening as they reflected on the attack, before they began their journey home the next day.

'You did well, my dear,' Thomas replied, 'springing at them like that. You are such a bold one.'

Emma looked at him, engaging his eyes with hers.

'Perhaps a little bold, Tom, but just a little. I did it for you, Tom, for I love you and would not see you hurt.'

Thomas blinked. Neither had used the word love in such an exposed way for many years now. It demanded an emotional response, but Thomas could not feign one and resorted instead to a safe platitude.

'You are a dear, Emma. What would I have done without you?'

Very little, Emma thought to herself. Most likely you would have been drawing plans for some building or another, but not writing, not writing.

Thomas reached over and placed his hand on hers, assuming the gesture would suffice for an answer. But Emma knew that Tom, her Tom, had changed, in a way she could not understand or countenance. And so it was in Milan, on their way home that, once again, he was happy for her to be left to explore the city on her own while he travelled separately to some historic site or other, oblivious to the effect his thoughtless neglect had upon her.

For months after their return from Italy, Tom busied himself in gathering up a number of his short stories which were subsequently published under the sobriquet 'Wessex Tales.' Encouraged by the book's critical reception, he decided to continue to work in the genre for the time being, ignoring pressing calls from his publishers for another novel. Despite Tom's insistence on wanting to return to Dorchester, to be back amongst his own people, they had few visitors. Mary, sometimes, Henry and Kate too, but Jemima and Thomas Senior only visited the once. Afterwards Jemima, having made a number of disparaging comments about the décor, the company, and the tea, swept out of the house and showed little interest in returning.

Of other family and friends, there were few who ventured to call and fewer still who were invited, even though the area around Bockhampton and Puddletown was awash with Hands and Sparks and Hardys. When other writers and literary friends called, many found the house inhospitable, and felt the impasse between Tom and Emma keenly, sensing the unhappiness that pervaded the domain.

When it came to his writing, Emma could accept that Tom had

recreated the geography and mood of his own town and its surrounding hamlets, yet paradoxically, she saw no living connection with the people that lived there. The characters of his books were not of the folk who gave them sullen looks when they passed, or ignored them altogether, but only the inhabitants of folklore fed through the gossip of his mother. Thomas placed the blame for their social isolation on Emma, saying that people were not inclined to call because she made them feel uncomfortable, or that she was not welcoming enough, as his family had frequently told him The truth was however, that it was he who was the native, and he who made no effort with old family or friends, appearing happy enough with his own company. Nor did he show concern when gossip eventually reached him that the locals saw him as aloof, deliberately distanced from those he once knew. He had not forgotten their traits and peculiarities, she thought, for his pen still fed off them, but he was uncommunicative for he saw little need to ingratiate himself with those he came across simply because of their proximity if they could not benefit him.

By the end of the decade he had written a number of unflattering portraits of noble dames, each based on some true story he had had recounted to him. Emma had not been asked to do any editing or transcription, so that when she read them for the first time, in their final draft, she was mortified at their content, and chastised him for insulting the County gentry.

'Why, Thomas, why upset those you look up to? What is the point of that?'

Thomas was immediately defensive. 'They will not know who the subjects of my stories are,' he replied, 'so it is mere speculation that they could ever think themselves the subjects.' Although he thought that the transparency of each profile might be visible to those nearest to them. Emma was right. On their publication, local reaction was hostile, especially amongst the gentry, but Thomas was too involved in his next project to worry much. In his heart, though, he felt a good deal of chagrin at upsetting such local eminences whom he was desperate to impress.

As the decade drew to a close, Thomas had begun writing another novel, having discussed the project extensively with Emma, who had provided a number of her own ideas to help augment the plot. For a time, they worked symbiotically, each contributing to the work in progress. It was in these rare spaces that Emma felt at her happiest. Yet it was also in that moment, when there finally appeared to be a semblance of tranquillity, that a book of verse arrived at Max Gate, enthusiastically dedicated to Thomas, from a young poet by the name of Graham R. Tomson.

Chapter Eleven

AN OLD LIKENESS

The London season soon exhausted Emma and, by the end of June, she had already returned to Max Gate, leaving Thomas to stay on in the city. He had persisted in walking everywhere, despite her lameness, and had found herself either excluded from various luncheons and dinners, or ignored by Tom whenever she accompanied him, which was even more dispiriting. He had appropriated her relative, Mary Jeune, and made her his own patroness, revelling in her flattery, enjoying her hospitality while being paraded like some pet lamb in front of her circle of friends.

Emma was none too happy travelling back to the house alone with only Thomas's family for company, but her presence, or lack of, seemed hardly to matter, as far as Thomas was concerned. Having surreptitiously encouraged her departure, Tom immediately turned his attention to the forthcoming Authors' Society dinner. He had established, by some small investigation, what he already suspected, that the poet who had sent the collection of poems entitled 'The Bird-Bride' was, in fact, Rosamund Tomson, a writer whose reputation and beauty made her much in demand during the season. He took it upon himself to organise that she would attend the dinner as his guest, having arranged for her to be sitting next to him. The fact that she was married was no deterrent for Tom, whose fascination with his erstwhile admirer was alerted by her reputation as a new woman, attractive and modern, but also by the interest she had first shown in him. He knew he was not prepossessing in appearance, but he also knew by now that he could trade on his burgeoning reputation as a writer to hold anyone's attention long enough for his words to settle, if not beguile. With a bare modicum of modesty, he understood that in order to gain his admirer's confidence, it was useful to employ some false modesty as a lure, accompanied by flattery and the occasional 'bon mot'. Despite

99

such mental preparations, however, Thomas was unprepared for the confident young woman who walked boldly towards him, her hand out-stretched.

'Mr Hardy, how grand to meet you at last. I am honoured.'

Mrs Tomson was every bit as striking as her reputation had suggested, and Tom struggled momentarily to find an appropriate reply.

'My dear, it is I who am honoured meeting such a fine poetess, even if she masquerades under a man's name.'

She laughed.

'It is a man's world still, Mr Hardy. I write fair poetry I think, but to get published, I do what many women do, and resort to a nom de plume. Mind you, it didn't seem to work very well if you have unravelled it.'

'Your poetry does not need to be delivered by some Trojan Horse, my dear, for it is fine as it stands – much finer than what purports to be poetry, written by too many poets who feel inclined to share their verse, even when we sensitive souls would rather they didn't.'

Rosamund laughed at his reply. 'I can see we are going to be very good friends, Mr Hardy, you and I, although I am not sure I am one of your "sensitive souls."' She paused. 'Mind you, I am not sure you are one either,' at which they both laughed.

Throughout the meal, they talked at great length of literature, of London, of family and writing, and by the time it came for the dinner guests to disperse, Tom had arranged to meet at a nearby tearooms the next day, ostensibly, to continue their conversation.

By the time Tom left London, he had met with Rosamund twice more. They had exchanged poems, had agreed to correspond, and Tom had even suggested that she and her husband visit them at Max Gate. Before he left he asked if he might have a photograph of her, a request to which she gladly acceded, delighted by the impression she had made upon this famous writer.

Tom was quick to talk of his new friendship with Emma when he returned to Max Gate, although he was selective as to what he told her. She was surprised when he said he had extended an invitation to Mr and Mrs Tomson, and somewhat relieved when it was not taken up. Having raised it however, the subject of Rosamund was not so easily bedded, as a succession of letters and occasional packages travelled to and from Max Gate.

'And Mr Tomson, Thomas, you say little about him?' she asked him when another book had arrived, neatly inscribed for Thomas, to which Tom was forced to admit he had not yet met the husband, but assured Emma that he would make a respectable guest, if his wife was anything to go by.

'And she, is she a beauty?'

'She is attractive, but dreadfully modern dear. I am not sure you would like that part of her.'

'And would there be a part of her I would like, Tom, or is that not important?'

Tom ignored her. Her jealousy was an irritation, especially as it was quite unwarranted, and her comments belittled her. Emma, he decided, was not at all attractive, when she was in this punitive mood.

Two days later, the discovery of a photograph of the young woman, tucked into a copy of a 'Selections from the Greek Anthology', reinforced Emma's feelings of disquiet. Mrs Tomson was indeed attractive, strikingly so. Emma reasoned that the woman's interest in her husband would likely be trivial enough, at most, she would be calculating how best to use him. Nevertheless, her influence on Tom would linger, for he was so easily smitten.

Since his growing fame in London circles, his susceptibility to flattery had become more pronounced, as had his interest in attractive young women of a literary bent. To Emma, his lecherous behaviour, as she saw it, had become deeply embarrassing. The fact that Tom could be so easily infatuated was even more hurtful for her. She wanted to talk to him, to warn him of the dangers of making a fool of himself, as he done when he had offended the Earl of Ilchester with his 'noble dames', but he would not talk to her, insisting he was busy with the manuscript for *Tess*. Despite this, she noted, he still found time each day to write to the poetess.

There were occasions when she felt impelled to challenge him, for the devotion he showed to his coterie of hostesses and admirers, upon whom he had come to rely for their inflated opinions and sycophantic comments. And in the person of Carrie Balestier she at last found an ally.

Carrie Balestier had come to England with her brother, Wolcott, whose intended business was to help protect the copyright for British authors in America, while enabling authors to promote and syndicate their books abroad. For Thomas, as for many other British authors, his arrival was a godsend, providing the possibility of financial security for the first time.

Whilst in London, Nellie Gosse had persuaded Emma to call on the family at Balestier House, situated nearby in Kensington. Emma, normally so guarded and reticent in unfamiliar company, surprisingly found herself faced with a similarly strong-minded woman, in the person of Carrie Balestier. She also met a young writer of exotic background, Rudyard Kipling, who Carrie had evidently taken a shine to, and the three of them spent as enjoyable afternoon as she could remember away from the smothering blanket of her husband.

In Carrie and Mr Kipling, Emma unwittingly found two allies in her determination to persuade Thomas to be more suspicious of those who sought to ingratiate themselves with him. In contrast to Thomas, who revelled in the attention paid to him by the denizens of London society, Kipling was deeply cynical, talking scathingly of the shallowness of society life, with its 'fawning old men and lion-eating hostesses.'

'Why do you not see what Mr Kipling sees?' Emma put forward to her husband. 'He observes just how superficial these people are, how they will make use of you and swallow you up, every last creative bone and then spit you out.'

Thomas felt himself tense. He hated having to answer for something he was happy to partake of, for it was a harmless pleasure and reassuring, if not easy to defend, on either count.

'Because they are not like that,' he answered. 'Besides, your Mr Kipling is an odd cove and is hardly a good spokesman for our kind of people. He seems to have some sort of inferiority complex, probably from living abroad all that time, that makes him behave in such an ill-mannered way.'

He paused, raising his eyes to look at her. 'One shouldn't be in thrall of those who want to celebrate our success for their own ends, that I agree, but to turn one's back on so many kind and generous invitations for some suspicion that they are using us in some way is ludicrous. Besides,' he would continue after a moment's reflection, 'where would we meet our friends, the Whistlers, Mr Stoker, Mr Meredith, and the like, if not at these occasions?'

Emma thought to herself, 'but these are not our friends, Thomas, they are just sparring partners, for you don't have a kind word about any of them when at home.' Instead, she bit her tongue, and said nothing, for she could see that he was too blinded by the excesses of London's literary life to change anything.

Aside from the shallowness of society, they found themselves disagreeing once again about all manner of things. Often it would be related to matters of theology and the irreligion that permeated his later novels, but increasingly, Tom's wandering eye, and his hurtful friendship with Mrs Tomson, became a prime target.

'You are a fool sometimes, Tom Hardy, preening yourself and carrying on so,' she would say accusingly, while Tom would reply that she was being foolish for such literary friendships were invariably platonic.

'Platonic perhaps for you,' she sneered, 'but she is making you look foolish. What must the Jeunes think of you?'

'There is no reason to think ill of two writers sharing their craft, Emma. You must not be so suspicious.' And eventually, against her better judgement, Emma would desist, sometimes more convinced than she should perhaps have been, of the supposed innocence of the liaison.

The spring brought news of the death of Tryphena Sparks. It affected Thomas deeply, though he tried hard to keep his feelings to himself. He was keen not to let Emma see the extent of his grief, yet she could sense and probed him mercilessly. 'It is a pity about your cousin, Tom, but she was hardly a friend of ours.'

Emma had just brought in a tray from which she took two cups and proceeded to pour tea from an ornate, but inadequate teapot. She paused and looked straight at Thomas. 'Perhaps you should write to the husband. I trust you had got over her, and aren't still pinning for old times?'

'Of course not, Emma,' he answered. 'She was family, that's all.'

'Family's family, I'd vouch,' Emma replied, 'but not that close, not now at least.'

Thomas winced, but said nothing. She had set herself out to make his life miserable of late, and he could not deduce what he had done now to deserve her disapproval. He could only sigh, resolving to be more circumspect when talking with her. But despite Emma's encouragement, Tom declined to go to the funeral. He had no wish to see Phena's distraught husband and children in mourning. Instead, he wished to remember her, and the secrets they shared without the encumbrances, as she had been with him, young and impulsive. He wanted to remember their lovemaking and the way they had cared for and understood each other, as family.

On the day of the funeral he completed a poem he had started only days previously. It was with his pen that he could express his grief most aptly, Tom thought, and it was with his pen that he could fantasise about what might have been, but he was not immediately satisfied with the draft, and put it aside.

Whether it was carelessness on his part, or whether it was simply blindness to the potentially compromising nature of his lines, he left the fledgling poem on his desk. Emma, suspicious of his sudden spells of solitude and more curious than usual, picked it up and begun to read it before him.

'What is this, Tom?' she asked, waving the sheet of paper in her hand.

Tom looked at her. Too late, he realised he should have been more careful when she was on the warpath. Still, it was futile now to ask her not to read it.

'It is a poem. A poem for Phena, as a way of a memorial.'

'You sound upset not to have part of her with you, Tom.' She began to read on. 'A bit of hair? Why would you want a bit of her hair, Tom?'

'It is my acquisitive nature, Emma.'

But Emma had fallen silent. 'You describe her here as your lost prize, Tom. Your lost prize? Where was the loss when you won me instead?'

'I meant nothing by it, Emma.'

'There's a lot in your nothing, that's all I can say,' Emma answered grimly, placing the poem back on his desk.

It may have stopped there, until Tom blundered on, 'the strange thing, Emma, is that I started writing this a week before she died, so it was not at all from the shock of what happened.'

Emma stared at him incredulously. 'You started writing a poem to Tryphena Sparks for no other reason but that you suddenly missed her after all these years?'

Thomas realised, with a sinking feeling, that he had only made matters worse for himself. 'It was not like that, Emma. Sometimes the idea for a poem just comes to me.'

'You cannot just call up the muse whenever you want, Tom, without a reason, and the reason here, I dare say, is some romantic notion you still harboured for the woman.'

'She is dead, Emma, and was probably dying as I wrote it. Perhaps it was some sixth sense. Anyway, she can do no harm now.'

'Dead for sure, as we are likely to be soon too, Tom.' She glared at him.

'Do not be so sure she cannot do us harm still, for dead souls don't so easily let go.'

She waited for him to say something, before carrying on. 'All this nonsense. It seems to me that whether your women are dead or alive, you are ready to humiliate me, with your sordid imagination. If you had stayed with the church you would know the error of your ways, Tom.' She started to leave the room, before suddenly stopping, turning to face him again.

'You remind me of nothing more than a ship without an anchor, Tom, drifting aimlessly,' before concluding, 'heaven knows what rocks you will end up upon.'

Despite the impasse in their relationship, after their first years at Max Gate, Emma felt that she had made some small progress in laying out the gardens and lawns, putting in a small orchard and furnishing the house. But life was about to take a decided turn for the worse. Whatever fragile calm they had cultivated was shattered, when Emma received news that her father had died. She made immediate plans to travel down to Portsmouth for the funeral. While it had not come as a shock, for her father had been frail and in ill health for some time, Emma was deeply distressed.

'I am sorry, Emma,' Tom had proffered by way of sympathy.

'Why?' she had replied blankly, 'why should you be sorry, knowing the ill he spoke of you?

'For you, of course. A father is precious, whatever one feels.'

'Not that precious, Tom. Not my father. But I want to go for mother's sake. It is she that has had to put up with him.'

'Then you must. And I will accompany you, should you so wish.'

Emma stared at him, incredulous. 'Accompany me? Accompany me? I should think that would rouse my father from his coffin, should you appear Thomas. Have a little sense!'

After two days' absence, Emma had sent a telegram to Tom, saying that she would be staying on with her mother for a few weeks and that he would have to look after himself. But instead of staying at the house on his own, Tom seized the opportunity to take his younger brother, Henry, to Paris, in appreciation for building Max Gate. Their trip took in quite a different set of sights than those enjoyed on Tom's previous trip. Watching the can-can at the Moulin Rouge and drinking in the bars into the evening, were not things that he could ever have entertained doing with Emma. Tom realised with a start just how much he relished being apart from her, and not having to be held to account.

Emma was now over fifty. Her own aspirations as a writer had come to nought, and she was feeling increasingly frustrated and unfulfilled. Instead she immersed her interests in women's franchise and the church, as well as her pets, a varying number of cats, and Moss, the dog they had bought when they first moved into Max Gate, but it was little consolation for the loneliness of an unsatisfactory marriage.

Early on in the following year, Emma's mother died. She had not recovered following the death of her husband the year before and, once again, Emma travelled alone, to mourn with the diminishing core of her family, while Thomas stayed at Max Gate, finishing his final draft of Tess, indifferent to her grief.

What to do? Seventeen years they had been married and while they still shared a bedroom, the lines of their relationship were clearly delineated. She wrote to Helen, with whom she had grown closer to following the death of both of their parents, but her sister's response was guarded, even to an invitation to visit her at Max Gate. Anchored as she was in Dorchester, within the confines of that house, Emma felt the loneliness of the outsider acutely. How to cope?

She was distressed at Thomas's indifference toward her, but it was more than that alone that upset her so. It was his indifference to the Church, to common decency, to the institution of marriage that she felt so keenly. There were only two courses of action, she felt, that she could take, in order to cope with her wayward husband: she resolved to befriend any woman that Thomas became infatuated with and thereby disarm them, for, she reasoned, it is much harder for a woman to be flirtatious with a man when the wife also seeks her friendship. Second, and sinisterly, she would begin another diary, a darker, secret diary, in which she would record the hurt she had been subjected to. It would be written by way of a private solace, as if by writing her grievances on paper she could somehow diminish them. Regardless of whether that might truly be so, she was resolved to try.

And so, that evening Emma pulled the seat up to her desk and besides the diary she scrupulously entered every day, she started another, a book of recrimination, that she entitled *What I think of my Husband*, so that in time, Tom would be able to read of the damage he had wrought in her.

Chapter Twelve

THE POISON

The publication of *Tess of the D'Urbervilles,* immediately prior to Christmas in 1891, signalled a sea change in the fortunes of Tom and Emma. The novel became a best seller on both sides of the Atlantic. For the first time since he had committed to his writing, Thomas could feel financially secure in the path he had chosen.

While Thomas was delighted by the success of the novel, which would push him to the forefront of the literary world, Emma could only wonder at the effect this popular acclaim would have on them both. She knew how Tom was easily affected, and now it appeared that every grand house in London was opening their doors to him. His critics were taking his work seriously, writing on his art and even the few damning reviews of *Tess,* lambasting its morality, views which she often shared, seemed to have no effect upon him. She disliked the effects of his success upon them, and the people he was mixing with, for it was not only grand people, aristocrats, who unnerved her, but new people, with modern ideas and philosophies.

One such person was Edward Clodd, a banker and free thinking philanthropist, with keen literary interests and pretensions who Thomas had met some two years earlier. He had taken Thomas under his wing and had invited him to his house in Aldeburgh the previous summer, leaving her at home. She was aware, more than ever, that Thomas had acquired numerous sanctuaries to which she was not welcome, either by diktat, as with his London clubs, or through such dubious friends as Mr Clodd.

The success of *Tess* saw other changes in Tom. Gone was the beard. In its place he had cultivated a fashionably waxed moustache. Of late, he had taken to wearing a tweed jacket and matching knickerbockers, and while he had always been a meticulous dresser, Emma could see that changes were afoot in his person. He was an unabashed romantic in his views of womanhood, although, she grimly observed, they did not carry over into his marriage. He was also a fool. Rosamund, of course, may have been to blame for playing up to him, but she knew the fault lay within, for there would always be Rosamund's, so long as Tom conducted himself in so shameless a manner.

The request, therefore, from another attractive admirer to visit the famous author at home, was to provide Emma with a new challenge, one she was determined to meet head on. Responding to their overture, Emma invited Miss Owen and her sister, Catherine, to tea in the garden, even deigning to share her home-made damson jam with the two ladies, for their cakes and bread.

Once the pleasantries were over, it was soon evident that Rebekah's interest in Tom was in his work, and she wasted no time in asking several questions about his texts that showed an expert knowledge, an interest which both delighted and intrigued Thomas.

'Why omit that wonderful passage of Henchard and the goldfinch, Mr Hardy? I couldn't understand it when I picked up a copy of the book in England and found it wasn't included.'

Hardy chuckled.

'You are observant, Miss Owen. I am worried you know my books better than I. We discussed the matter, – that is my editor and myself – and felt it better left out, knowing the sensibilities of the English reader, but I will look at it again.'

Emma tried to engage Catherine, but with little success, for the sister was painfully shy. All in all though, the afternoon was a success, and Emma felt able to invite them on a picnic to nearby Bindon Abbey. Indeed, by the time that they returned to America two months later, Emma felt that she had found two new friends that she and Tom could both share. Moreover, she sensed in Rebekah a moral rectitude that consoled her, although she knew that for Tom, meeting a new admirer in the first instance in the presence of them both, had a profoundly limiting effect on the manner in which he responded to the inevitable praise, and he had been much more measured and circumspect in his response.

But this period of euphoria was brought to an end, with the death of Thomas Hardy Senior. Emma had always felt kindly towards her father-in-law, and had often wished that she could have known this gentle old man better. She wrote a note of condolence to Jemima but received no reply. When Thomas visited to make funeral arrangements, she was not invited to accompany him. Nor was she to go to the funeral for, as Thomas explained, 'it is best this way. He would not have wanted any dissension in the church, even in spirit.'

It was a bleak time for Emma. Even the few short weeks they had spent together in London prior to the death had been compromised. Tom had revelled in the success of his book and entertained in lavish style, but often at places where she was excluded. Together, they visited the Gosse's at Delamare House and Emma and Nellie would occasionally visit Carrie before she, too, disappeared off to America with her new husband, for, as Nellie unkindly put it, she had succeeded in ensnaring Mr Kipling.

Tom had also become increasingly secretive. She suspected that he was still seeing Rosamund Tomson, although she never felt compelled to ask. It was if his soul had been turned from the sweet, shy man who had courted her so avidly at St. Juliot, to someone altogether too worldly, too avaricious for her. When Clodd persuaded her foolish husband to join him as a founding member of the Omar Khayyam Club, her disillusionment deepened, sensing in Clodd someone determined to wrest Tom away from his provincial life and his rural upbringing, towards the irreligious and profane. Assailed by the new furore that *Tess* had created, and the new philosophies embraced by her husband, Emma retreated into her own world, one with no defence or shelter for her.

The onset of the new decade, and the changes it had wrought in Thomas, were markedly visible. The glamour of being a famous writer had made him contemptuous of his previous life, as well as of her. While in London society he could rest at ease, freely making play with his comments and observations, especially to those 'despicable creatures', as he called them, whose demeanour and dress marked them out as flirts, although he was not above flirting outrageously in return. It was a falsehood, an artifice, a transient life, without scruples or honesty which she knew would prove ultimately unfulfilling, yet he could not, and would not see it. She had sought only to be his perfect companion, to be one with him, but he had wearied of her, and her offerings, in the face of the new opportunities of fame, were paltry and meagre.

And though Rosamund became less visible, both in thought and spirit, and with no discernible threat from the earnest Rebekah, she could only wait for the next crisis that would befall her. With both parents gone, she felt more vulnerable than ever. But if she had hoped for more sympathy from her husband, it was not forthcoming. She and Thomas talked, but sparingly, and any attempt to engage him beyond the trivial ended up achieving nothing.

Sometimes she would try to take him back through the passage of their marriage to the north Cornish coast. 'Tom,' she started one day, 'do you remember our first walk on Beeny Cliff?'

Tom, who had been busy revisiting a manuscript for the new book he was working upon, paused and looked at her.

'That I do, Em. It seems a lifetime away now. Yes, I remember walking it, although my memory tells me you did no such thing.'

'I was on the mare, for sure, Tom, but we were together, that was the main thing. We were on the cliff together.'

Thomas reflected briefly. 'Together Em – yet apart, even then. And that's how we've grown really, like two disparate people locked in an old-fashioned union.'

Emma fell silent, wounded by the callousness of his response. Tom felt compelled to carry on, to try and ameliorate. He reached over and took hold of her hand.

'I do remember, Em. You were such a sight in your robe flying about you, as you rode like a fury across the crest of the hill.'

'And do you remember when you first told me of your wish to be a writer, and how I encouraged you so?'

'You were a constant encouragement, Em. I give you that. You believed when others didn't.'

Emma looked earnestly at him. 'Then why have you changed, Tom? Why have you changed towards me?'

She could sense Tom immediately stiffen.

'I've not so much changed so much, Emma, just grown up. I have a different world-view now, for when I look back on those times, I think what a narrow prig I was, and with no understanding of the world.'

'You were honest and decent then, Tom,' she answered, biting her tongue as she remembered the deception over Phena.

'As I am now, I trust,' he replied, 'for if I am not, you must tell me.'

Emma hesitated, not knowing whether to continue, for it was as long and civil a conversation, as they had for some time.

'Then, Tom, you must not be seduced by all these admirers, by all these people who want to use you for their own ends. You must keep to what you believe is true.'

'But I do that Em. For goodness sake, why do you go on?'

'Because I have seen you, Tom, and I have heard your views and I am afraid.'

Tom snapped at her. 'Afraid? Afraid? Afraid that I might start to enjoy my success? Afraid that others might find me less tedious than you? What are you afraid of?'

And Emma could only look at him pitifully and answer, 'I am afraid of losing you, Tom. I am afraid of losing you.'

But if she had hoped the conversation had had any effect on Thomas, their trip to Dublin as guests of Lord Houghton would soon dispel any such notion. Lord Houghton, being a widower, had called upon his sister, Florence Henniker, to act as hostess for the Hardys during their stay, a decision which delighted Thomas. Florence was herself a writer, and the pair soon struck up a close friendship that once again pushed Emma to the periphery.

Here was a woman who posed a real threat, Emma quickly deduced, and although she was happily married, so she professed, that did not stop Tom flirting outrageously with her throughout their visit. By the end of their stay, it was clear that some compact had been agreed, as they both became more cautious in their conversation when about her.

Florence was perplexed by Emma and when out for a walk about Dublin, told Thomas so.

'Your wife, Tom, is rather unusual.'

Thomas looked at her, unsure how to respond. His response, in the face of any criticism of Emma had always been defensive and loyal. This time, however, he felt no such inclination. Not only did he concur with Florence, but found himself entering upon a path of explanation, in order to elicit sympathy from his new friend.

'She has unusual flair, Florence, that I'll grant.' He had quietly tried to tell Emma to dress more appropriately, but he was aware that her appearance when they had arrived at the Vice-Regal Lodge, dressed in a muslin dress with exaggerated blue bows and lace trimmings, with two curls prominent, turning in on each other in the centre of her forehead had been met with suppressed amusement.

'It is not her appearance, Tom, and I would never want to be rude, but her manner towards you. She seems to be always correcting you, as if she was the most important person here.'

Tom laughed. 'In her mind, Florence, she is.' He paused. When he spoke again, it was with the utmost seriousness.

'The truth is, Florence, we do not really live together as man and wife should. We were married before we were properly ready, and have different views on life. But . . .' and he thought for a minute before continuing, '. . . she is a good soul, and means well.'

Whether Florence took this admission as anything more than Tom getting something off his chest, their correspondence began as soon as they left Ireland. Before two weeks were out, they were at the theatre in London, watching 'The Master Builder', while Emma remained at home.

What Rosamund and Rebekah had not managed, Florence achieved, unwittingly and without guile. For Emma, initially unaware of the growing intensity between the two, was left as a bystander yet again. The flirtation went on, while she lived with the residue that followed soon after they had returned to Max Gate. It was more than she could bear. She sensed Thomas's ardour for his new friend, and felt powerless to affect it, although to watch it unfold before her was deeply upsetting.

If Emma was feeling distressed though, Thomas too was irritated. Emma had failed to accept his new circle of friends which, in his position, celebrity demanded of him. When she asked him when they had last been happy, his reply had been that he was happiest now, save her nonsensical bitterness towards him.

'I think not, Tom. You may be happy, but we, we Thomas, when have we been happy since those early days in Cornwall?'

'We have had many happy times, Em, in Sturminster Newton, in Wimborne . .

'No we did not. You may have, Tom, for you were too oblivious to notice anyone else's feelings, but not me, Tom, never me. I was as lonely there, as I am now. There was nought there that I look back upon with any fondness.'

'But we are comfortable now, Emma. We have a home and can enjoy London at our leisure and without discomfort. What is there that concerns you so?

'Just you, Tom. Just you.' She looked at him, forehead creased, face lined. He seemed older, despite the extra care he was taking with his person. His beard was neatly trimmed, his hair cut and his clothes tidy and well-fitting, yet he looked no better for it. The rustic man was not to be so easily hidden, she observed cruelly. And with that thought presiding, she retreated to her room.

Tom lacked the capacity to respond to her despondency in any way. He knew he could write words that affected emotion, but he could not speak them. Emma deserved better from him, that he could plainly see, but he was unable to give her the solace, the affection due her, and his inability to do so troubled him. She had accused him once of preferring Tess to herself, that his characters were treated with more affection than those he was supposed to hold most dear – bar his mother, she added bitterly, after a moment's thought. The promising seeds that had been scattered at St. Juliot had turned out to be barren as their marriage, which now felt bereft of all the love he had once professed to feel for her.

Chapter Thirteen

THE ANTIDOTE

Emma's separation from her remaining family, as well as the death of her parents, had isolated her from the world she had once known. She longed for a correspondent with whom she could confide, and when a Cambridge scholar and aspiring writer, Alfred Pretor, visited Max Gate to visit Tom, she appropriated the young gentleman as a literary friend of her own.

Despite the encouragement from her new friend, especially through his assurances about the public knowledge of her contribution to many of the novels, Emma felt trapped and frightened by the direction her life had taken. She still wrote regularly to the Holders, the Dashwoods and the Serjeants, yet apart from her sister, she reasoned, they would not be unduly sympathetic to her, should her marriage falter. It was only to her sister, Helen, that she was able to confide about her husband, although knowing her sister's prejudices, she felt disloyal in saying anything. Yet at times, the indignity spilt over nevertheless.

'He has become so unfeeling,' she wrote, 'and insensitive. You know how much I encouraged him by writing his manuscript for his first novel. I made so many changes and suggestions that at times it felt like I had written half the book for him. But he has never acknowledged me, ever. There is no dedication in any of the books he has written, no comment on the contribution I have made to his career in his prefaces, nothing. And now, with mother and father gone, at a time when he could be a little com-passionate, he has more or less abandoned me, at least emotionally, and seems hell-bent on making a fool of himself, with these fawning society ladies he mixes with in London. He has become vain and selfish, although I hope people who knew him previously will remember him otherwise. I fear he will destroy himself and us both. If only his head was not so easily turned. Sometimes these women are like poison and I, I feel I am the antidote, although I fear that even when dying, he may choose not to use me.'

Helen was non-committal in her reply, for she knew better than to come between husband and wife, but she was consoling to Emma, encouraging her instead to take up riding again, to show Tom the woman he knew when they first met at St. Juliot. She suggested that she get away on her own, to visit family what family was left in Launceston. 'If it is good enough for 'His Nibs' to go off and leave you on your own in that ugly house, then I think it only right that you do the same.' But she carefully avoided making a personal invitation to her sister, for there was part of her that had derived some grim satisfaction at her younger sister's plight.

Emma hated to think people were talking of her, of them, in disparaging tones. Once, when she caught one of the servants smirking at her after some caustic comment from her husband, she turned red, in a combination of rage and shame, and berated the poor girl. It seemed that Tom had removed her from his world. He no longer felt he had to act in accordance with the vows they had taken together in front of her uncle, the Bishop.

Whatever she thought, Thomas was not unaffected by Emma's unhappiness. Although increasingly frustrated by her, he still felt the residue of an old affection. But he had changed and could not ignore the fact that his life was different. Instead of joining with him in his success, she had reacted negatively towards him, had rebuked and criticised him for his views, his writing, and, most unfairly of all, for enjoying the fruits of the society that would have once shunned him. The division between them was not new, and the fault, he felt, lay with her, not him.

But at heart, he knew Emma had reason to suspect otherwise, and that reason was Florence Henniker. He had been entranced by her, her warmth and candour, her chestnut hair, and her eyes, (for he always noticed a woman's eyes first), a soft greyish-blue. That she wrote herself and was interested in him, despite their differences on matters of religion, he found compelling. He tried at one time to set out in a letter his views on life, including his agnosticism, his hatred of vivisection, his views on women, but she laughed at him in such a way that he was confused, derailed, yet could not feel offended. Nevertheless, Emma, who did not know of the letter, was acutely aware of how intense her husband's feelings were, and rebuked him for his transparency.

'She is a married woman, Tom, and while you might think it appropriate to take her to the theatre while in London, innocently enough, so you tell me, her husband might think otherwise.'

Moreover, the constant stream of letters and small gifts, including various books and even once, an ornate inkstand, that regularly arrived from Mrs Henniker seemed much at odds with Tom's protestations of innocence.

'This is how her class of people conduct themselves, Emma. They are exceedingly generous and supportive of writers. Remember, she is one too, so knows the trials of writing a book.'

'Then she should know the trials of being married to a writer, Tom, for they are as great.'

'Only because you do not embrace all I do, Emma,' snapped Tom.

She glared at him. 'Nor, I dare say, would I want to embrace all that you embrace, Thomas.'

And with that utterance, the conversation was finished before it had begun. Tom was left there alone, reflecting in a sudden flush of guilt and suppressed pleasure, on how he and Florence, on returning from the theatre the previous month, had been caught in a hansom cab for some fifteen minutes during a heavy summer rainstorm. With the notion of travel impossible, she in her terra-cotta dress, pressed tightly against him until he felt he had no resolve left in him at all.

In May, Thomas's latest collection of stories, 'Life's Little Ironies' appeared, though it was simply a precursor to the novel that Thomas had been working on for some time. He had spoken of it to Emma, but had felt disinclined to share it with her, an act in itself, that had made her suspicious.

'Why,' she exclaimed one day, seeing the manuscript upon his desk, 'the draft is almost complete, Tom. How is it you haven't offered it to me to read through?'

"I wanted you to see enough to form a picture of how it will be, Emma, as close as can be to my own satisfaction. It will not be too late for any suggestion that you might wish to make for I have lots to add and amend."

Emma took the manuscript and set to reading it that very afternoon.

By the end of the next day she had finished it, driven to reading by a mounting anger. Finishing the last page, she stormed in Tom's study and threw it down on the desk before him.

"If you are to publish that," she said, spitting the words at him, "then I will repudiate any part in it. It is an unsuitable book, Tom, in all ways. It is immoral and irreligious, and while I guess I have not seen the worst of it, there are people in it who are all too recognisable."

"People? What people?" Thomas asked, feigning surprise.

"She is in it,' she accused. 'She! From all you tell me of this woman and from all I hear, you have modelled Sue Bridehead on her! How dare you."

He tried to defend himself. "Emma, you are wrong. If there are characters in my novels that seem to share a resemblance to those we know, it is because I study people, see their traits and write of them, but not the people themselves.'

'Do you deny Mrs Henniker has influenced you then? Do you deny that she doesn't exist in the book?"

"Not Mrs Henniker, my dear, but I might possibly use some of her traits and characteristics, as I might use some of yours. You know that I am a squirrel, writing down notes and observations, but once I've done so, they are anonymous, just words. Do you not see?'

Emma was not at all convinced by Tom's response.

'Well, I only implore you to change it, Tom. It is not a story which will bring you any credit; on the contrary, it could undo you."

Tom sighed, nodded and agreed to heed her advice, but with no intention of doing so. What was more, she had seen none of the passages he knew would indubitably upset her. But he had no intention of excising them now. It was better, he felt, to prepare for the response to the book's publication now, for at home at least, it was sure to be savage.

For the emerging London season, Tom and Emma took a house in South Kensington, along with servants they brought with them from Dorset. While there, Tom took himself off to Strafford House on the seafront at Aldeburgh, once again enjoying the hospitality of Edward Clodd, of whom Emma was deeply suspicious.

'I don't think that man likes me,' she remarked to Tom, as he was preparing to depart.

'Why do you say so, my dear? He hardly knows you.'

'That is because he would rather not know me. I know his type, who seek the bonhomie of fellow men, yet who talk in seditious tones about their womenfolk.'

'Emma, that is paranoia. He is interested in literature and that is what his guests have in common. He is a generous patron, Emma. Give the man his due.'

Emma soon tired of the frenetic pace of life in London. After the success of *Tess*, they seemed to be swamped by invitations, but often it was Tom who went out alone for lunch, and invariably again in the evenings. He attended dinners hosted by Lady Carnarvon, Mrs Pitt-Rivers, and others, often ending in an intimate tête-à-tête with one admirer or another. In one instance, spent in the thrall of the nervous and delicate Lady Yarborough, he returned home in high spirits. She found him writing a trifling poem of her pretty pink dress at 2.00am, still dressed in his evening suit.

It was just as Emma feared. Thomas was overwhelmed by the attention he was now receiving, and seemed content to behave in a way that was both discourteous, and deeply humiliating. It was all innocent fare, he protested, and part of the life of a successful author. The hold that Florence Henniker had over her husband, however, told her otherwise. With little explanation, she decided that she had had enough of London, and decided to return to Max Gate after a few days by the sea at Hastings, to purge herself of all the sycophancy and falsehood of the city.

Often now, her thoughts turned to her own family. She was proud of her uncle, Canon Gifford, and her links through him to the Bishop of Peterborough. She shuddered to think what they made of her husband's attacks upon the church, but it was thoughts of her immediate family that preyed upon her. A few years previously, her elder brother Richard had been admitted to the County Asylum in Bodmin, suffering from melancholia and delusions. She had wanted to visit him, but the thought of having to tell Tom of the incidence of instability in her family had dissuaded her. Now, she had heard that, after a period in and out of asylums, he had been admitted to the Warneford Lunatic Asylum in Headington. While Emma was comforted by the fact that he was now in an asylum, opened specifically for the accommodation of lunatics selected from the higher classes of society, his presence there, far away from his remaining family in the south-west preyed deeply upon her.

Worse, still, his illness raised dark memories of her father, whose drink had led to his committal to Bodmin Asylum, around the time that she had left home. She wondered how much Tom had really known, when she assailed him with talk of her family's superiority to his. But they, at least, had not interfered. She had had to marry without their blessing, and she had been cast out, but they had not interfered. Tom's family, on the other hand, were pernicious in their influence, with tendrils everywhere. Emma was aware that Tom's sisters were now both teaching in Dorchester. Tom had brought them a house nearer to Max Gate, but there was hardly any contact between them. While Emma had written to both sisters previously, her impasse with their mother had infected them also. It was Jemima who never had, and never would accept her, who encouraged her son, on whom she doted, to look first and foremost to her and his own family, even though it was this same precious boy who had thwarted her request never to marry, most certainly not to the wife he had taken in a moment of defiance.

Florence Henniker continued to fill Tom's time and thoughts. There was a frisson between them that excited him, and, for a time, she seemed responsive to his overtures, seemingly encouraging a closer liaison. They were corresponding ever more intimately and Thomas kept the photographs she had sent him tucked inside his desk drawer, or in a cupboard which he kept locked with his favourite, one of Florence seated beside a bird cage, so that he could steal a glance in the evening, before turning in. They started to plan a joint story; their letters were full of personal asides as well as matters of literature, but increasingly, Tom felt he was battling against the impediments of her marriage and her faith. Her declaration that she had read parts of his effusive letters aloud to her friends in Dublin had dampened both his ardour and his confidence in her. He had hoped it was himself rather than his literary persona that was most desired, but not for the first or last time, he was feeling disillusioned, by the possibility that this was not the case. Still, he resolved to retain Florence as one of his most valued friends, even if it meant settling for being merely one of the rank and file of hers.

When, therefore, he met Agnes Gove, the daughter of General Pitt-Rivers at a country dance at their Wiltshire home in Rushmore, he was immediately smitten by her beauty. Having danced with her, he proceeded to keep hold of her hands as they sat there deep in conversation, to the considerable embarrassment of Emma, when she heard. Nor was his hostess impressed by Hardy's behaviour. But once again in the ensuing correspondence, Tom had the sobering experience of realising that what he perceived was seen by others as something quite different. His appeal was simply that of a literary adviser, a conduit, a prestigious reference point, without the intimate affection that he had sought. Perhaps Emma was right, he reflected, of use only for what he had become, not for who he was, for who knew him thus? He was aware of becoming old, his skin wasting, and worse, his heart constricting.

For the first time since the euphoria of *Tess*, Tom was drawn to reflect on what he had lost, and on the superficiality that fame had brought him, when measured against his life with Emma. He realised, with a start, that despite all her foibles and her eccentricities, he minded that her heart had grown so cold to him.

Chapter Fourteen

A WALPURGIS NIGHT

The publication of *Jude the Obscure* was met by widespread condemnation by many literary critics, but none of the criticism could match the vitriol that Emma unleashed upon her husband. Not only had Thomas included those unseemly passages that she had objected to, but a great deal worse.

As the number of unfavourable reviews mounted, she accosted her husband angrily. 'Why, Tom, did you choose not to listen to me?'

'Because you have missed the point of the story, Emma. It is not the degenerate book you suggest. It is a work with a strong moral themes and a social purpose.'

'Moral! Moral? That is not what people are saying.'

'Then they are wrong.' Tom's voice was raised, his chin set.

'All of them?'

Thomas sighed. She had lambasted him since the book had first appeared and, worse, had no compunction about letting others know, including his own family, what she thought of the depravity of the narrative. 'It is the most dark and depressive book of the human condition I have ever read. There is no light, no joy, no hope on any of the pages.' She glared at her husband. 'It is a pitiful depiction of humanity, as befits the pen of a non-believer, when even a modicum of Godliness would have made it a much better story.'

Tom fell silent. He had to concede that the backlash had been considerable, both in and out of the home. Some of the correspondence he had received had been extreme, even to the point of the bizarre. The previous day, he had received a parcel from Australia, which turned out to be a packet of ashes. The writer of the accompanying letter claimed it to be 'that foul book, *Jude the Obscure*'. Tom was amused at the gift, and remarked blithely to a stony-faced Emma that, from what he had read in *The Times*, in a report on a cricket match between the two countries, the exchange of ashes seemed to be the fashion. More serious though was the denunciation by the Bishop of Wakefield, whose response to the book had been equally incendiary, stating in a letter to the national press that he had burnt the scurrilous work. He was now publically campaigning for the novel (and others from this immoral author) to be removed from library shelves.

Tom was shaken, although he maintained a brave front. He admitted his novel was a mass of contradictions, and had some deeply unpalatable scenes in it, but laughed off most of the unpleasant and personal comments even when *Jude* was described as 'immorality and coarseness beyond belief'. As the criticism showed no signs of abating, however, it began to weigh upon him. In responding to one critic, he took the approach that they could say whatever they liked, as his personal respect for his own writings and reputation was so slight. But it was an assertion that neither he nor anyone else believed. Henceforth, he privately resolved that he was finished with writing novels.

For all the criticism he received, it was that of his nearest and dearest, that hurt the most. The first attack that wounded him deeply came about when lunching with Edmund at the Savile Club. Edmund had supported Thomas through all his writing, and had rallied to his friend's defence when *Tess of the D'Urbervilles* had been under attack, but now, here he was, his oldest literary friend, saying that *Jude* was the most indecent book he had ever read. Thomas angrily turned on Edmund. But his subsequent apology for offending his dear friend by his honest appraisal did little to assuage the insult, and it would be some time before any cordiality was restored between the two men. Compared to Emma, however, Edmund's comments were mild. Rather than resorting to words, which never served her well in arguing with her husband, Emma had made a number of persuasive attempts to stop the novel from being published. Instead of galvanising support from Thomas's family, her outburst had served as another example of her unsuitability to be his wife. Without reading the novel, Tom's mother reacted angrily to Emma's prejudice against the book, especially as her criticisms had been picked up in the local community and then by the national press. Her disloyalty to Tom did little to lessen the wound that had been festering between Bockhampton and Max Gate, and now showed signs of haemorrhaging.

Despite her own feelings on the matter, Emma still found herself feeling protective towards Thomas. The savage criticism may well have been deserved, but it did not stop her sympathy for her husband. It was unnerving to her how intellectually she could side with those who railed against Tom, but emotionally could not bear it. Tom's ability and reputation deserved better, and his mistake, she reasoned, had been in trying to exclude her from the writing of the book. If only he had listened to her, and ignored the pernicious influence of others, notably Edward Clodd and the ungodly friends he kept, none of this would have happened. She wondered a little at her own vacillations on the matter, and whether the shingles that was causing her such discomfort at the time had affected her judgement, but she knew that was not so. When Tom left for the City early in the new year, she was sad not to be going with him, even though the London season always brought its own difficulties for her. By remaining at Max Gate, she was acknowledging what Tom had never dared tell her in person, that she was an encumbrance, a lame embarrass-ment, one that her husband was only too keen to leave behind, while he prepared to ride out the storm and restore his damaged reputation.

Over recent months, Emma had taken up bicycling and was keen to persuade Tom of its merits. Having tried it, under her tutelage, around the lawn at Max Gate, he was persuaded that it was a pursuit that he would enjoy, and on his trip to London the following month, he found a Rover Colt, a particularly sturdy bicycle which he determined to buy, so that he could begin exploring the district further afield from Max Gate than their walking allowed. Whilst there, he continued his social rounds, staying for a time with Lady Jeune, collaborating on a project to dramatize *Tess*, and at the same time, attending various luncheons. By the time he was ready to return home, Emma had gone, having taken herself to Brighton, to ease her prolonged recovery from shingles and nurse the scars of her failing marriage.

While Tom had been in London, Emma had also received a short, terse note from Mary Hardy, written on behalf of her mother and herself, crit-icising Emma's disloyalty to her husband, and telling her that the role of a wife was to support her husband, especially such an eminent one as Tom had become. Such a scurrilous attack was more than Emma would tolerate. Having been subjected, first, to Tom's indifference and then hurt caused by his wandering eye, she wrote a letter to Mary which, when told its contents, Tom felt was ill-judged and provocative, and that he 'would inevitably hear about it.'

As predicted, Mary was so incensed at receiving Emma's letter and that when Tom next called at Upper Bockhampton, she thrust the envelope in front of him. 'Do you see what this lady you married thinks of us, Tom?'

Thomas took the letter and read it, his heart sinking as he realised the breech that would inevitably ensue, from the vitriol of Emma's response would be nigh on impossible to close.

'Do you read what she called me, Tom? A liar, a witch-like creature!' And to emphasise the gross slight, she added angrily, 'and not just me, Tom, not just me, but Kate and mother too.' She took the letter from him and read on. 'Apparently, so 'Lady Emma' says, we are all to be raising a storm on your Egdon Heath, next Walpurgis Night.'

Tom looked at his sister and wondered how such things had come to pass. What had made his family take such a dislike to Emma, so that she would write such things? He knew her social pretensions were irritating and that she was uncomfortable around his family, but she had a good heart, surely that much was evident even to his family.

Mary, however, was not finished with the epistle yet. She drew his eye back to the part of the letter he had glossed over, whether deliberately or not. 'And you, Tom, do you see what she says of you? That you have been outrageously unkind to her. Not that we know Tom, unless you want to tell us otherwise, although no-one here would blame you had you been so.'

'She is upset, Mary. Leave her be.'

'Leave her be! Leave her be! I'll leave her be, Tom, for I will not foot in that house of yours while she's there, and I think you can take it for read that the same will stand for Kate and mother too.'

The rift weighed heavily upon Tom, but had the unexpected effect of galvanising in him some sympathy for his wife. Emma could be cantankerous and disagreeable, but she didn't deserve this opprobrium. That he would inevitably have less contact with Mary, his dear sister Mary, who had always been his best friend and confidant, was an unfortunate consequence that he would have to bear although he hoped that time would ameliorate the situation somewhat. His first instinct was to try and dampen the flames, but Mary was disinclined to have hers put out; neither was Emma unlikely to simmer for long, before another retaliatory outburst.

'Why do you not stand up for me against their carping?' she asked him, after he had related the extraordinary difficulties of his meeting with Mary.

'You do not make it easy for me, Emma. They see you criticising me and see what I have provided for you and deem you ungrateful.'

'But that is not the truth of it, Tom. You must tell them. The only things I say are to protect your reputation and to stop you making fools of us both.'

'Ay, but that is not how they see things, Em.' He looked at her solemnly. 'When we at Riverside and you and Mary were writing so favourably to each other, I had hopes that we could live harmoniously with all my family – and yours too,' he added a little belatedly.

'Your mother would never countenance such an idea, Tom, as you well know. She resents me for taking you from her. Imagine, she'd still have you cooped up in that little house, writing novels on the same window seat if she could.'

If he had resolved to write another novel, Tom thought, it would have been about a battle of strong-willed women, for he would never doubt of their invective. But that was now of no matter for the uproar over *Jude* had finally convinced Thomas that his interest in writing would henceforth be restricted to his first love, the writing of poetry, and that was what he intended.

Once again, he and Emma moved to South Kensington for the summer season, from where he continued to advise Agnes Grove on her 'journalese' and catch up with his literary coterie. The aftermath of *Jude* had dampened his spirit somewhat and after a short break in Brighton, at Emma's instigation, they returned to London. As previously, despite resolving otherwise, Tom found himself going out on his own, especially in the evening, and while he recounted most episodes to a waiting Emma on his return, some – including those of his dancing with Agnes Grove at the Imperial Club – he did not.

Although her views on living in Max Gate remained as ambivalent as ever, Emma was relieved to get Tom out of London, where she felt his health was often affected, and onto his bicycle. The summer was glorious and packing up a picnic lunch, tidily stowed in her front basket, she persuaded Tom to widen their range, riding significant distances around Dorset and beyond. For Emma, it was like having Fanny again, and the mobility that her mare had given her. Despite the fall-out with his family, which she knew would still be troubling Tom, they were doing something together, something that brought them both pleasure. Whether there was hope of a respite, however, whether Tom would actually give up the position he now lauded over her, was unlikely. Men change, she thought, more than women, because they are better able to. Their lives are more active, their pathways greater, their opportunities more numerous. Yet even in saying so, she knew it was not because of these reasons, but the fickleness of a man's love, that determined the fate of women such as her. Tom was fickle, she knew, and had none of the commitment marriage required of him, for it was not in his make up. His father and his father's father no doubt stayed married out of habit, out of a desire to be cared for and nourished, but they had not been subjected to the temptations that Tom had known. It hurt her now, wondering why she was not enough for him, how the couple that they had once been had disintegrated, and the shock was that when she asked the question, she could not entirely exonerate herself from blame either. I know what men need for way of nourishment, she thought to herself, this mixture of allure and pampering, and being supported in their views and prejudices, but he has become a fool and I cannot ignore that. Worse, she concluded, a fool that's made a fool of me also.

It was not as helpless as she sometimes thought it, for they had the occasional contented times too, but she could never feel that such times would endure. When they visited the Powys family at the Rectory in the village of Montecute at the invitation of the Vicar's son, John Cowper Powys, she felt a happiness she had not known for a long time. On the train journey from Dorchester, Tom had squeezed her hand when pointing out a deer running from a copse of trees, and Emma started, such was her surprise. On arrival, the family were charming, and while John and Llewellyn took Thomas off, she enjoyed tea with the vicar and his wife on the delightful lawn that sloped north in the direction of Montecute House. Next time they would bicycle here, she resolved, as she exchanged pleasantries with the family and for a few brief moments, when she saw Tom coming back to join the group, an eager young man on each elbow, she felt proud of him, proud of her husband, proud to be his wife. But the moment was fleeting. As she looked harder, there was no joy at the end of the garden, for the garden was already starting to resemble a wilderness and become overgrown with grasses and weeds. No joy at Max Gate either. No joy with Tom – or even with her. She realised she could not give of herself as she once had, for she sensed that state of matrimony, once compromised, was hardly ever retrievable, although she was loathe to say 'never' quite yet.

As the summer faded into a distinct autumnal pall, Tom organised another visit to Belgium, to research an epic poem he was proposing to write on the Napoleonic wars. They visited Waterloo, Emma riding the bicycle she took with her and Tom walking beside her. It was, he thought, reminiscent of their first walk on Beeny Cliff nearly thirty years before, with her riding beside him. Does she not feel it too, he thought, looking at her? But there was no sign of recognition, none of the playful banter that had once sat between them, just this stout and serious middle-aged woman sitting in judgement upon him.

Chapter Fifteen

THORN IN MY SIDE

H ad Emma seen the letter Tom wrote to Florence Henniker while in.
Liege, addressing her as 'my dear little friend', she may have looked
upon their trip to the continent with less of a romantic eye. For she would
have known they were not alone, were never alone as long as Agnes and
Florence, and a hundred other ghosts inhabited their marriage. Even those
that seemed buried and out of sight, like Rosamund, were prisoners in his
verdant imagination, and she knew that he could wheel them out at will
in one of his cursed poems or stories to belittle her.

If Tom had understood the unhappiness he wrought in Emma by
parading his bevy of society ladies before her, he gave no indication of it.
She resented the affront to her pride, her dignity and the daily embarrassment she felt from the smirks and asides from the servants, resulting from
his unseemly behaviour. Even so, she could deal with that, she reasoned,
rather better than the haunting of his past. When 'The Well-Beloved' was
published early in the following year, she immediately recognised the
visage of the now dead Phena and her two sisters, buried in the story's
theme of the transience of love. It was as though Tom was trawling
through his life and laying tributes where he saw fit, with scant disregard
to the signals he was sending to his readers and to her. Humiliation. That
was all Emma could feel, and any dormant affection that had arisen,
however momentarily, was inevitably quashed.

Despite Thomas's protestations, what he had described as an innocent
little tale was savagely attacked on both sides of the Atlantic, for its immorality and its complete negation of human love, leaving him to fend off,
and Emma to bear, the inevitable opprobrium.

'Do you believe what you write, Tom? Is this how you think of marriage?'

'No, Emma, it is not. But there is some truth in it too. From what you have your read, can you not see it is about the human condition, the idea that love resides on shifting sands over which we have no control? And it is an idealised love I write of, Emma, an idealised love, not real love.'

Emma let the words sink in, before asking, 'so what is the difference between your idealised love and real love, Tom, assuming they start in the same place. What makes love last?'

Tom thought for a minute.

'Idealised love is the purest for it allows no impediment. It might be irrational and illogical, but in all its naivety, it is also wildly optimistic.' He paused and added, 'It is the stuff of writers.' Emma stared at him.

'But for love to be real,' he continued unabashed, 'it must become habitual. That can only be achieved in my view when one person allows their ambition to be subsumed by the other. If you begin your marriage with that understanding, it is possible, certainly. But most couples don't agree this or establish a modus operandi by which they can grow, one through the other. It seems they remain the same distance apart from where they started, like railway lines that never converge, until the end of their unsatisfactory lives. I believe there is no way of closing the gap once the journey has begun, not in this life, not ever, and therein lies the tension. For such people, marriage becomes a series of adaptations and compromises which will almost certainly turn sour and putrefy although, I grant, may provide companionship and happiness of a sort, but I do not believe ever, represents real love.'

'That is a dismal view of marriage, Tom, and disagreeable. I have read your book, twice now, and I suspect you implying to your readers that it is so with us.'

'How?' Thomas started indignantly. 'That is not so?'

'I read Pierston talking to his friend on the decay of love, Tom, how the perfect, divine creature one first falls in love with, ends by making the same person absolutely miserable in the end.'

Emma stared at her husband.

'Is this not us, Tom? Is this how you see us too?'

'Not us, dear, not us, of course not. Pierston is the type of man not to be admired for his views.'

'Then not you, Tom.'

'No, never. You are blurring what is a figment of my imagination, views that I just float by you like passing clouds, for the story's sake. The trouble is you wring them out and then pour the accumulated water on me like some biblical flood.'

He lowered his voice.

'Were we not together when we married? Were we not one?

'I don't know,' Emma replied. 'I used to think so, but now I am not sure.'

After the ordeal the previous year, Tom was reluctant to commit to going to London; indeed, he felt he had grown rather tired of it, and in one rash moment had told Florence he would not mind never setting eyes on London again. By way of compromise, he and Emma decided to take lodgings at Basingstoke, about an hour west of the City, from where they could take the train in and out of London two or three times a week, visiting their old haunts, staying, as always, with Lady Jeune, attending concerts at the Imperial Institute and attending the theatre, with Ibsen being their penchant for the summer.

Yet when the rest of London, and England, prepared for Queen Victoria's Diamond Jubilee, Emma and Tom deserted the City for the continent, to escape the inevitable hubris. They spent the time in Switzerland, mainly in Lausanne and Geneva, long enough for the celebrations to wind down before returning to Max Gate. From there on, they spent much of the late summer bicycling further and further afield, to Wells, the stately home at Longleat, and to Salisbury.

It seemed that in the twelve months since the Jubilee and 'The Well-Beloved,' there had been an easing of tensions at Max Gate. It was true that none of Tom's family communicated with Emma now, or would ever deign to visit, but the silence was something Emma would endure happily, should Tom be similarly contented. If there was to be a time for rapprochement, he would have to be the one to make concessions, not her. That was the view of Emma. And, paradoxically, if ever the matter had been discussed, it was also the understanding of Tom that he was he who had to give way.

But what was there to concede? On this point, neither of them quite knew. They shared their joy of exploring the countryside on their bicycles, and when away from Max Gate, their conversation lightened and they were able to enjoy the other's company. For how long would it remain so, Emma thought, for how long?

The lull, in fact, lasted for a few months only, for in the following December, when *Wessex Poems* were published, containing so many slights and allusions to other lost loves, Emma knew she had deluded herself to think that Thomas, the writer, could ever subjugate his imagination and his writing for the greater good of their marriage. Undignified, disloyal, traitorous were all epithets she used when challenging Tom, who as usual, let her batter herself out on the rocks of his indifference, until the fury of her words subsided when she had no energy left to sustain them. He could blame her, by saying her heart had grown cold towards him, but she soon opted for the weapon of silence, as the only means possible to answer the accusations of her poet-husband.

She wrote, of course, to Pretor, to the Owen sisters, regaling them of her circumstances, telling of her dislike of a number of his poems and of their own life. 'He should be the last man to disparage marriage,' she wrote to Rebekah. 'I have been a devoted wife for twenty years or more – but over the last four or five he has betrayed me constantly. The thorn, I fear, is in my side still.'

That the thorn, which meaning they could only guess, continued to cause her such distress made her friends fear for her. They tried to reassure her that the writer would always attempt to seek out and embellish tales of their early life, and of their imagination and that she should not despair of it, but rather sit in his reflected glory. Emma could not find it in herself to do so, reading and re-reading the poems, looking for clues about his feelings for her, now or past.

She grimaced particularly at the inclusion of the poem she had found him writing to Tryphena, not for the lines alone, but more for the thought of him sitting there, pen in hand, thinking of her. As for the poetry, she had hoped, nay imagined that he might have written something for her, but she was to be disappointed. He writes only of the unattainable or those he doesn't ever have to reckon living with, she thought bitterly, for I'd challenge any of his pretty muses to deal with the man in his hearth.

When Elspeth Graham wrote to Emma seeking advice on her recent marriage to Kenneth Graham, and in particular, the trials of living with a literary husband, Emma could not disguise her feelings, vitriol dripping from her pen: 'At fifty, a man's feelings too often take a new course alto- gether. Eastern ideas of matrimony secretly pervade his thoughts, and he wearies of the most perfect and suitable wife chosen in his earlier life. Of course he gets over it usually, somehow, or hides it, or is lucky!'

But Emma had not been lucky. When she wrote those words, she could scarcely think that proper and enduring love was in the nature of man. It was not the consolation that Elspeth had been looking for, but having opened the floodgates, she had to bear the brunt of what poured forth.

There was much to deal with. Emma had been both encouraged and saddened by one of Tom's poems she recognised as having been written after they had attended a service in Salisbury Cathedral, a few years previously. He had written in such plaintive tones of his regret that he could not find the joys others had found, of being blind to sights his brethren saw, and being denied the ease that believers knew. Encouraged she resolved to give him a Bible for his 59th birthday. She was gratified that having done so, he marked the Old Testament reading from that same service, but any hopes that this would signal a late conversion of her non-believing husband were short-lived. It was a blow for her, as she had written in the same letter to Elspeth, and she believed that occasionally 'marriage proves to be the happy state which it was intended', noting pointedly that only if both husband and wife are believers, that would be the case. With their marriage in a state of disrepair, she was adamant that Christianity was the only oil that could provide a salve to their troubled relationship, but Tom, for all his spiritual vicissitudes, would not budge in the direction of the Church.

Tom's poems had snuffed out the last vestiges of feeling between them. Emma reflected on what she had left: a recalcitrant husband, with his coterie of admirers; a loveless marriage; no children; and no acknowledgement of her pivotal role in his success or of her talents. He had attacked her through his novels and now seemed determined to humiliate her through his poetry. But she would not buckle. She would not. Nor would she continue to share a bed with him, but would move up into the attic bedroom and stay there until he came to his senses and so might entice her back. But she was not hopeful. He had treated her as an underling, a protagonist. She would let him know what she was capable of. She would become the fantastical wife he had first married with a head full of sparrows perhaps, but now armed with a sharp beak to peck him with as well.

After the celebrations of the Diamond Jubilee, the outbreak of war in South Africa had come to dominate the news. The dogged resistance of the Boer farmers came as a surprise to the Government, and before long soldiers from the shires were on their way to reinforce the troops that had come from Britain and its Empire. Tom and Emma were ambivalent about the justification for war since, like many progressive thinkers, they felt sympathy for Boer farmers, mixed with a suspicion of the motives of the Government. Emma was particularly outspoken and wrote to The Times, railing against the war, and alleging that while the Boers fought for their families and homes, 'we fight for Transvaal funds, diamonds and gold', exhibiting a boldness that disconcerted Thomas.

Despite the moral quandary he found himself in over the rights and wrongs of the war, Tom was moved to write a number of poems, published in newspapers and journals, bringing the broad karoo home with his Wessex born 'Drummer Hodge'. He even found it in him to write to Major Arthur Henniker on his departure for the colony with his battalion, and asked Florence for a photograph of her husband to frame and put on his wall of dear and notable friends, she already being amongst those so mounted.

For Emma there was a final blow before the century was properly put to bed, which came with the death of her sister Helen. Emma had nursed her intermittently for almost two months, although Tom resented her prolonged absence from her role at Max Gate. When Emma did return unexpectedly for a few days rest from the stress of nursing Helen almost constantly for several weeks, she found Thomas missing. Rebekah Owen and her sister had been making one of their regular visits to Dorset over the past few days, and Tom had spent time bicycling with them and sharing his poetry. The night of Emma's return, Rebekah had expressed a desire to see the slum area of Dorchester that appeared in *The Mayor of Casterbridge*, but only after dark. Gallantly, Tom had offered to walk her home and did so, only to find Emma in high dudgeon on his return. For, as she told him in front of an amused Lillian, he was not to be trusted, to which he indignantly, but fruitlessly protested. Her presence established, and the household reinvigorated, she disappeared again soon thereafter to comfort Helen until she died two weeks later, severing their last links with St. Juliot. There was nothing Tom could say by way of sympathy, and he was not invited to accompany Emma to the funeral held at Lee-on-Solent, where Helen had been living since Caddell's death. Staying behind, he deigned only to lower the blinds at Max Gate on the day of the burial, before returning to his work.

After Emma moved into her own rooms, life at Max Gate unexpectedly became more settled. They ate their meals in the dining room and occasionally walked or cycled together, while sharing in the company of their growing menagerie. With Tom's family, there was no contact, no discussion, although Emma knew that Jemima would never desist from blackening her name at every opportunity. She, herself, had also become more outspoken in her criticism of her husband, and the pervasiveness of his family. She blamed the interference from others in their marriage for its demise. Thomas had hurt her deeply, but she could have accepted being ruled by him, were the decisions he made more often than not, still emanating from his family. His great failing was that he was weak, weak in that he had let others persuade him into thinking ill of her. It was his lack of fight she could not forgive. And it was his mother, most of all, who was to blame, with her poisonous tongue and blind prejudices. If only the old woman had died instead of her husband and given them some respite, it might have been different. Tom had always been so loyal to his mother, defending her against reason. The very fact that he spent so much time with his mother and siblings, who no doubt shared with him their intense dislike of Emma, would mean she would always be compromised. She had hoped for so much after the hurt and humiliation of the past decade, but like Tom, she was starting to accept the reality that 'twice-over cannot be.'

Chapter Sixteen

BEFORE THE VISIT

As she had grown older, Emma's memory of her years spent at St. Juliot was more often coloured by a romantic nostalgia. She yearned for the simplicity of living in the comfort of her sister's marriage, the freedom she had enjoyed to ride, to roam and to busy herself with those easy pursuits she enjoyed with brush and pen, to be her own creation.

Yet she also remembered, after the first wash of memory passed over her, the loneliness of life as a thirty year old woman, isolated and dependent, before this small, diffident would-be writer appeared unexpectedly, on the doorstep of the vicarage. Memory is such falsehood, she thought, in suggesting that time passed could be reclaimed in the future, still had an existence. But there was no way back, not ever. The past – its physicality, its moments, its inhabitants, she knew, was a graveyard and all in it were dead and buried. It was only the spectres that occasionally came to haunt her.

The new millennium had started uncertainly. The war in South Africa kept rumbling on, and she and Thomas, who agreed on little else, shared an increasing disquiet about the righteousness of it all. They had not long read of a new social experiment in which the families of Boer soldiers had been gathered up in what were labelled, 'concentration camps', ostensibly for their protection, but which conversely seemed to be adding substantially to the number of civilian casualties.

The death of Victoria in 1901 added to the maudlin spirit of the nation, wringing further verses from her husband. Unlike Tom, who felt that a song of joy emanating from an aged thrush presaged something better to come, and would dispel the bleakness of the world, Emma had little confidence that this century would start any better than the last had ended.

She was sixty years old now, beset with bouts of shingles, back pains and failing eyesight and restricted by her lameness. She had lost both parents and her sister, another brother was in an asylum, while three of their cats had strayed from Max Gate to their death upon the nearby railway. It had been a dark year.

The end of the war and the coronation of the new King went some way to dissipating the fog that had befallen the country since the turn of the century. At Max Gate, however, clouds still pressed down upon the house, suffocating any nascent joy. Emma had seen the momentary hope of bringing Tom into the fold of the church pass by, and while his muses had aged with them, seeming to affect him less emotionally, he seemed bound to keeping up a constant stream of correspondence with both Agnes and Florence. He was starting to age, though, thought Emma, and his libido too, and she speculated whether the time of these hurtful infatuations which had dogged them since *Tess*, were becoming a thing of the past.

The past was never truly far away, however, as Emma discovered, with the publication of her husband's second volume of poetry.

That he had adopted poetry as his first voice disturbed her too, for, despite the moral unravelling in his latter novels, she had felt more secure behind the more structured and superficial prose form. Poetry, by contrast, and especially his, was so exposed, so transparent. She read them cautiously, the war poems, the homage to Victoria, the travelogue through the Low Countries, Italy and Switzerland. There was despondency in his banishing of love, in his puerile revisiting of young infatuations, and his intimations of the more recent. She read 'The Broken Appointment' with a chilling realisation, if not a certainty, that this was directed to one of his recent muses, and his rejection of the memory of her faded beauty wrought bitter tears, of pity and regret and of the sheer waste of it all.

Why? Why had it happened this way? What if she had stayed at St. Juliot and never known of the promise and the hurt he was to bring her? But that would have been impossible, simply impossible. For despite herself, despite him, she still hoped for an enduring affection, however slight, now that the pretence of love had subsided.

Tom had started work in earnest on *The Dynasts*. He had refuted a charge of pessimism directed at his 'Poems Past and Present', arguing as ever that every man's philosophy should come from his own experience. Emma, meanwhile, had been left to deal with the death of her brother,

Willie, an event which cast extra responsibility upon her and Tom, for their niece and nephew, Lillian and Gordon. She wrote short stories and poems and kept up her diaries, intermittently adding to the one entitled, *What I Think of My Husband*. It was never faltering, but more often now spoke of bemusement, of one perplexed by life's turnings.

'I am convinced,' she had written, 'that Tom is by his very nature unable to see himself as others see him. It is a great irony that he is so fearful of being forgotten that he neglects the hearts of those dearest to him. He has been habitually disloyal to me and merely excuses himself by hiding behind his literary persona. Such nonsense. He is just weak. It was a deceit, his abandonment of Christian faith, for he was a believer when we first met and courted. He will be damned, for that is what he deserves. And he thinks I don't know the extent of his infatuations, of his betrayal of my person, of the vows we took together. He doesn't realise how I watch him with Lady Grove or Mrs Henniker and see the way he conducts himself. He looks ridiculous, but that doesn't make his behaviour any less hurtful. He writes to Mrs Henniker most days and her brazen letters are brought into the house without a care as to their propriety.'

And she would close up the notebook, tying up the closely folded pages with red string, placing it beside her bed, safe in the knowledge that it would not be disturbed, so little interest did Thomas ever show in her.

More and more, their lives had separated. They not so much lived in Max Gate, but had become an intermittent part of its furnishings. The house had never accepted her. Although the later alterations had made life a little more comfortable, Emma never deigned to call it home. The sitting room, where visitors were entertained, was cold and austere. Guests coming into the room found themselves watched over by a bust of Sir Walter Scott, above the large oak dresser. Portraits of Shelley and Keats, purchased after the trip to Rome, were mounted on either side of the fireplace, while two sketches by Thomas completed the wall's décor. Of Emma's quite adequate watercolours there was no sign, nor of anything that spoke of her presence. It was as if she had relinquished the woman's traditional role as an arbiter of taste, in deference to her famous husband. That the house contained nothing of her, simply reiterated that in his eyes, she did not matter.

In addition to her husband's indifference, Emma was constantly being reminded of how isolated she was. She no longer enjoyed going into town where she felt people sneered at her and she ran the risk of running into one of his family. Their time in London reduced each year and for Emma, the City had little to commend it anymore, with her presence at anything never seeming more than a courtesy, often reluctantly given or shared by her husband. The coronation the next year gave them both every reason to abandon the season altogether. The following year, it was Tom, alone, who took bachelor rooms, while Emma, in the company of her niece Lillian, absconded to Calais for three weeks. Their marriage vows, long since threatened, were nearing absolution.

The publication of *Jude the Obscure* did little to endear the Hardy's to the local populace. One local bookshop refused to stock the book for its scurrilous content, while many townsfolk felt that the Hardy's had adopted airs above their station. At home, Emma's relationship with the servants was often strained, and she was constantly snapping at them for their coarseness and sluttish habits, for they were of the same social background as Thomas and shared all his inadequacies.

As time passed, Emma had withdrawn into herself, in a last, attempt to preserve the remnants of dignity. She knew her trip to France had unsettled Tom as she hoped it would, and was not surprised to hear that he had taken himself to London, then returned, ill, to Max Gate where he anxiously awaited her return as he did not like to be alone. She knew she had not done as Pretor had once advised her, to accept that her life was best lived in the shadow of her husband, where she could vicariously enjoy his success. She was far too headstrong for that, too opinionated, too contrary. But he should have acknowledged her instead of dismissing her in his writings, for that had turned her, made her provocative. He owed her a debt, one that thus far, he had refused to acknowledge, but she felt certain her time would come when he would come to his senses. Perhaps now love was immaterial, for that emotion had gone, but she was still deserving of some acknowledgement of the partnership which had bound them together and provided every impetus for his career.

Thomas made regular visits to the cottage at Higher Bockhampton and spent as much time as reasonable with his ailing mother, but even so, the news of Jemima's death when it came, while not unexpected, given her considerable age, affected Tom greatly. For most of his life, he had lived in the bosom of his family and his birthplace and she had been a formidable presence in her son's life. Tom grieved and took to his poetry for solace. Despite suffering at her mother-in-law's tongue, Emma strived to be charitable, to be properly Christian to her nemesis and, where possible, to console him, although he was as difficult to penetrate in grief as in any other state of being.

Even so, she would not, could not, attend the funeral, and it was some days before she felt she could speak to Tom about his mother, without the immediacy of emotion strangling their words. She wanted to properly express her sympathy for him, for one's mother was dear and should be decently mourned, although she had thought, in a flash of bitterness, he seemed not to have thought so, when her own had died. But this was different. His mother had been as a marionette, had lavished unnatural affection upon him and never released him to her keeping. She had, thought Emma, simply ruined any chance of happiness she and Tom might ever have had.

Emma encouraged Tom to take a short walk in Thorncombe Wood with her, despite her own discomfort in walking far before returning to afternoon tea, which she had brought out to them in the garden. It was a surprisingly warm spring's day and as they looked at the spring growth, she heard a thrush call, as if to presage what lay ahead.

She wanted to know. She wanted to know what hold Jemima had over him, and why she had acted as she had. Was the fault simply hers, that she was to be blamed for her better breeding, for her son falling in love with her, for her higher intelligence?

They sat, drinking tea, without a word being spoken for some considerable time, before she gathered up the courage to ask what had most troubled her all these years.

'Why did your mother want to keep you to herself, Tom? Why did she not give us a chance?'

She could see Tom's hackles rise and the words gather in his throat, ready to defend his mother. But he said nothing. Instead of turning on her, his shoulders dropped, his head also. Emma looked at him and noticed a tear upon his corrugated cheek.

She reached out her hand to cover his.

'I am sorry Tom. I am sorry for your mother and sorry for the impertinence of the question.'

Tom said nothing for several seconds before answering her. 'No, Em, you are right to ask. You have been patient with her, I know. She was my mother and was dear to me, but her first instinct is to protect her children, and that was her abiding wish for all of us.'

'Protect you? Protect you from what Tom?'

He sighed and lowered his head. 'It is complicated, Em. But I will try to explain to you, for you at least deserve that.' She looked at him, his head still down and waited in silence for his words. 'My mother said many strange things to us when we were young, Em. You knew she and father had to marry?'

Emma started. She did not, though such an occurrence was common enough. 'No, I did not Tom, but there was no shame in such things back then.'

'Perhaps not, but it affected her.'

'Affected her? How?'

'She beseeched all of us not to marry, Em, for she felt we carried bad blood, which she wished us not to pass on.'

'But that is ridiculous Tom. Did she have any justification for feeling so?'

'For years I thought so. But it seems it was just superstition rather than anything of a medical nature. I was never inclined to challenge her, for she was never one to give on such matters.'

'But your siblings. Is this why they never married?'

'Perhaps. I don't know, Em, for I have never cared to ask, nor have they ever spoken of it. She wanted us to look after each other, me for Henry, Mary of Kate, for our lifetimes. That was her wish.' He looked away, towards the ring of fir trees before uttering in tones almost beneath hearing, 'I fear she wanted to bewitch us all.'

Emma stared at him. 'But you did marry, Tom, and the heavens didn't fall upon you.'

'Mother thought differently Em. She cursed our marriage.'

'I know that, Tom, for I felt the lashings of her tongue more often than not.'

'No Emma, you don't understand. She cursed us and our marriage and while I don't believe in such superstition, the fact that you were barren made her feel she was vindicated in feeling so.'

Emma stood up angrily. 'And who is to say it was I who was barren? With your philandering, one would have supposed an accident somewhere, Tom. It could as easy have been you that failed us.'

'I'm sorry, Em, you are right to be indignant, but I know it to be so. But please, there is no blame,' he beseeched her.

'And you can prove this thing, Tom? This accusation you make?' She stared at him. 'I cannot believe you think she cursed us and that was what was wrong with us. You believe such a thing? You?'

'Of course I don't believe in the curse, Emma. All I know is that she cursed us and we have not been blessed with children which is perhaps just an unfortunate coincidence. I just lament the end of our bloodline, that's all.'

'But why would she have even wanted such a thing?'

'There were reasons, Emma, which she never shared, but she believed in absolutely. Don't forget, her life was of another age. She felt things deeply and feared no-one, but where we were concerned, she was deeply suspicious.'

For several seconds they sat there in silence, their tea grown cold. Emma looked across at her husband. The conversation appeared to have sapped everything from him.

'Thank you for talking to me, Tom.'

He looked at her, eyes wet and rheumy. 'I am not saying it could have been otherwise, but I am sorry Em.'

It was only later that she recollected the admonitions of Great Aunt Drusilla's in the words of warning she visited upon Jude Fawley, and realised where they had come from. So like Tom to take the machinations of his mother, and to use them as the plot in a novel, even one that railed against the tenets of common decency.

The conversation affected Emma in another unexpected way. She had often wondered at their childless state, and as much as she had wanted a family when they were younger, she was grateful that they had ended up childless. The reason, however, was not the one that Thomas had given. While he had known something of her father's instability, he had little idea of how her family had been so touched by the illness. She had just heard that her older brother, Richard, had died, after fifteen unspoken years in the Warneford Asylum. She said a silent prayer and blessed her barrenness, and whether it was the result of his mother's curse or not, she cared very little.

With Jemima's death, there was a respite of sorts. Both bereft of parents now, they clung to their cats and were more solicitous, each to the other. While the rift of the heart could never be papered over, Emma was determined to be a better companion for her husband. She knew his foibles now, accepted the benign correspondence he had with Florence and Agnes and determined to let him be. She sensed he would not fall to humiliation again for he, also, was feeling his age. He turned down the opportunity to go to Edward's to recover, preferring to stay at home and embroil himself in the writing of his epic poem. Perhaps, some equanimity was attainable, some solace in their old age.

It all seemed imminently possible. And then, as if sensing an outbreak of peace, a letter came from a new admirer, praising Thomas's writing with such scented phrases that he acceded to seeing the correspondent, a young teacher from London. He did not see fit to tell Emma of the invitation he had proffered, or to organise the visit when his wife was about. It did not do his correspondent any harm that she shared her Christian name with that of his dearest friend, Mrs Henniker. He would see her, at home, and when Emma was absent, for he had deemed that was for the best. That way, she had no cause for worry when there was naught to worry about.

Chapter Seventeen

VERY AFFECTIONATELY YOURS

Emma had been an active supporter of the suffrage movement for over a decade and, tacitly, at least, she had carried Thomas along with her. As with the other public cause she championed so vociferously, that of vivisection, she saw herself as the active partner, with Thomas making the right noises for public dissemination, but without any of her conviction.

After all, she reflected with some cynicism, when Tom was being praised in the newspapers for his views, it was she that had opened up the drawing room at Max Gate to meetings on vivisection, even as *Jude* was being published with all its carryings

on and it was she who had written to *The Times* about the treatment of Bengali tigers, when Thomas could not bother to lift his pen to help the poor beasts. Now that she had resolved to be her own person, she would be answerable to no-one, and especially not Tom. On such issues, she had became emboldened, speaking for them.

'And what of Mr Hardy,' she was once asked at a meeting, 'what does he think about the emancipation of women,' and she had answered, barely keeping the scorn from her voice, 'Mr Hardy only understands the women he invents; others, sadly, not at all' adding by way of afterthought, 'he is a man like any other in this respect, though perhaps you are right to think he, of all people, should know better.'

Visitors to Max Gate were aware of the subtle changes that had occurred, particularly over the past year. In what seemed a comparatively short time, Emma appeared to have shrunk, her stout frame diminished and aged, the full-blooded, rosy, jovial freshness of her youth replaced by a grey, uneven pallor. Even her cascading hair, once her pride and joy, had grown thin and white although it retained its ability to startle through her manipulations. Only her kiss curls, once so beloved of Thomas, remained, though now looking slightly ridiculous as they peered out from under any one of an array of bonnets while her fixed smile and her preternatural round blue eyes made her seem prematurely senile and unworldly.

Thomas, also, appeared more wizened, more gnarled and much subdued, seldom venturing out. He was engrossed in his research for *The Dynasts*, and wrestling with the magnitude of the task he had set himself. Yet between them there was equanimity, an acceptance, one of the other, that produced surprising accord. Both read avidly, whether books or newspapers, and now that the emotion had been wrung out of their relationship, they found it easier to compare notes on new authors and books, and to share their observations on the state of world affairs. Henry James and Tennyson were favourites of them both, and each provided tenuous scraps on which to build a conversation where no other pretext existed.

Even the contentious issue of the Zionist movement appeared to unite them, with Tom having a letter to Israel Zangwill published in The Times, supporting the creation of a Jewish state in Palestine, only to have his correspondence trumped by that of Emma, who wrote directly to Mr Zangwill with a donation for the movement, albeit only of token proportions.

Their lives, however, were lived tangentially. Despite the unspoken truce, neither felt any need to give account to the other. They moved about Max Gate respecting each other's pathways, acknowledging the other when circumstances required it, but making their own plans nevertheless, without any cross-thought or consideration.

Earlier that year when Thomas was invited to travel north to Aberdeen to be conferred with an honorary doctorate by the university, he did not consider asking her to accompany him. Whether he ever wanted her to come, or whether she had any desire to do so, he reasoned, was but a moot point, for he told himself that her failing health would have ruled the possibility of such a strenuous journey out. While she still cycled, for it seemed the one activity in which she was not bodily impeded, her lameness and eczema were causing her considerable discomfort, adding to the mood of gloom and introspection she often found herself in.

The recent losses of her parents and of her sister Helen and brother Richard, were now compounded by the death of her uncle, the Archdeacon Gifford of Oxford, to whom she had so often referred as a measure of her family's social standing. The grief of bereavement, of family and of her hollow marriage weighed heavily upon Emma. There seemed little enough that she could offer to Tom, and even less that he seemed to want of her.

It was with some effort then, that Emma had steeled herself for another London season, determined not to allow Thomas to continue making a fool of himself in the backwash of London society, not for his sake, but for hers. They skirted many of their old acquaintances, went to the theatre and concerts, attended dinners hosted by Lady Jeune and others eager to meet and parade the great man, yet both seemed strangely out of sorts. Even when hosting a multitude of journalists at Max Gate late in the autumn, some two hundred in number, neither Thomas nor Emma did anything to make the assembled company feel especially welcome. It was not an act of rudeness, or indifference, but of social awkwardness, that meant that the journalists left after cake and tea little the wiser about the house and its inhabitants. With only Emma's rather peculiarly flamboyant dress and garish green bonnet, adorned with extravagant scarlet velvet bows to write about, they returned the next day, slightly bewildered, to their desks in Fleet Street.

For much of the time, Thomas was ensconced in his study putting the finishing touches to the second part of *The Dynasts*. Emma was aware of the work, but existed apart from it, although conscious of how much it meant to Tom. The publication of the volume the following year, however, offered little relief, as if the author had now begun to fear that his ambition might exceed his life span, and so he spared little time before beginning the third and most challenging part.

Once again he and Emma travelled to London for the Season, lodging, as was their habit, at Hyde Park Mansions. For the first week or so, Thomas set out daily to do some reading at the British Museum for the last part of his epic poem on the Napoleonic Wars, but found the rigour and minutiae of research dispiriting. He resorted instead to taking lunches with Edmund at one or another of the London clubs his friend frequented in a relentless round. They made one trip to the theatre to see George Bernard Shaw's latest production, 'The Doctor's Dilemma' which Thomas felt a trivial script, and to the National Gallery for Emma to see the work of the Venetian artists, particularly Titian's 'Bacchus and Ariadne' about which she had been reading. But before long she was complaining that she was tired of the seasonal games of London society, and that the City made her unwell, before taking herself back to Max Gate.

Although freed from the guilt she invoked in him whenever he took himself off on his frequent rounds of publishers and clubs, lunches and soirees, Thomas found himself growing weary of the mannered extravagance of the company of society ladies and even tired of the laden tables of partridges and quails, of ham, tongue, chicken, beef, lobster, truffles and oysters and the like, that increasingly were arrayed before him and which suddenly struck him as decadent and gross.

Occasionally, and now without the censorious Emma to frown upon him, he would dine with Lady Jeune, while eminent hostesses, such as Mrs Ronald Greville and Mrs Edith Lyttleton also sought him out to grace their tables as a literary centrepiece, although he suspected the truth in Emma's words now, that he was invited not for who he was, but as some rustic amusement, some showpiece to adorn and give gravitas to a social gathering.

Nevertheless, there were still some whose company he was glad of and would endure much for. On one occasion, he visited Lady Burghclere, the wife of a prominent Liberal Peer, when he heard that the Lady Agnes Grove, recently returned from a period of convalescence abroad, was to be there. After the recent electoral success of Campbell-Bannerman's Liberal Government and their rebuff of the suffragette movement, Tom thought it best to avoid saying as much to Emma, who was as antagonised as ever by the rule of men and viewed the new government, and its members in the House of Lords, as bigoted scoundrels. Nor was he sure that to mention Lady Grove's presence would be wise, even if, in Emma's own words, such dalliances were for his sake only. It was with a start that he realised how desperately keen he was to meet with Agnes again, and would gladly have taken the risk in doing so had the opportunity existed.

When he returned to Max Gate in late July, there was little communion between them. Lillian had been staying for some short time, although she had moved out when she heard the master was returning. Occasionally he and Emma rode in the vicinity of the cottage, she on 'Grasshopper', her sky blue bicycle which occasionally she had trouble controlling whenever the paths were ridged or rutted, he on his Rover Cobb.

Yet in August, when Thomas went with Henry on a cycling tour of Lincoln, Ely, Cambridge and Canterbury to study the cathedrals, Emma was left behind. Instead, in protest, she rode about Dorset, ignoring an unseasonable heat wave that had driven everyone else inside, painting local scenes of Bulbarrow and Durdle Door, knowing as she did so, that they would only be hung, if anywhere at all, in her own secluded part of the house.

Emma was a very capable artist and had once sold paintings to aid the restoration of the church at St. Juliot, but while Thomas had praised her then, he had given little encouragement thereafter. She often wished that Thomas would speak of her talent, but she had learnt that Thomas would never notice, let alone encourage any other person, apart from occasionally, the scribbles of his latest paramour, and even then only until he tired of them, for he was too consumed by his own genius to bother with the incipient gifts of another.

They had seldom talked at any length apart from on matters literary or relating to the house, since their unspoken truce of two years before. Emma had made the attic rooms a sanctuary and spent an increasing amount time on her own. Thomas showed little inclination to engage with her and less still, to visit her room. When the occasional visitor called, they would both meet them cordially at the door and be perfectly civil to each other whilst in company, generously sharing their menagerie of disparate cats and the conversation more or less equally, even it was only Thomas that people had come to see.

Occasionally they would walk from the conservatory past the Druid Stone, a menhir Thomas had had set on the north-east perimeter of the property, and down Nut Walk, an alley of low and bending boughs. They talked of what was in the news that interested them: Alice Perry, the 'kerfuffle' that accompanied the erection of the Anti-vivisection Brown Dog statue in Battersea, the Grantham rail crash that followed so closely on a similar disaster at Salisbury station and, of late, the actions of the suffragettes in disrupting the State Opening of Parliament. They debated the militancy of the women, she supportive, but only to a degree, he firmly opposed to such lawlessness. They had left the subject long behind them, when Thomas added, after they had stopped, as if by afterthought, 'I see there is to be a march next year.'

They had been sitting together on the cast-iron bench that was situated in the near corner of the lower lawn, in a reflective pose, before Thomas had interrupted the silence.

'A march?' Emma glanced at Thomas who sat bowed, his head downcast, staring at the patch of grass between his knees.

'It is your lot, Emma, your dear Millicent, Mrs Fawcett who has called it. She thinks it time for government to see the will of the people – by whom I assume she means women.'

'Then I will join her.'

Thomas started. 'You will do no such thing, Emma. For a start, you're in no fit state to do so.' He looked at her sternly. 'Have you forgotten what the doctor said to you, after your fainting fit in the summer? Nothing strenuous, nothing to excite you, and certainly nothing as absurd as this.'

Emma stared at him. She had not forgotten the fright her fainting had given her at the time, but she would not be deterred from making the decisions she chose, and, especially now that he had provoked her.

'The time is long gone, Thomas Hardy, when you can instruct me as to what I can and cannot do.'

With that the conversation ended, a brief moment of social intercourse was terminated and, as Thomas told himself glumly, normal relations, such as they were, resumed.

And so, in early February, despite Thomas's reservations, and the inclement weather, Emma took the train to Waterloo, staying at the Carlton Hotel where she met up with some of the march's organisers, including Lady Strachey and Lady Frances Balfour. She had made a red and white scarf which she wore down to breakfast the next morning while carrying a homespun banner, with 'Votes for Women' scrawled upon it in bright scarlet letters, propping in the corner of the room. She entered the dining room boldly, excited by the day's mission and was hardly conscious of several pairs of eyes turning in her direction, casting glances at her ensemble, when a voice called out to her. 'Why, Mrs Hardy, do come and join us.'

It was Mrs Fawcett who had addressed her. She was one of the march's organisers and waved Emma over to her table, at which sat two other women, both considerably younger than she, and both, as she was to be informed, students of the new school.

'Mrs Hardy, Miss Beddeford and Miss Weston. Both have joined us from their university studies, and we are delighted to have them marching with us.'

Emma leant across and shook both woman's hands, before settling down beside Mrs Fawcett who was busy drinking from a large cup of tea. 'It is dreary and damp outside, Mrs Hardy, and I fear the route will be cold and uncomfortable. Still, we are not going to be deterred now, not with the world's press watching.' She paused and looked at Emma, now with a cup of tea of her own held tightly in two hands.

'Are you planning to walk or follow in a carriage?'

Emma started. 'Why, walk of course. I have most certainly not come all the way from Dorset to trail behind some carriage. This is an important day, ladies, and I intend to be part of it.'

'You have warm clothes, then, and waterproofs too, for we will all need them.' They lapsed into silence as the rain continued to fall, albeit a little more intermittently on the pavement outside.

'And your husband, Mrs Hardy, is he supporting you today?'

Both Miss Beddeford and Miss Weston sat up, realising simultaneously that this was in fact the wife of Thomas Hardy, a fact that caused both of them to turn their heads towards the older women, in sudden close attention.

Emma grimaced and put down her cup. 'Mr Hardy professes to be for women's rights, to be sure, although he is not so inclined when it comes to mine. Still,' she continued, aware that the three women were now staring at her, 'in that he is like most men who have no idea either what they do or what they don't do until it impacts upon them.'

Miss Berresford, with youthful impetuosity, was quick to respond. 'Why, Mrs Hardy, I would have thought that you being here would say that he was a sympathetic husband, for many men have not let their womenfolk out.'

'You might well call it sympathetic, young lady,' Emma replied somewhat tartly, 'others might call it indifference.'

There was an embarrassed silence. Miss Berresford, if she had been afforded more years, might have desisted, but she was not so blessed as to have aged prematurely, in this respect at least.

'But I have read your husband's books, Mrs Hardy, and am a great admirer. He writes so knowingly of women and their treatment. Tess was . . . '

'Tess was a fallen woman,' Emma interrupted, 'who deserved the punishment visited upon her.'

'That is too hard, Mrs Hardy, surely. And in *Jude the Obscure*, your heart cannot help but bleed for how he supports the downtrodden. He writes with such sensitivity, Mrs Hardy.'

Emma glared at the younger woman. 'For Jude, perhaps, but not for the womenfolk. They all are conniving and shrewd or as ignorant as peasants or have lost the faith. I'd not march for Sue Brideshead, nor for Arabella nor Eustacia Vye or for any of them. Flawed women, that's all Mr Hardy ever wrote about.'

Without waiting for a response, Emma stood up from the table, gathered her shawl about her and walked haughtily from the room, indignant that even here, in a refuge for similarly minded women, her husband was held up as some paragon, not for who he was, but for some fiction he had cared to write.

The march started in Hyde Park and soon after nine, a large and voluble crowd had gathered. The rain had stopped, but by the time the procession of several thousands set off, they were being lashed by icy sheets, more like sleet than rain.

The streets along which they walked on the way to Exeter Hall, were blanketed in a clinging mud that sucked at the underside of their shoes yet was still viscous enough to splatter their clothes, and cold enough seep into the extremities of their limbs. It took the shouts of support from by-standers along the way to keep their spirits high.

Emma however, found the going difficult, with her lame leg causing her a good deal of inconvenience, but the sense of sisterhood, emboldened her and when she joined hands with other marchers at the end of the walk, as they stood to listen to Mrs Fawcett's exhortations, she felt a spirit she had not felt since riding the brow of Beeny Cliff a lifetime ago.

Thomas was none too pleased with Emma on her return. While he had told her he had long endorsed the cause of women's suffrage, his support didn't run as far as having his wife pilloried in the newspapers the next morning, as one of the new breed of suffragettes. Emma protested, pointing out an article that expressed a certain sympathy and admiration for the marchers, written by a brave reporter in the *Manchester Guardian*. Thomas was not deterred.

'But here, Emma, here in Dorset, what do you think the country folk think of it all? You are 66 years old, for goodness sake. Where was your sense of propriety? Did you not think it undignified to be walking with these young militant women, when others of your station at least had the sense to follow discretely behind in motorcars and carriages? Did you think of me, for one moment?'

To which Emma answered, almost shouting as she did so, 'and why should I think of you, Tom Hardy, when you think of no-one else?' an admonishment Emma delivered by jutting out her chin, rotating sharply within the circumference of her dress, and striding haughtily out of the room.

After their rather heated exchange, which left the servants whispering in corners and shuffling about the house, lest they be embroiled in some unnatural conflagration, Thomas was strangely out of sorts. *The Dynasts* had been consuming him and he had become curmudgeonly to a degree usually reserved for Yuletide. The research for the last part of his momentous saga, which involved a series of engagements and battles leading up to Waterloo, required considerable investigation. He had resolved, as he now told Emma, to find an assistant who could do the work for him. Gosse had been a considerable help in this and had located a suitable person, who not only had the instinct needed for research, but was a proficient typist as well and he expected, might well be employable as his secretary in time, should she prove herself capable.

Emma had long been removed from acting in any literary capacity for Thomas. She used to remember how he had once depended on her for her editorial advice and for proof-reading his work, but since *Jude*, she had resolved no more, even if she had been asked, which was never likely. She would be pleased that Thomas had someone whose expertise he could call on, so long as it kept him from complaining, and her from his faithless writing.

In April, Thomas had gone to the City alone, in preparation for the London season. Once he had settled into Hyde Park Mansions, and re-established himself at The Athenaeum, he sent for Emma, who arrived some days later. She was conscious that word had gone round of her outburst against her husband three months back, and she worried about how people would view her, but the stream of invitations to the couple seemed to flow unabated. Emma continued to hold luncheons and soirees, although never a dinner, for Thomas would not allow it. As he explained to her, dinners were the domain of the London hostess, to embellish the standing of their distinguished husbands, not for a country writer, although she always suspected it was undoubtedly the cost that deterred him.

Once they had settled, a number of friends came to call. Edmund and

Lady Grove were frequent visitors, with the latter eager to preside over their social gatherings, alongside or instead of Emma, entertaining and amusing guests in a way that she could not. Thomas had agreed to edit the final proofs of the book she was soon to publish, and Emma conceded, by way of explaining to herself the woman's constant presence, that if she was not there in a self-bestowed social role, she was there in another, as just one more protégée, leaning on Thomas for his professional advice and encouragement.

Emma viewed such arrangements with equanimity in the main. She knew how vulnerable her husband was to the woman's attentions, and it seemed to her that Agnes played the old man shamelessly. Yet she was still surprised how jealous she could feel of another's youthful beauty, knowing full well how easily manipulated her husband's emotions were. Nor was Agnes alone in preying on her husband, for she was conscious of the letters that flowed backwards and forwards between Florence Henniker and Thomas, usually signed off by her, and so she assumed in turn by him, 'very affectionately yours', when she herself now received no more than a curt 'yours, T'. It was envy, rather than jealousy, envy for those who could take one part of Thomas and not have to deal with the rest. And humiliation. He had humiliated her, with his meanderings, his roving eye, his pandering to those who wanted something from him, and saw her as no obstacle at all, in taking whatever he desired.

Nevertheless, when she found a half-wrapped copy of The *Rubáiyát of Omar Khayyám* with a card that read 'To Florence, ever affectionately, Tom' she was hurt that he could offer such an obvious love token to another married woman, whom he professed to befriend as only a literary companion, a fellow-novelist, rather than admitting to her as another of his infatuations. She had long suspected what had gone between Thomas and Florence was more than platonic. The little tolerance she had for the other woman, for she had worked hard to garner some over the years since they had first met in Dublin, dissipated into an irritation, which she gave voice to in her manuscript *What I Think of my Husband*. It was, she reflected grimly, now beginning to read like a charge sheet of accusations that he would never be able to answer.

Emma soon tired of the efficacy of London life. Her eyesight, which had been failing for some time now, and her gallstones were both troubling her, making her feel out of sorts in company. In June, they had attended the King's Garden party at Windsor, travelling out from Paddington to Windsor, where they were met by a number of landau to transport them to the castle. Emma was in considerable discomfort and Thomas insisted that she take the remaining seat in the last of the carriages, walking alongside, making solicitous conversation. Even so, he was pained at how she persisted in dressing so inappropriately, like a youthful Victorian mannequin, as if to draw attention to herself and away from him, which he sometimes, ungraciously, suspected, was her intention.

The publication of Lady Grove's book 'The Social Fetish' brought back all the memories of the author and Thomas, dancing under the Larmer Tree by moonlight, on the Green at Rushmore some twelve years past, as he had so insensitively recorded. Agnes was simply another woman with whom Thomas had been smitten, and the gushing dedication of the author to her husband, which included mention of their 'old and enduring friendship', only served to irritate rather than evoke any lingering feeling of dislike. Yet when Mrs Henniker sent Thomas a copy of her latest novel, 'Our Fatal Shadows', suitably dedicated to her husband, she was more ambivalent, fearing that her grip on Thomas was slipping further and further, even though she was unsure, when she thought about it, whether she really cared a jot.

When she reflected later upon it all, however, she realised what she mourned was not the love a husband, for that had long been trivialised and compromised, but the company, and the stinging reminders of what might have been. She looked at him that evening, his dark eyes restless, not able to settle on the meal or on her, the skin of his face as transparent, as venous as tissue paper on blue-vein cheese. He could hardly be happy, despite all his successes and the accolades his writing had brought him. He looked miserable, more miserable than she had ever known him. He might crumple, so frail did he look, but he would not crush her. She would outlive him, for she had promised herself that moment for redemption, the triumph of the believer over the agnostic.

Chapter Eighteen

THROBBINGS OF NOON-TIDE

The publication of the final volume of *The Dynasts* was met by critical acclaim, to the considerable relief of Thomas. His great friend, Edmund Gosse was particularly effusive, describing it as one of his most original and beautiful works, and that, after his invective on *Jude* delivered some thirteen years previously, which had threatened to derail their friendship at the time, meant a great deal. It had been a labour of love, and Thomas wished he could acknowledge the presence of Florence Dugdale in the latter stages of the work, for her research of the battle sites had been of considerable help. Her knowledge of, and feeling for, the animal world was just as an important influence behind what he felt was one of the most successful parts of the whole poem: the description of the effects of warfare on the natural world, that lay beneath the soldiers' feet at the Battle of Waterloo. How he would have liked to have broken the habit of a lifetime and dedicated the work to her, he thought, knowing that such an act was, of course, quite out of the question.

Emma was relieved that the project that had been many years in the gestation, and just as many in the writing, was finally put to bed. She felt more emotionally detached from this work than any of Thomas's major writings, and indeed, further from its author than at any time in their marriage, yet she shared that sense of relief that comes from living in close proximity with one who has finally thrown a load off their back or discharged some niggling obligation. She hoped that Thomas might be less fraught and that it would mark an end to the unhappiest time of their married lives. Perhaps now he would be less consumed by his writing, and become more companionable. She was grateful to Thomas's new secretary who had expedited the completed work, as she was for the fact that he now had someone else to deal with the growing volume of correspondence that arrived at their door each day.

Emma's health had suffered over the winter. For some weeks she was beset with a severe bout of bronchitis which lingered on, not helped, she felt, by Max Gate's draughts and the inadequate heating. Her eyesight, likewise, was causing her difficulties, and the cumulative effect of her infirmities meant she could not venture from the house, until spring had established a beachhead.

While she had worried about Thomas's health, in contrast to her general lassitude, he appeared to have taken a new lease of life, and allowed himself little time before launching into another commission. He agreed to undertake it, when he did, more from a sense of duty than from any reason, literary or pecuniary. The task was to produce a book of the poetry of William Barnes, the local poet whom he and Emma had last visited more than thirty years before, when he was the rector at nearby Winterbourne, not long before his death. It was a debt Thomas felt he owed to the old man, who had done so much to champion the language of the county.

To have something other than his own insipid poetry to busy him in was good thing, reasoned Emma. Her husband, whether she cared to acknowledge it or not, was a distinguished man of letters, and consequently there were more calls upon his time from an ever more appreciative public who wrote and spoke warmly and affectionately of his novels – even the horrid *Jude*, she noted with a shudder, and now, his mawkish and self-indulgent poetry. She remembered yet again Rebekah foolishly telling her that she should celebrate being in Tom's shadow, an opinion which at the time made her bristle with indignation, but she now saw that she would never escape it, so good a job had Thomas done on her.

By early spring, Emma had recovered sufficiently to host an occasional 'at home', and on one occasion, welcomed Lady St Helier and her select party, who had driven from Newbury to Max Gate and back again in a single day, for luncheon. Thomas was full of hearty bonhomie, keen to share the latest additions to Max Gate, including a tennis court and croquet layout. While Emma thought he was disinclined to share their visitors with her, she felt it was most unfair when he remonstrated her for making a spectacle of herself, with what he described as her 'ridiculous dress' and 'trifling conversation.'

Thomas was soon buried chin-deep in the proofs of William Barnes' poetry, trying to make sense of some of the Dorset dialect that the old man had employed and which, over the passing of years, he had grown so unfamiliar with. Dorset, old Dorset, the Wessex of his novels, he would sometimes opine, had almost disappeared, and with it, much of the local speech and customs. Thomas would occasionally talk nostalgically for what had passed, but in such a detached way that Emma, who was suspicious of most of what he said now, saw it as falsehood, rather than any yearning of the heart for time past. She wondered whether his heart had given out, not in any physical sense, but in its desire for the 'throbbings of noon-tide' as he had written in one of his damned poems, which had so sorely distracted him from the obligations of his marriage.

Soon after the visit of Lady St Helier, Thomas informed Emma that his secretary was visiting family in Bournemouth, and that he had invited her to Max Gate for a night or two, to familiarise herself with the house and his writing environment, lest she might ever come to work there. Emma had a room cleared out for her in the servants' quarters, and while she found the young woman agreeable enough in what brief moments she spent with her, she thought her excessively earnest, of an uncomfortably nervous disposition, despite the endeavours of both her and her husband to make her feel at home in their company. Still, she reasoned, if the woman reduced the paperwork and stresses of her husband, her personal temperament was of no consequence.

Since Christmas, it was noticeable that the correspondence between Thomas and Florence Henniker had dried up entirely, at least to her knowledge. She had been in Emma's mind often since the previous autumn when she had discovered the book that Tom had, presumably, long since sent her. Of Agnes, now her own book was finished, they heard nothing at all. London had done their marriage great harm she thought, London with its endless cavalcade of hostesses in their opulent homes, populated with self-important people who preyed upon her husband. While Thomas seemed perpetually glum at Max Gate, at least here he was safe from such predatory women.

Thomas, however, had every intention of continuing to enjoy the social life of the city, and was dismissive of the temptations, as Emma saw them. Having organised a room at his Club, in early April he caught the train from Dorchester, leaving Emma to manage the recalcitrant servants and deal with the various callers and tradesmen. In the time left to her, she would amuse herself with painting, by writing her poetry or filling her various diaries, by playing the piano vigorously when the mood took her, to dispel the gloom that was inclined to settle on the house during the long evenings.

He wrote to her very occasionally, expressing little enthusiasm for the constant social demands placed upon him, while hinting how dull it was without her. Yet when Emma wrote to him to offer to join him in the City, Thomas replied that the place was teeming with visitors and that while he had tried, he could not get suitable lodgings any closer than ten miles out at Richmond which was, as he had decided, of little use to a wife whose mobility was as restricted as hers.

In her absence, he had visited Lord Curzon at Hackwood Park, much to Emma's chagrin, for she viewed the former Viceroy of India with considerable distaste. The Hardys had met with George Curzon and his first wife, Mary, three years previously, and by the end of a single evening in their company, Emma had felt so desperately sorry for Mary. Her husband was such a pompous and opinionated man that when she heard of her premature death some two years later, Emma could see it only as a merciful release. Emma remembered the man's callous disregard for the plight of the Indian population during the famine, and his justification for the invasion of Tibet. She was irritated by his defence of both, but not as much as she was angered by his bigoted views on the place of women, and her discovery that it was he who was heading up the British Anti-Suffrage League, against which the suffragettes had pitted themselves.

On another occasion, Tom was at a dinner where he was intrigued to be shown a diamond pin by the Duchess of St Albans that had once been worn by Nell Gwynne. He attended a variety of lunches and crushes presided over by Mrs Frederick MacMillan, Mrs Crackanthorpe and their ilk. Nothing, however, prepared him for his reception at one of Lady Ottoline Morrell's famous Thursday soirees, held at her residence in Bedford Square. The reputation of his hostess's beauty was well-known, but even so, Thomas's first glimpse of his tall and elegant hostess, who floated ethereally down the hallway towards him in an extraordinary billowing avalanche of silk, wearing a headpiece that resembled a tableau of some pastoral idyll, replete with lambs, disarmed him to such an extent, that he was momentarily lost for words. Nor was the company at the party any less eccentric than the ensembles: Lytton Strachey, whose flamboyance and ambiguity of costume shocked him; William Somerset-Maugham, whose plays were everywhere; George Moore, the Irish writer who was part of the Irish literary renaissance, and who had his own coterie of admirers; and Vanessa and Clive Bell, there, no doubt, to size up Ottoline as a competitor in London's rich literary mileau, along with a group of disheveled bohemian types that put Thomas firmly in mind of his rustic roots. It was a sight to be seen, as he told Florence later, but not one to be repeated, and the disturbing undercurrent and gentle mocking that underpinned each conversation deeply unnerved him, making him feel every one of his 68 years.

Emma meanwhile remained back at Max Gate. She had written a long letter to 'The Nation', on the subject of woman's suffrage, in which she had expounded lucidly and persuasively on the importance of women being granted the vote, and the necessity for becoming part of government. For once, when reading his wife's words in print, Thomas felt a certain admiration for the fluency and logic of her well-constructed arguments, all the more surprising as he had not been aware of her writing it beforehand, nor had he a hand in its composition.

Emma was by now fully recovered from her early illness and felt Thomas had been on his own in London quite long enough. Since he still showed no inclination to return to Max Gate, she resolved that she would need to go, albeit reluctantly, to London. She also felt the need to get away from Max Gate which was an uncomfortable house to inhabit on one's own, attended only by servants, who were inexcusably rude and slovenly in the absence of their master. Furthermore, she had been upset by a recent letter from her friend Rebekah Owen who informed her that she had recently converted to Catholicism, a sin in Emma's mind, of considerable magnitude. Her suggestion, proffered for a second time that summer, was not met with any enthusiasm.

Thomas wrote back to her, telling her of his anxiety at the thought of her travelling to London, for the hotel in Russell Square had proved to be very noisy, and the heat outside was so great that he genuinely feared she would be prostrated. As if that wasn't a sufficient deterrent, he added, for good measure, she should wait until the question of her sight was settled, and take the time to see how much good the spectacles were going to do, with an enigmatic postscript stating he would rather take her to Cornwall than have her come to London.

Emma, despite herself, was hurt by the rejection. She did not, for one minute, think that his response was driven by any sense of consideration for her, but simply that he did not want her there. Had she known that he was writing at the same time to Mrs Henniker, stating that the reason they had not taken a flat was because she, Emma, was too weak to face the housekeeping, she would have felt was mitigated in her suspicions of Thomas, and them both.

Oblivious to Emma's feelings, or in spite of them, Thomas continued with his round of engagements, including a trip to Cambridge for Milton's Tricentary, visiting Lady St Helier, both at her home in Newbury, and in their new house in Portland Place. He was, so he wrote, busy meeting publishers and correcting proofs of Barnes' Dorset poems whilst posing for a portrait by Sir Hubert von Herkomer, destined for Max Gate, all tedious tasks as he explained to Emma, but necessary.

By the end of July, however, even his energy was exhausted and he decided to return home, appearing in uncharacteristically good spirits when he eventually arrived back at Max Gate, having spent the previous weekend with Edward Clodd at Aldeburgh. There, amongst the assembled guests, he had met Kenneth Grahame, whose book 'The Wind in the Willows', had just been published to considerable critical acclaim. Emma was relieved to have him home, if only for his health, although she had resolved not to show it. She had been asking for some alterations to be made to her bedroom, and Thomas, feeling the ledger was now firmly tipped in her favour, had consented, whereupon she promptly announced that her other related thought had been, that while the work was to be done, she would travel to Calais on her own.

Before that, however, Emma was once again prevailed upon to offer hospitality to Miss Dugdale, whom Thomas had cajoled to come to Max Gate to assist with the final proof-reading of Barnes' poetry, due at the publishers within the month. While there she would undertake the backlog of non-urgent correspondence that had gathered in his absence.

For the duration of her stay, Miss Dugdale was accorded the privilege by Emma, of sleeping in the second attic room, a decision Thomas considered querying, ostensibly because she might be a nuisance to Emma, but really from a concern about what impression Emma might make upon her. Still, he thought better of saying anything against it. As it was, each woman handled the proximity of the other with due consideration and decorum, and by the end of the week, which Miss Dugdale spent mostly ensconced in her husband's study, a bridge of sorts had been established between the two women, across which words meandered in a rather light and inconsequential way. Mealtimes were remarkable only for the lack of conversation, save for the occasional prosaic observation by Mrs Hardy, usually about one or other of the cats, Comfy, Marky and Kitsy, who were accorded personalities only the Hardys could begin to recognise or comprehend. Miss Dugdale was disconcerted to find that Marky spent mealtimes sitting on the corner of the dining room table, observing each mouthful of her food in transit from plate to mouth, but the absence of any comment from her hosts led her to deduce that it was the custom to ignore the cat's presence altogether. Instead, she spoke of her parents and sisters, and a forthcoming trip to Ireland, where she had gone regularly over recent years, to nurse an ailing woman for a distinguished Irish family she had become very fond of.

Thomas was clearly not happy with the information, or to hear of his secretary being shared for some domestic chore and spoke darkly of the Irish and their families, although in this he was ignored by both guest and Emma, who seemed in tacit agreement that the author was in a prickly and judgemental mood and should be humoured until his spleen was vented. For Emma, such complicit and intuitive support was welcomed, and her opinion of the young secretary's intelligence and powers of perception rose accordingly, along with a determination to be more familiar with her, should she return in the future.

Soon after Miss Dugdale had departed, Emma took herself off to Calais, while the builders moved in to undertake the renovations she had requested, leaving Thomas on his own at Max Gate. He seemed out of sorts when she left, for no reason she could easily discern.

Whatever it was, she was disinclined to care. The journey was long and tedious, but Emma took pleasure in every mile she travelled away from Max Gate, and the spell of independence that lay ahead. With Thomas as devoted to the cats as she was, she felt reassured that her only possible worry, that, with her being absent for a period of time, their safety and well-being would be met by her housebound and not always reliable husband.

The past year had reinforced her feeling that anything more than co-existence under the same roof was beyond them, and that what remained was little more than the memory of a promise that had long lapsed. She had put up with living in the pocket of his shabby family, and in a style that would have made her grandmother turn in her grave; she had encouraged him to give up his work, helped him in writing his earliest and best works and now, now, he had nothing left to say, he seemed determined to embarrass her. He had been a fool many times over, susceptible to flattery, to modern ideas, to the whims of pretty women and she had tolerated all of it. But over recent months, she had been disturbed by a suspicion that had been gnawing at her, of a detached shadow she could no longer fix to him, and a demeanour as evasive as it was remote. She thought darkly, not for the first time, of Mrs Henniker, and the hold she had had over her husband for more years that she cared to remember.

It had been difficult coping with it all, all the points of difference associated with faith and family, all of his betrayals and his coldness towards her. 'What was he?' she had asked herself more than once. Who was this man, who was her husband? Had he always been the weak, pliable person she knew now? Or was he conniving, always playing a game with her and with rest of the world? He was not unkind, nor kind, not bad, nor good, not true, nor false, just neutral, living his own closeted life, keeping himself to himself. Despite all his flirtations, all his dalliances, there was so little emotion to him. She had resolved not be cowered by him, but would hide behind her mild eccentricities, her unusual garb, her banal words. They would comment about her, for they did that already, but she would cope, and by coping she would triumph.

For the following weeks, Thomas remained at Max Gate while the work that was being carried out by his brother Henry went on around him. He didn't much care for being alone in the house, even less so than Emma, but dismissed his own suggestion of following her to Calais, insisting the coastal town was little changed. It had been called 'sluttish and monstrous' in the time of James the First, and he stated frankly, yet insensitively since Emma was by now in situ, that any visit did not seem worth the journey. Otherwise, he wrote to her of the cats, of the leveret Kitsy had caught (and they had eaten), of persistent rain and a local outbreak of scarlet fever, of the deaths of two acquaintances and of a woman in Dorchester who had murdered her baby, all prefaced with a refrain as to the dullness of life, in short, nothing that would compel her to return prematurely.

The publication of the selected poems of William Barnes that occurred during Emma's absence had freed Thomas from his long-standing obligations, and allowed him to turn again to his own writing. He retired to his study to write for long periods of each day, oblivious to Emma or the rest of the household. They went out rarely. Once it had been to see the burghers of Dorchester dramatizing and acting out 'The Trumpet Major', while he lay in bed with influenza; once, together, to visit Mrs Baskett at Evershot, but when the opportunity presented itself in December for both to travel to London to attend the Milton banquet at the Mansion House, it was soon 'agreed' by Thomas that he would travel alone.

Emma had however suffered a more singular slight whilst abroad. In her absence, the Prime Minister, Mr Asquith, had written to Thomas with the offer of a knighthood. He declined it, after some considerable vacillation. Emma was furious when she found out, for, as she reflected, it would have been some recompense for the trials and travails of the preceding thirty four years; an acknowledgement, however belated, of the important role she had played in her husband's career. But when it came to sharing any honour with her, even one that would have detracted nothing from him, Thomas, in her view. showed not one ounce of generosity. It was as if to do so would have deflected some of the honour which was rightfully his, to another. One, he could not help but see as an impediment to the body of work he had produced, despite her omnipresence.

It had been an unhappy year and ended in like fashion, with the death of Comfy, who had been ailing for some time. More irritating for Emma, however, was the card that arrived from Newbury, ostensibly from Major-General Arthur and Florence Henniker, but adorned by a photograph of Mrs Henniker alone, standing in front of the house and wishing them both well, although, she sensed, the wishes were never meant for her.

That he still held a light for her was evident by the prominence he gave the photograph upon his desk and by the fact that the card was separated from others sent to the couple. He kept it instead, upon his study mantelpiece.

Chapter Nineteen

A HINT OF ROSE

The snow, which had started falling soon after Christmas, covering the hills to the north of Dorchester and blocking the roads through Cerne Abbas and the Piddle Valley, lingered for much of January. The County froze beneath a white blanket, under which there lay a sheet of treacherous ice that restricted movement, and discouraged anyone from venturing outside who had no imperative to do so.

Thomas had succumbed to a further bout of influenza over New Year, and his recovery was slower than usual. Occasionally, now that the days were showing signs of drawing out, he would come out of his study and sit by the fire in the drawing room, from where he could look out over the garden, and towards Came Woods.

He and Emma had fallen into the habit of talking in a curiously oblique manner, with one offering a thought then waiting while it was digested, batted back, or else completely ignored, and replaced by a different subject altogether. If not in the conversational, they would settle down and read a mixture of books, often new editions, but more usually religious tracts, for Emma or philosophical subjects for Thomas. He lacked the patience of Emma, and at regular intervals would walk to the window, gazing outwards, often for minutes at a time, before returning to his book, which he invariably left perched on the overmantle beneath their ornately framed Venetian mirror, a reminder, if one was ever wanted, of travels once shared. Occasionally Emma would play on the piano, positioned in the corner of the room although her playing style was an unfortunate mix of fortissimo and staccato, usually delivered furioso. It inevitably drove Thomas, after a respectable lapse of time, to pointedly replace the book he had taken to read from the marquetry panelled bookcase, and leave the room, without making any response to the provocation.

When they did speak directly, it was usually about some national event, some local passing, or some new author. One such subject, that generated conversation without the usual circumlocution, was that of the recently passed Old Age Pensions Act. Only that week, their gardener had indicated his desire to retire, now that he had reached seventy years of age and was earning below the permissible limit, a fact he spat out through his remaining teeth. In order to be considered for the pension, however, his employers had to vouchsafe that he was of good character, something Emma was loathe to do, for she had found him obnoxious and not at all civil towards her on account of the cats. 'It is a foolish Act,' she commented, 'taking the work of the Church and giving it to politicians who have no interest in caring for the poor.'

'It is an attempt to right wrongs,' Thomas countered, 'and will help clear the streets of vagrants, if nothing else.'

'It will do nothing of the kind,' she retorted. 'Those that need help most and are unable to help themselves, are excluded.'

'Who are excluded?' Thomas had not read the detail of the Act, since he had deduced that it would be of no benefit, and hence no relevance, to him.

'Those with convictions for drunkenness, or who don't have the habit of work – that is according to those who profess to know about work,' she answered cuttingly, adding after a pause, 'and worse, those committed to asylums as lunatics.' She turned on Thomas. 'Why should they not receive something?'

To this, Thomas had no answer, other than trying to get Emma back to the request of the gardener and the benefits of assisting his departure, if he really was as difficult as she had painted him to be.

By April, Thomas was already ensconced at the Athenaeum where he spent a jolly evening in the company of another of its members, Sir Arthur Conan Doyle, and caught up with a variety of writers and artists who used the Club as their London home during the season. Later on, as was his habit, he travelled to Aldeburgh, where he stayed with Edward at Strafford House, enjoying both the sea air and the lively company, before returning to London and starting on a seasonal round of readings, lectures, lunches and dinner parties. He related little of this to Emma though, instead filling his letters home with domestic matters and instructions on what to do with his mail, restricting anything that might be seen as evoking emotion to enquiries as to the well-being of the cats.

It was state of affairs they had tacitly agreed to, and was acted out by Emma's expressed disinterest in her husband's affairs, where he went or whom he met; but while that was her intellectual position, it was a contrary view to the one bequeathed to her by her sex. She might not love Thomas as she once had, but she resented others assuming they could do so, and remained particularly ill-disposed towards those who imagined they saw qualities in her husband, qualities she knew from bitter experience were not there. Could a woman ever escape feeling some sense of proprietary, she wondered, some small inkling of suspicion, that someone else could see something of value or elicit some sliver of affection from her husband that she could not? It was not jealousy that she felt, for she knew that to be a wholly irrational emotion, but a fear that any sympathy for Thomas from another woman would be a judgement on her own failure, as a woman, as a wife, however the odds had been stacked against her, however unjustified. It was that malignant thought, she realised, and the implication therein, that she didn't like one little bit.

Thomas stayed in London for the next month, during which he heard of the death of his old friend George Meredith, who had first befriended him some forty years previously. The passing of Meredith drew from his protégé a farewell poem which, as usual with Thomas, mixed a respectful tribute with an introspection that dwelt on a growing awareness of his own mortality, despite the twelve years that separated the two men.

Whilst at the Athenaeum, Thomas had been introduced to Baron Frédéric d'Elanger whose opera, *Tess*, was due to open at Convent Garden a fortnight hence. He had kindly been offered a box by the author and wrote to Emma to inform her of the fact, but more as a courtesy, than an expectation that she would attend. He was then rather disarmed by her enthusiasm to do so. He tried hard to dissuade her, citing a long list of reasons why it may not be wise to venture into the city, when it was so hot and crowded and would make her fatigued, but to no avail. Emma had resented his frequent attempts to contain her at Max Gate, to keep her out of the public eye, and it was therefore as much out of sheer bloody-mindedness than any interest in the opera, that determined she would attend.

Thomas met her at the hotel when she arrived there by hansom cab from the station. He tried to be enthusiastic about her being there, but was patently not, and any attempt at warmth soon dissipated when they entered their rooms. They had an early supper at his club, shared in near silence before making their way to Covent Garden.

Emma derived little enjoyment from listening to Thomas's miserable story sung in a shrill Italian libretto. Thomas told everyone afterwards that he had enjoyed seeing *Tess* set to music, although he seemed ill at ease, fidgeting and appearing distracted throughout the whole performance. Emma had worn a long green cloak for the occasion, with a deep and expansive fur collar, and a hat whose topography lacked any consideration for those sitting beside her or for that matter, her husband. During the first scene, she had produced with great ostentation, a pair of mother of pearl opera glasses that she loudly insisted in calling Galilean binoculars, and proceeded to use them with no obvious success, but considerable flamboyance, for the rest of the evening, with the result being that she saw little of the performance. During the intervals, when Thomas went out for some fresh air, she turned her glasses on the audience and noted, with some pleasure, several other members of the Lyceum which she had recently joined in attendance with their, or someone else's, bored husbands. She was also gratified to see Miss Dugdale there, in the company of a gentleman who she thought she recognised, but could not place, which had the effect of raising the status of the young lady, in her eyes.

After the performance, Emma was shrill in her comments to those about her, on one hand congratulating the author for making her husband's sad little story into something significant, while on the other, complaining about the ghastly Italian singing and the pretentiousness of the whole thing. Thomas was relieved to get her back to the hotel, and more so to pack her off the next morning back to Max Gate, with his admonishments ringing in her ears.

Emma was aware of how her presence had troubled Thomas, and was glad of it. He was soon off to Aldeburgh for ten days and she would no doubt be expected to await his return alone, and therefore, to her mind at least, he deserved little sympathy. Thomas, meanwhile, had been disconcerted by Emma's presence, which now seemed to throw the duality of his life into cold relief, and caused him considerable anxiety. He had closed off much of his life to Emma over the years. Many of his more recent friends hardly knew of her, still fewer had met her. She was becoming determinedly more outspoken, more eccentric, more maddening, but whether by design or through the natural attrition of growing old, he could never be sure.

By late September, Thomas had made his way back to Max Gate, re-establishing his authority in the household, at least with the cats, although he held little sway elsewhere. Despite his time at the coast, he appeared to Emma in particularly low spirits, and as one familiar with the symptoms of depression, she grew unnaturally concerned for him. Perhaps he had realised how shallow his faithless life had become without any order to it. Having shunned and neglected his wife for so long, she hoped he could now see the price they might both have to pay, in living out their days, remote and unfeeling, together and separate. If she hoped for some rapprochement, however, it was not forthcoming, and after a few restless weeks, Thomas was off again, this time with brother Henry for a tour of the northern cathedrals of Durham, York and Edinburgh.

December saw the publication of a further volume of poetry, that Thomas entitled *Time's Laughingstocks*. Emma read it with a jaundiced eye, although after his shameful insinuations in *Jude the Obscure*, she felt there was little that could shock her. Nevertheless, she found the final two lines of one poem he had written some years previously, 'Too fragrant was life's early bloom / too tart the fruit it brought!' both sad and tasteless. The lines sent her back to her diary, to write more on what she thought of her husband, a volume growing in length as well as in its acidity.

Emma felt her absence from London for most of the summer had been a mistake, and resolved to make a greater effort the following year, if her health permitted. She had resigned from the suffragettes in reaction against what she perceived to be their growing militancy. Some of her older friends no longer bothered with the season, but she still had her London club from where she could meet other like-minded women, women whose own considerable talents, like hers, had been subsumed by avaricious and egotistical husbands.

Christmas was a quiet affair and as the New Year began, both Thomas and Emma were conscious of the imminence of their allotment of three score years and ten. Occasionally they talked of family matters, of their niece and nephew, of contrary neighbours and dead pets. Once, they rode out together through Puddletown and on to Athelhampton House, where they commented on an early rising of bluebells, punctuated by a precocious bursts of daffodils that filled the gardens leading up to the house and fell away on either side into the woods, before returning via the graveyard at Stinsford, where they paid a rare visit to his parents' graves. But by the time they remounted their bicycles, whatever hint of companionship that had built up over the dozen or so miles they had ridden had been stripped away, as Thomas fell into a maudlin state that started to descend upon him before he had closed the churchyard gate, closing her out of any private thoughts he may have been harbouring. She reflected on how he had always kept his emotions to himself, and been reluctant to share any of his deeper feelings with her. So when, two days later, he told her he had decided to make a personal pilgrimage to visit Swinburne's grave on the Isle of Wight, having earlier missed his funeral through illness, there never was any question of her accompanying him.

By early April, he had gone again, first to Aldeburgh and finally London. Once in the City and settled into his Club, he spent several days looking for a flat, where he and Emma could spend the summer season. It was a time-consuming process, and, after much searching a flurry of correspondence to and fro with Emma, about the need for a servant to accompany her, about the provision of sheets, napkins and tablecloths, the requirement for their silver teapot and the ordering of fuel for the fire, he found one that he deemed suitable in Maida Vale, and signed on for the following three months.

Before Emma could travel to London, however, the King unexpectedly died, which created little private dismay to her, but resulted in public outpourings of grief that caused disruption in the City. It had the welcome effect of persuading her to delay her journey, until the funeral was over.

This time, she was determined not to sit about in the flat, but to make the most of her time in London, visiting her club when she could and hosting a number of 'at homes'. Amongst other new acquaintances, she planned to dine with Lady Alda Hoare, who she had met for the first time only a few short months earlier and with whom she had already begun a close and intimate correspondence. It was heady stuff, and for the first time in several years, she felt a little of her old spirit returning.

Emma had wasted no time in complaining to Alda about life with Thomas. She had confessed to her new friend how angry he would have been had he found her sitting in his study chair writing her diaries and going through his desk drawers, while he was waiting for her in London. What she didn't admit to, for to do so, she felt, would not reflect well on her, was going into his study cupboard which was kept locked. It took little time for Emma to find the key for in such practical matters, Thomas had no imagination. He had placed it under a vase and thereafter, such was his under-estimation of her, she had even less compunction about opening it and rifling through the correspondence. There were signed photos, from Agnes, from Rosamund, from Florence and a raft of letters, wrapped in bundles. The largest, she noted with some irritation was that of letters from Florence Henniker, laced with gentle and harmless endearments intended to humour him, yet clearly written in response to intimacies penned by her husband. Of the other bundles, the most voluminous were from Lady Grove, Mrs Tomson and Lady St Helier, although there were others, including a number from Edmund. In returning the bundles she found at the side of the cupboard another solitary letter, a request from a young admirer whose name she recognised, written some five years previous, asking if she may visit Max Gate to meet the author. She stared at it for several minutes wondering if such an assignation had ever taken place before dismissing the thought, for she was sure she would have remembered it.

They had quickly settled in to the first floor flat in Bloomfield Terrace, which, she was pleased to find, was as commodious as Thomas had promised. It boasted three bedrooms along with a dining room and drawing room, and Emma was soon busy sending out invitations to a lecture she was giving in the Lyceum, on 'Tennyson's Use of Classical Allusion'. She was especially pleased when Thomas asked her whether Miss Dugdale, who was still doing some typing for him in preparation for the new editions of his Wessex novels, could attend, as she was 'most fond of the late poet laureate', a request to which Emma gladly acceded.

The lecture went far better than Emma could have hoped for, and afterwards Miss Dugdale had made much of the older woman's excellent grasp of her subject matter, and the ability she showed in imparting the same with such richness and clarity. Buoyed by the younger woman's interest and enthusiasm, Emma invited her to tea the following week at Bloomfield Terrace.

When she arrived at the flat the following week to be let in by Thomas, Miss Dugdale was surprised to find herself ushered into a roomful of distinguished literary ladies, including Lady Grove and Lady St Helier, both of whom Mr Hardy had warmly spoken of in the past, along with May Sinclair, who she recognised as one of the leading writers for the Suffrage movement and an earnest feminist. The afternoon programme was orchestrated and led by Emma, first in the welcome she extended to everyone, thanking them for coming to such a humble soiree, with such profusion that Thomas had to leave the room. While she had the floor, she announced that she wished to share with her dearest friends (at which description one or two guests looked mildly surprised) her plans to publish a volume of poetry, before concluding her talk by reading out two of her efforts to polite applause. Immediately, as she finished the second reading, although Emma suspected probably at Thomas's prompting, the servant girl Daisy, who they had brought with them from Max Gate, pushed a trolley from the kitchen into the drawing room, loaded with a sumptuous cream tea, signalling the end of any formalities. Daisy briefly raised her eyes at seeing Miss Dugdale sitting by Mrs Hardy as a guest of the family, having shared with her part of the servants' quarters at Max Gate some twelve months prior, but any awkwardness during the afternoon was reserved only for Thomas, who appeared quite adrift, as the only man in a room of strong-armed suffragettes. He was soon further lost in the ensuing discussions, on a mixture of fashion, marriage and general tittle tattle in which Miss Dugdale – or Florence as Emma now insisted on calling her – was eagerly contributing.

Soon after Emma caught another unseasonal cold that threatened to aggravate her already delicate bronchial tubes, and so, reluctantly, after ten weeks in London, she decided to return home. It was of particular disappointment to her that she could not accompany her husband to the Palace, for the receipt of the Order of Merit which had been bestowed upon him, having longed to be part of such an occasion. With Lady St Helier back in Newbury, and no other woman she would trust with her husband, she turned to her new acquaintance, Miss Dugdale, to accompany him to the Palace, and to look after him until his journey back to Max Gate at the week's end, insisting that she should also follow for a weekend with them as soon as she was able.

Chapter Twenty

TOO TART THE FRUIT

Within a matter of days, Florence had written to Emma to thank her for her kind invitation to visit Max Gate, which she now had great pleasure in accepting. She hoped that while she was there, she might also be of some help to Mrs Hardy with her forthcoming collection of poetry, although she added, politically, that should Mr Hardy have some typing to complete she would be happy to do that too.

Her visit was of a quite different nature than her two previously, as this time she came as Emma's guest. From the first day, the women spent most of each morning talking about Emma's poetry and a short story she had written out in longhand. Florence took it away to type, and, apart from an afternoon excursion to Maiden Castle with Mr Hardy, her few short days were spent in the drawing room, which Emma had seconded as her working space.

As Florence was preparing to return to London, Emma suggested that she return the following week while her husband was away with Edward at Aldeburgh, particularly as it was the occasion of her 70th birthday, an occasion from which her husband had chosen to absent himself. Florence demurred, apologising profusely that she could not, explaining that her father had written to say that her mother was unwell, and she felt she should return to Enfield to help look after her. She could not, therefore, get down until the week after that if that would be possible, a suggestion to which Emma acceded.

When Florence returned to Max Gate she found there was another guest staying already, in the person of the Scottish painter and engraver, William Strang. He had come to draw a portrait of Tom for the Royal Library at Windsor Castle, a task he had previously undertaken for other recipients of the Order of Merit. While Thomas was too vain to enjoy the honest brush eye of the artist, he clearly enjoyed the company of Mr Strang, who had first painted his portrait some seventeen years previously. On that occasion, he had taken a shining to the younger man, and his opinion was strengthened further when he discovered that Mr Strang was, like him, the son of a builder, and that he had provided illustrations for books by Samuel Taylor Coleridge and John Bunyan, amongst others.

The next day, when she walked into the conservatory, Florence found the two men in an animated discussion about Rudyard Kipling and Carrie, his American wife, who William was describing in most humorous terms from the time he had stayed with them, when illustrating one of Mr Kipling's books. Mr Strang had not long finished his preliminary sketch of Thomas, which Florence picked up to admire.

'You have captured him very well indeed, Mr Strang,' she commented.

The artist gave a low bow in mock deference. 'Thank you Madam.'

Thomas came across and studied the sketch closely. 'I think I have aged a little since your last portrait, Mr Strang.'

Florence looked closer. 'Perhaps, Mr Hardy, but you are less wistful than you were then.'

Thomas shrugged: 'I only notice how far my hair has receded since and how grey my moustache has grown.'

She laughed. 'I never knew that men suffered the vanities of my sex, Mr Hardy, but it is reassuring that it is so. I like it. It is so much more dignified than the oil painting.' She then realised that what she had said could be interpreted by the artist as critical of his earlier work, and turned to him, quickly adding, 'of course, it is not the artist's job to bestow dignity on a sitter – only time can do that,' and they both laughed, as they turned to Thomas to gauge his reaction.

'You are right, Miss Dugdale, it is the more flattering likeness. I like it. William. Thank you.' He paused. 'Now, could I prevail upon you for a favour?'

'A favour? Most certainly Thomas, as long as it is in my gift.'

'It most certainly is. Do you think' – and at this point he looked at the other with a surreptitious grin – 'that you could sketch Miss Dugdale? I know her family would enjoy a portrait by an eminent artist, and I am sure you'd agree she would make a most suitable subject.'

'That she would, Mr Hardy. And of course, I'd be delighted to do so.'

Florence sat dumbly during the whole time, bewildered that such a conversation about her could transpire, without her even being acknowledged, although she felt a surge of excitement at sitting for such an eminent artist.

The next morning, while Emma went to Dorchester, as was her habit on market days, Florence sat for Mr Strang who, when he had completed the sketch, passed it to a grateful Mr Hardy. He expressed his delight with the excellent likeness, and gave a knowing nod to the artist before taking it upstairs to his study for 'safe-keeping.'

Emma, meanwhile, monopolised Miss Dugdale – or 'Florence' as she now insisted on calling her – and the two spent some days working on the draft of her short story, 'A Maid on the Shore', which she had set in Cornwall. Emma was busy correcting as Florence was typing the final draft, while promising Emma she would do what she could to help get it published.

'It will not be easy, Florence,' the older woman said, 'not because of the story good or bad, but because of him.'

'Will Mr Hardy not help you?' Florence asked.

'He helps pretty women with whom he has one of his infatuations, but only until they run their course.' She put her pen down, stood up and walked across the room to open a window.

'He ignores the fact I contributed a good deal to his early work, which were always his best novels. As a result, he seems determined that I should not be seen to rival him. It is so difficult getting into print without a patron, no matter how good the book, but Thomas, I fear would not only decline to help to get me published, but he actively hinders me in doing so.'

'Mrs Hardy, I could not think of Thomas doing such a thing.'

Emma looked at her, her small blue eyes pinched, making them appear even closer together than usual.

'Mr Hardy is capable of a great many things that would surprise you, Florence, but nothing, I fear, that would surprise me.'

Florence appeared unsettled by Emma's steely gaze, but eventually answered, 'then I will see what I can do,' said Florence, 'for I have a friend who may well be able to help.'

Another pause settled in, as Emma raised herself out of her chair, and allowed her face, and voice, to soften.

'You are a kind soul, Florence, to humour an old lady so. I know it is not a particularly meritorious story although it is an honest one. I think in the time we have we should get back to the poems.' And with that, she picked up the manuscript and placed it in the large envelope she kept it in, walking slowly from the room.

Watching her leave, Florence felt desperately sorry for her. She was a sad, deluded old woman, but she deserved to be helped, not pitied, and she resolved to do so, whenever the opportunity presented itself.

Thomas remained in his study for most of each day, settling before nine. Apart from the short time he allowed himself for a light lunch, he did not re-emerge until supper. From time to time, Florence would spend a morning with him, helping with the papers, although Emma was a demanding hostess. Sometimes, she and Emma took a carriage into Dorchester, and once on an unseasonably warm day for late autumn, travelled to Weymouth where they walked slowly the length of the esplanade, before taking tea by the quay.

If Emma was otherwise indisposed, she would sometimes walk with Thomas, starting from Max Gate and usually heading east, to Winterbourne Came or north, traversing the Roman road that ran through Puddletown Heath, and near to his childhood home at Higher Bockhampton.

After a few weeks of unbroken residence, Florence had begun to feel herself a part of the Hardy household, and moved freely between husband and wife, helping where she was needed. And when Thomas was accorded the freedom of the City of Dorchester, she was invited to join the family party, that consisted of him and Emma, along with Thomas's three siblings, Henry, Kate and Mary. She noted that while they conversed freely with her, it was never so with Emma.

As November began, so the temperatures dropped dramatically. The cold air had resulted in freezing fog and ice that stayed about week after week. The cleaning out and re-lighting of the fireplaces in the drawing room, the dining room, study and bedrooms became a major part of the morning routine for the maids, as well as dealing with the laundry and general household chores. Being Wednesday, they had gathered up the bed linen from all the first floor bedrooms and when leaving Florence's, a small posy dropped from the assemblage, which Daisy picked up and placed on the table downstairs, en route to the laundry at the rear of the house. As chance would have it, it was Emma who noticed it first. She picked it up, unsure of where it came from or, indeed, its significance.

It was, as she examined it closely, a tiny bunch of dried flowers, no bigger than a book mark attached to a card on which were written the words ' Maiden Castle' and the date '25th September, 1910'. For some moments, Emma could make neither head nor tail of it, before thinking back six weeks or so to the excursion Thomas and Florence had made to the iron-age hill fort, on the pretext of some research or other.

So he was at it again. This time, it wasn't one of his fancy ladies, but a poor girl he had taken advantage of, who would not know what to make of her husband's flirtations. She had hardly been in the house for a week, she calculated, before he had sent her this most inappropriate trinket. What must she think?

It was only later that she wondered about Florence. After all, the girl had known Thomas for some time now. Had she had to endure such overtures before? In which case, it was a shame that she didn't repulse him more forcibly.

The following day, when Thomas was out for a walk, she made the decision to re-visit the locked cupboard in her husband's study. She was not at all surprised when she found the key in its usual place – in fact, she would have been more surprised had he taken the trouble to move it – and unlocked it, careful not to disturb anything in doing so.

She did not have to look far for on the very top was the portrait of Florence drawn by Mr Strang. Emma stared at it. It was a very good likeness, and while it flattered the woman a little, it most certainly should not have been here. She found herself asking and answering questions of herself, When? Why? How? in such rapid order, that it took her but a few minutes to arrive at her unshakeable judgement on the matter.

Thomas had cajoled Mr Strang to do this for his own ends, but Florence and the artist were at least in part complicit. She accepted it may have been difficult for Florence to extricate herself from a situation her husband no doubt had placed her in. After all, the girl was not to know that Thomas had not asked the same of Mr Strang on her account (and he most decidedly had not). But she should have, at least, insisted on keeping the portrait for her, for her family, for her young man, Alfred, of whom she had told so much Emma about.

She returned the sketch to the cupboard and resolved to say nothing of the matter, although she was deeply shaken. She would need to be watchful, both her husband, for he was incorrigible, but also of poor Florence, who was clearly being subjected to the old man's lechery.

Emma's resolve was soon tested. The next evening, she sat in the corner of the drawing room, listening to her husband blithely talking to Florence of Mrs Henniker's recent letter, about Lady St Helier's recently published reminiscences. She was disturbed to find in the flow of the conversation that the two women knew each other and that Thomas had, in fact, introduced Florence to Mrs Henniker, when she wanted some secretarial help of her own, and that the two women were also in the habit of communicating by letter. It seemed the whole world was complicit in some pact against her, and she left the room shaking in anger, a fact which neither of them appeared to notice.

Later, after Thomas had gone to his room, while Emma and Florence were preparing to go upstairs, she turned to the younger woman, asking, in all seriousness, whether she felt her husband looked like Dr Crippen, the accused wife-murderer who had recently been captured in Canada, having fled there with his secretary.

Florence was taken aback at the question and started to make a measured response, saying that 'apart from his declining hairline and similar moustache, he was much too youthful,' before realising that the question was meant as rhetorical. Rather than listening to her reply, Emma was staring at her as if distracted, though in a way that thoroughly disconcerted her.

The next day, Emma had recovered, quite back to normal, and seemingly unaffected by whatever had upset her the day before. Florence was engaged in typing out some of the poems that Emma was assembling, for a collection of her verse that was to be published under the working title of 'Alleys'. She had prevailed upon a local publisher to print two hundred copies for her, half of which she intended for a local bookshop, for public consumption, the remainder to be used for her own munificence, for close friends, and to give to future significant visitors to Max Gate. Florence was encouraging of her writing, even when Emma herself was dubious of its worth, constantly flattering Emma for her poetic gift. She spoke enthusiastically about 'A Ballad of a Boy' and 'The Trumpet Call' and one or two others, although she felt too many were lost in the artifice and stiffness of form that affected much of her poetry. She was careful though, not to communicate as much to Emma. Yet as Florence read some of Emma's naïve and wistful verse written indubitably for her estranged husband's eyes, she recalled the graphic conversation of the night before, her mind becoming so confused with Emma's extraordinary question that she wondered if she, like Dr Crippen's secretary, Miss Le Neve, was merely an accomplice to a great crime.

Unsettled by the past few days and weary of the constant pull on her time and goodwill, by both husband and wife, Florence decided to return to Enfield, although only after she had consented to the entreaties of them to return to Max Gate for Christmas. Emma tried hard to persuade her to go away with her on holiday, and would not accept anything less than a deferred promise to do so. Thomas said little, but Emma could see he was distressed at the thought of her departure. The next day, he accompanied her to the station in Dorchester. By the time he returned to the house, Emma had disappeared to her rooms, and a hushed silence had fallen over the house.

Florence returned to Dorchester, as promised, in the week immediately prior to Christmas. She seemed frailer than before, more pallid, more subdued, as if the winter was not agreeing with her. For the past three weeks she had been staying with her parents, nursing her ailing mother, supporting her father and catching up with the three sisters. She had spent so little time with them over recent years that what had once been familiar to her was subtly changed, and she felt less certain about her family and how they would relate to her, and her to them. Her older sister, Ethel, who had her own family, called in for tea once, for she lived several miles away. But she was so preoccupied with her own husband and children that the conversation never ventured beneath the skin; Florence could talk more easily with Constance, who now taught at her father's school, although their words only served to remind her how different they were; while her youngest sister, Margaret, still only thirteen, seemed like someone from outside of the world in which she had grown up, so little did she recognise her.

Christmas at Max Gate was a more solemn affair altogether, and without the presence of children, centred about Church and some ill-regarded traditions. After an almost silent breakfast and the strained exchange of Christmas wishes, they went together, she, Thomas and Emma to the Christmas service at Stinsford Church, sang the requisite carols, and as Florence stood with them briefly, they placed a small bunch of flowers on the grave of his parents before returning to the house for a Christmas meal, traditional in fare, but joyless in spirit.

After they had dined and were about to rise from the table, Thomas informed the two women that he intended to do what he always did on Christmas Day, which was to visit his siblings at the old home in Higher Bockhampton. Having stated the fact, he turned to Florence and asked if she would like to accompany him, for he was sure his siblings would like to see her also.

Before she could answer, Emma jumped to her feet.

'No Thomas, no. Miss Dugdale doesn't need to be subject to the scurrilous gossip of your family. You know they will speak ill of me.'

Thomas looked up, alarmed.

'Hush dear, it is Christmas. Do you really think that people would talk uncharitably of others at such a time?'

'I do. Your family are vipers, Thomas, vipers, full of poison and bile. They have always envied me and lose no moment to disparage me. They spread stories about me in the town, for I have heard them. They think that Daisy and the others don't have ears. I forbid her to go.'

Thomas also stood, turning puce, and raising his voice in a manner Florence had not heard before: 'Forbid! Forbid! You are exceeding yourself, Emma. The woman shall do what she wishes.'

Through all this, Florence sat rigid in her chair, not knowing how to respond, or if, in fact, a response was even required of her. Certainly it was not now.

'Then she must make up her own mind.' And with that, Emma thumped the end of the table, making the cat jump onto the floor, and strode out of the room, leaving Thomas and Florence looking at each other, neither daring to utter a word until they heard the door slam shut at the top of the stairs.

After she had disappeared to her attic, clearly not planning to return, Thomas spent some considerable time persuading Florence on the best course of action.

'She is like this at Christmas, when she has not the support of her family, those of them that are left and capable.'

Florence looked at him inquiringly.

'I mean her niece, Lillian and nephew, Gordon. They were meant to join us this year and she is upset they have not. That is all. She will get over it.'

And by that and similar entreaties, he persuaded Florence that it would be best for them all, if she did, in fact, come with him. Independently, Florence had been reasoning her own position, recalling that she had visited the cottage with Thomas once before. While clearly Emma had not been told of this, the thing she was railing against had already happened, and it had not been as Emma described, for her name was not mentioned by anyone. So, on the balance of it, she felt it ruder to stay than to go, and agreed to accompany Thomas.

The walk through the woods took a good hour during which time Thomas was full of excuses for his wife's behaviour.

'She is not always reasonable, Florence, and has these outbursts from time to time,' to which Florence answered darkly, 'and who made her un-reasonable, Thomas, who made her so?' and Thomas would go quiet and not reply.

Night had fallen by the time they returned to Max Gate, although not late. They had had a merry time in the company of his siblings with mulled wine and mince pies, and felt warmed and decidedly more cheerful than when they had arrived. The nearer they got to the house, however, the mood changed, and little passed between them until they reached the head of the drive.

'I have determined to go home tomorrow, Thomas,' Florence started. 'I feel it is best to do so,' and despite all the pleading and inducements he could lay upon her, Thomas was unable to persuade her otherwise.

The house was quiet when they entered and only Jane, one of the house-maids, was about. She had prepared them a light supper, which they ate in silence. Soon after, Florence excused herself, determined to pack that evening in anticipation of catching the train to London early the next morning. Going into her room, she sensed something was wrong. The drawers were not closed properly, her chair had been moved, her suitcase left half open,, but it was only when she pulled back the bedspread that she saw the copy of *The Rubáiyát of Omar Khayyám* that Thomas had given her two years previously, lying there with the card that he had written placed carefully upon it.

Chapter Twenty-One

THE LAST PERFORMANCE

Emma had been writing her recollections for some months now, unbeknown to Thomas, revisiting her early days in Cornwall and their time together at St. Juliot. She had such dreams then, although one dream, the fear of being left on the shelf and becoming an old maid, never quite left her. How desperate was she for Thomas to be her saviour back then, to take her away from the disintegration of her family, and from this place that lay at the back of beyond? How much did she dream, of Thomas, or them both, of the promise of a family, of writing together, of a distinguished life like the one her father had wished for her? How desperate the remedy had been, marrying someone beneath her, in the hope of making him a gentleman, when all his life told her otherwise? There was, she concluded, no escaping the determination of one's birth, the allocation of place, for those things were immutable.

As she put one diary away and pulled out another, she looked at the heading page and frowned, her brow knitted, her hand tightening around the barrel of her pen.

New Year's Eve had always been, in Emma's life, a sad and melancholic time, when minds inclined to the maudlin, hearts dwelt in regrets and souls on the relentless march of mortality. That is, except for Thomas who carried on, as if he was convinced his writing, somehow, assured him of immortality. It was to help right this misapprehension that she now had picked up her diary entitled *What I Think of My Husband*, which carried all the accumulated pain and vitriol that she had experienced ever since the publication of *Jude the Obscure*, and which she had recorded her feelings in at regular intervals, fed by his faithlessness, both to God and to herself.

Her hand shook as she wrote, her letters tight and spidery, sloping awkwardly across the page:

'31st December 1910: One would have thought the occasion of our seventieth year may have effected some change upon our lives, but alas, no. He has carried on as selfishly as ever, oblivious to those around him and determined to embarrass us all. Stupid man! Does he think the servants don't talk, that Dorchester doesn't notice, that his friends don't smile at him? And now he has pulled another weak creature into his web. Poor Miss Dugdale, how galling to watch her being subjected to his predatory affection and she, being so utterly without guile and lacking any breeding simply unable to cope with him. I fear she is quite unlike those society ladies of his who take what they need and spit him out, whereas she clings to him and his inducements and is persuaded that he is a great man who needs her, for that is what he will be telling her. I do not blame Thomas entirely, even though he cannot help but to behave disgracefully. The fact is that women, too, have a choice, even one as susceptible to flattery and bribes as Miss Dugdale clearly, which is, to desist when they know the man has a wife. Miss Dugdale has the round open eyes of one who is habitually untruthful, and yet convinces herself that she is honest and can defend every falsehood. She has not been open to me, I know, and may even be a serial adulteress for all I know, but I am forgiving of her for she is of a certain class that knows no better. She will come to realise her error. In his books, they always do. I only hope for her sake, it is not too late.'

She closed the diary. It was past ten and she could hear Thomas still at work in his study below, his chair scraping occasionally on the floor. He would see the New Year in, she thought, for he was superstitious enough to want to do so. She would sleep now and, God willing, wake up for the first breathe of January in better fettle.

Since her departure on Boxing Day, she had heard nothing from Florence. Thomas had been as taciturn as ever, still blaming her for the scene the previous week. News of their argument had got out via the servants into the town, with various embellishments added that were both rude and humorous, and which eventually came back to Thomas through Henry, who was always goaded about his famous brother and had a sufficient sense of mischief to pass any slanderous comments on.

In April, Thomas and Henry went to look at the cathedrals at Hereford, Litchfield and Worcester. Emma was unaware of their itinerary, so that, when she was asked where Thomas was, her answer was so vague, as to be of no use at all. He went from there to Aldeburgh, for his constitutional in the sea air, before going on to London where Emma briefly joined him at a reception at the Foreign Office which she had been determined to attend, much to Thomas's irritation.

Soon after, he was back in Dorset, enjoying his 71st birthday in the company of his siblings. One of the servants had heard from a sister working on the farm at Higher Bockhampton, that Miss Dugdale also turned up at the Cottage, but, knowing the local capacity for tittle-tattle, and with the sure knowledge that Florence would have called, had she been in Dorset, she was dismissive of such an idea.

In May, Thomas was back to London again, attending a play in the company of Mrs Crackanthorpe, and lunching with Lady St Helier and Lady Lewis, before London cleared out in readiness for the coronation. From there on, Thomas, along with Henry and Kate, travelled to the Lake District while the royal circus, as he called it, was in full flow. It was a relentless schedule for Thomas. Occasionally he complained of feeling 'fagged', but two or three successive days at Max Gate seemed to be a sure cure for that, and he was soon away again with his sister Kitty, visiting the north coast of Devon and Somerset, travelling by coach across Exmoor, by steamboat to Ilfracombe, and train to Exeter, before making their way back home.

For Emma, life at Max Gate kept to its usual seasonal pattern. She enjoyed walking in the grounds, often with her cat following behind her, and took her pleasure in overseeing the gathering of produce from the kitchen gardens and orchards, along with the allocation of any surplus. Late in the afternoon, she would work in her flowerbeds down on her knees with her trowel, until the sun disappeared. Thomas rarely went anywhere near the working gardens, preferring to sit in the wrought iron chair on the conservatory lawn for a time each morning, if the weather allowed it, after his regular stroll down the nut walk. Between her and Thomas, little was said and without consciously avoiding each other, they had instinctively established their own routines, their own spheres of activity and habitation, that ensured their paths rarely crossed.

When they did sit down together, they skirted anything that other than the inconsequential. Emma has noted that the letters from Florence Henniker, which had ceased for a while, had started up again, and when she made some cryptic remark about his 'friend', Thomas snapped at her that she had been so for some eighteen years now and in that time, had befriended them both.

His anger always lit something in her, as now, and she could not resist retorting that she didn't mind one bit and counted the lady as a friend of hers too. But, she had noted darkly, she herself never seemed to be the recipient of any of the mail that came to the house. There was no respite, no concession, no opportunity to spill blood that was not taken, and even the arguments which were downright irrational, as was this one, were nevertheless wrapped around the shaft of an arrow, to be fired at the other in the hope of puncturing the skin.

In the early summer, Emma had written to Florence Dugdale about the suggestion of the previous year, for the two of them to go away together. Florence had read the letter with a good deal of trepidation having wondered about the old woman's sanity, following their last meeting at Max Gate. It had been more than six months since Florence had left the house on Boxing Day, and she had not seen her since. Nor had she heard one word from her, despite having written to thank her hostess for her hospitality.

Emma was insistent, however, and so plans were made for them to go to Worthing, where they would stay at the Burlington Hotel situated conveniently on the esplanade. Both women arrived separately, Emma from Dorchester, Florence from London, but took little time to settle in and establish a daily routine that they would follow throughout their fortnight. For much of the time, they either read and exchanged views on a range of literature, or else dealt with the challenge of getting Emma's poems ready for print in good time for Christmas, a task Florence readily helped her with.

They visited Highdown Gardens and the ancient forest at Titnore Wood and sat upon the beach when the weather allowed, never in a hurry, for the days were warm and accommodating.

Emma seemed in good spirits, happy to have Florence to herself, yet there was something about her manner that made Florence uneasy. She sensed a volatility in the older woman that unnerved her, as if there was a purpose to them being here, that Emma wanted to show or tell her something, although what that might be, she had no choice, but to wait and find out.

185

After a week of benign conversation in her company, Florence had relaxed sufficiently, to feel warmly towards the old lady. She had talked a little of her childhood in general terms, of her early life and education in Plymouth, of the gentility of her upbringing, and her distinguished family links with the Anglican clergy.

'My life,' Emma started in one evening, 'was a fortunate one, By the time I was ten I had learned to paint watercolours, which, if I may say so, were very fine for one of my age. And I had acquired a proficiency on the piano which has afforded me a great comfort in my life, and had taken dance and ballet lessons.' She stopped as if dragging on her memory. 'My father made us learn about Shakespeare. We would all join together after supper and declaim scenes that he would give us.' She sighed. 'Who would have thought I would end up as I have, not as a lady, but as the unwanted wife of a unprincipled writer.'

Florence looked at her, choosing her words cautiously.

'But Emma, surely that is not so. Thomas is a great writer. He would not have been given the Order of Merit had he not been considered so great a writer.'

Emma said nothing. Her gout was giving her trouble and she spent some seconds adjusting the cushions, moving the footstool into a more convenient position.

'I fear you don't know my husband as well as you suspect. It is not for me to tell you, but suffice it to say that he is without anchor, having jettisoned his faith and the sanctuary of his marriage. He thinks I don't know about his goings on, but he is as transparent as tissue paper. All this carrying on, all his vanities, all the words and compliments people have paid him, have puffed him up to near bursting. How much did you know of my assistance in helping write his early books? I will answer my own question. Nothing. Nothing. Nor will you ever, for by sharing his reputation with me, he fears it will diminish him. He sacrificed me in the cruellest possible way, by parodying me in *Jude the Obscure*, by humiliating me, by making others laugh at our union'.

She paused again, taking a tissue from her sleeve.

'And after I had given up my life for one who was bereft of any appreciation of culture, other than what I have taught him, living in the bad breath of his cantankerous and poisonous family.'

She paused yet again, wiped her nose once more.

'Mark though, I have never abandoned him, nor given up hope of reforming him, for that is the duty of any wife, to try and better their husband, and his lot.'

A maid had brought in a tray laid out for tea, which Florence stood up to pour. She seemed strangely nonplussed by what Emma was telling her, unsure if there was need for her to contribute although she deduced not.

'Men!' Emma spat out the word with such intensity, that in the long pause that followed, it seemed to Florence to stay suspended in the air like a body on the gallows, swaying and resonating with an otherworldly presence.

'You must not trust men, Florence, for they will always let you down. They may flatter you, defer to you, humour you, appease you, but they will never do anything to jeopardise their position of authority. It is easy to be magnanimous, when you know whatever concession you make is never going to weaken yours. This is why even getting the vote will not be enough, neither will getting women to sit in the Houses of Parliament. We need to challenge the natural order of things, Florence, or else they will continue to behave disgracefully.'

Florence looked at the older woman and ventured a comment.

'I do know some decent men, Emma, who I believe in. I know my father . . .'

'Even fathers let you down at some stage, Florence, mark you. Even fathers.'

'But there are others. There is my dear Alfred.'

'Alfred?' She thought for a moment, 'Oh yes, your young man friend in London. Does he still write to you?'

Florence bowed her head, paused, took another sip of tea before answering in a hushed voice.

'Not of late. I fear we have fallen out of correspondence, but his heart was always for helping another.'

'Another being you?'

Florence blushed. 'I think so.'

'Then it is good you have that memory of him and have moved on before he has left a scar as men inevitably do.'

'I do not think it is in him to do such a thing.'

'Then you are still too gullible to know the capacity of men for doing the unthinkable.'

Emma picked up the embroidery that had lain beside her, waiting patiently for her attention. She looked at Florence, her voice softening.

'Florence, I don't blame you. Wherever you go, in any settled manner of life, there is always a Judas trying to make it less so, for people are not forgiving of the happiness in others. I had the misfortune to marry a weak man, but my dear, one thing I have learned is that all men are weak in their own way. Just be careful, Florence, be careful.'

Florence blushed deeply. From superficial cordiality, the conversation had plunged into a pit of intimacy, full of writhing snakes, which had both disconcerted her and made her mindful of her position. She slept fitfully that night, but by the next morning, Emma seemed as good as normal, and so she felt it best to dismiss what had been said as the ramblings of an old woman, disheartened with her lot, unable to see that much of her unhappiness was of her own making.

Thomas appeared pleased to see Emma on her return to Max Gate, but only in that she provided a semblance of order to the household. Meals were prepared on time, fires lit, the house aired, the staff more attentive. He made his usual visit to Aldeburgh in October, from which he always returned uplifted and bullish from the company Edward Clodd provided for their amusement before returning to Max Gate, and burying himself back in his study.

In November, Emma heard from Florence Dugdale, a rare letter, to inform her that her dear friend Alfred Hyatt had died, and stating, whether cryptically or not, with undoubted sadness and an undercurrent of undeniable remorse, that she could think of him, hereafter, as an exception to her critique of mankind in general.

Emma was not sure how to read the letter, although the pain and guilt felt by Florence, for not having seen her friend for some considerable time was very evident. She noted, as she replaced the letter in the envelope, that the letter had been sent from Weymouth and wondered at the woman being so close and not calling on them. She reasoned, not unnaturally, that she may well have frightened the poor girl away, by raising the spectre of her insidious husband.

When she told Thomas he seemed indifferent to the news, or to her, she was never certain which. Unless of enough moment to generate a poem, or personal grief to wallow in, he was strangely unmoved by death, or even by its residue on those he purported to care about. And when Emma responded to Florence to express their condolences, she included a recently published copy of her poems, 'Alleys', that Florence had helped her with, adding in her note that she hoped, within, she would find some verses that might give her comfort.

Christmas and the New Year passed without incident. Lillian and Gordon stayed for almost a week and moved around the house silently, aware of the bristling tension, doing their best not to ignite it. When Thomas disappeared to his siblings on Christmas Day, they took Emma out for a carriage ride to Bournemouth. The sea air was sharp and penetrating, and, after taking tea, they made the long journey home, for Emma complained of feeling unwell, only to find Thomas again cosseted in his study with the door firmly shut.

Emma was unusually stoic, but not by choice. She had given up complaining about her health, for there was no one to complain to, at least no one who was at all sympathetic. Her shortness of breathe, her eyesight, her gallstones, all affected her general disposition, although it was the depression of day to day life with Thomas that weighed her down most of all.

News came in February of the death of Major General Henniker which awoke old demons in Emma. Thomas was prevailed upon to write some verses which Mrs Henniker, with the assistance of Miss Dugdale, gathered together into a book of tributes to her late husband, with various obituaries and reminiscences. Emma, however, wondered whether Mrs Henniker, having lost her own husband, would try to appropriate hers. Miss Dugdale, had her own sad news which she conveyed to them that Sir Thornley Stoker, whose wife she had cared for in Dublin over a number of years, had also died, a loss that appeared to affect her greatly.

Meanwhile Emma wrote. Each day, after breakfast, when Thomas had disappeared into his study, she went into her attic and took out her diaries. She wrote schizophrenically, first, nostalgically of the idyllic time at St Juliot and their courtship, along with the affection she and Thomas felt for each other; and secondly, dipping her pen into another inkwell, this time full of vitriol, continuing with her diatribe against her husband.

The same month, Emma's exposition of great truths, entitled 'Spaces' was published by the same Dorchester printer who had produced her slim volume of poetry. Thomas deigned to make no comment at all, although when he looked at the copy of the book she had pointedly left in the drawing room, and read the headings of the four sections: 'The High Delights of Heaven', 'Acceptors and Non-Acceptors', 'Hell' and 'Retrospect', he sensed another attempt to shame him back into the fold. He sent the gardener down to the local bookseller in Dorchester, with instructions to buy up as many copies as they had available, which he determined to hide away until a convenient time arose to add them to a bonfire.

In June, W B Yeats and Sir Henry Newbolt came, to present the Gold Medal of Royal Society of Literature to Thomas. It was an awkward lunch in which Thomas was clearly on edge. Emma was in truculent mood, having been lectured about what she could or could not do or say, which merely served to aggravate her, ensuring that the ceremony would not be an easy one. Emma was irritated because she had read much of Yeats's poetry and was intrigued by his interest in mysticism, spiritualism and astrology, and was keen to discuss these with him, but Thomas was adamant that when the meal was finished she would leave the room, before the simple ceremony of presentation he had planned was conducted, with only the three men in attendance. She had objected at the time at her banishment, and Messrs Yeats and Newboldt spoke up for her, but Thomas would not relent and picking up her cats and without looking back, for her eyes were stinging with anger and shame, she departed the company without a further word.

Emma was beyond caring now what Thomas thought of her. She would live her life according to her own precepts and to hell with the man. In the late summer, she took a party of children from Fordington to Lulworth for a picnic, before taking them back to Max Gate for tea and presents, while Thomas remained in his study, opposed less to the deed itself than to she who had organised it.

Not long thereafter, Thomas's old friend, Edmund Gosse visited with the poet, Arthur Benson. Emma had met them at the door dressed in a lace blouse stuffed under a light blue velvet jacket with a scalloped collar, topped by a straw hat, a dark velvet ribbon done up round her neck as a bow tie and a gold watch on a long chain, pinned to her left breast. Thomas, when he saw her, remonstrated in hushed, urgent tones, visibly embarrassed by her presence. Eventually, he managed to persuade her to leave the three men on their own, which she reluctantly did, but not before making an indelible impression on the odious little man, who looked at her with such disdain that she felt angry beyond words. If only Thomas had accorded her more respect, they would not dare to look at her as they did. If only Thomas had not pushed her into a dark corner and had showed her some affection, she would not have felt the need to dress so. If only he had loved her, it could have been so different.

She was growing tired. In October, she played the piano, but without enthusiasm and closed the lid saying she would not play it again. Her stomach was causing her problems and her legs were so swollen, that even mounting the steep flight of stairs to her bedroom had became an effort for her.

In late November she celebrated her birthday alone with her young maid Dolly, who had organised with the cook, a small cake, which she brought up to the Attic bedroom. Once, she came downstairs when Rebekah and Catherine Owen called with their customary timing, although so intent were they on listening to Thomas's every word, she might as well not have bothered.

Two days later, she felt unusually tired by the late afternoon and took to her room as outside a storm was gathering force. By late evening, a strong wind was stripping the remaining leaves from the trees and rattling the slates and windows and the temperature had started to drop, leaving her cold and shivery.

That night she took her diaries down from her cupboard and read what she had written of her first sight of Thomas some 42 years before, which she remembered 'as if in a dream', and what they offered each other. She recalled finding in him a perfectly new study and delight, while he found in her a "mine." She sat there for some minutes reading before closing the book, and sitting in silence with tears welling in her tired red eyes, until she had recovered herself and slowly replaced the book, taking out instead the frayed copy in brown paper bound in red string, entitled *What I Think of My Husband*, and began to write in it as she had done for more than fifteen years.

'I pray I might outlive him,' the sentence read, 'for were he to read this, he would be so consumed by guilt, it would overwhelm him. It surprises even me that I would not wish that upon him, although others might feel that is what he deserves. That decision will not be mine, thank God. All I know of him after a lifetime is that he has not loved me as a husband should love a wife. If only he knew how much I know of his shameful life, of his betrayals, his faithlessness, his deceit, the unwitting cruelty he has perpetrated on me. If only he knew the hopes I had for us. I ask, can a writer ever be a good husband? I don't know. All I know is that the only compassion, the only kindness, his only love he showed came through his pen, not from his heart. And alas, there was never enough left for us. She paused, before lifting her pen one last time.

'Poor Florence, for she is a most unlikely adulteress. I have tried to warn her for she is ignorant and desperate and cannot see what lies ahead of her. The Good Lord will see she gets what she deserves and I fear for her it may be Thomas. I hope that when he is dying, I will be there to ask him was it really worth all those stories, all those poems to have arrived at this?'

And with that thought, she closed the diary and placed it back in her cupboard. Outside the wind had picked up to an unrelenting roar, bending the branches in the orchard and causing a pane of glass in the conservatory to come smashing to the ground.

The next morning her maid found her dying. Thomas was called to her, but not for the first time, he was too late, for she was beyond speech. And would be forever thereafter, although he would do his very best to make amends in the only way he knew how.

AFTERMATH

The death of Emma on the morning of 27th November, 1912 unleashed in Thomas a sudden outpouring of grief and remorse. The shock of her sudden passing drew from him memories and poetry that was incomprehensible to those who had witnessed the disintegration of their marriage over the previous decade. Thomas, who had so often dismissed his wife's writing, found that in death, her words caused a convulsion in his life. The mixture of nostalgia, through her 'recollections', and guilt, invoked by her diary *What I Think of My Husband*, combined, to plunge him into a period of mourning that was to stay with him for the remainder of his life. Just over fourteen months later, Thomas Hardy married Florence Dugdale, with whom he was to remain until his death in 1928.

He was 73 years old when he married Florence, who was less than half his age, and throughout their remaining years, the spectre of Emma stayed with them both. Thomas kept his desk diary fixed on the date he had first met Emma in March 7, 1870 and every year, on the anniversary of her death, especially after Thomas's, Florence would be overwhelmed by the presence of Emma that seemed never to leave her, for the voice kept calling to her.

Some sixteen years after Emma's death, a dying Thomas asked Florence to read to him a verse from The *Rubáiyát of Omar Khayyám* that he had given her as a gift more than twenty years before. She read the words in a hushed voice, holding his hand as she did so:

> 'Oh, thou, who man of baser earth didst make
> And ev'n with paradise devise the snake:
> For all the sin wherewith the face of man
> Is blackened – man's forgiveness given and take!'

She closed the book at his request and kissed him gently on the cheek before making her way downstairs. She had not long been there when a cry came out that brought both her and the doctor rushing back into the room, only to hear his last uttered syllable, 'Em'.

Florence, with her heart already scarred, had next to endure an even more desperate moment with the burial of his heart at Stinsford, in the same grave as Emma. There were few mourners and only a few she did not recognise, one, a small woman of around sixty, who she had never seen before. It was after the interment that she looked at the small posy of flowers she had left and looked at the attached card, that read 'Mr Hardy, from one of yours' and after staring at it for several seconds, removed it and ripped it into a dozen pieces.

For Emma, however, there was to be a glorious resurrection with the poems of 1912 – 1913. Overwhelmed with guilt, Tom wrote a series of moving elegies to his lost love and set in train a haunting from which the new Mrs Hardy would never escape.

It was left to Kate Hardy, Thomas's remaining sibling, to have the last word. After she had returned to Tabothays, following the opening of the reconstruction of her brother's study at the Dorset County Museum in early 1939, she sat down and ruminated on all the platitudes that had been laid at her late brother's feet, before turning to the assembled company:

'If only they knew,' she said. 'If only they knew.'

BIBLIOGRAPHY

As with the novel *Florence: Mistress of Max Gate,* to which this is a prequel, *Emma: West of England Girl* is essentially a work of fiction which nestles into a framework provided by other writers on Hardy. At times, events are taken out of context of time and place and mingled what may have happened, but the timescale and the people are, in the main, based, if only in name, on real persons and places.

To that end, I am most grateful to the many biographers of Thomas Hardy and the legion of other writers who either wrote on aspects of Hardy's life, edited his work or collections of letters or who helped develop the Wessex mythology. I have consulted primary sources where possible to give a sense of realism to the story and have used phrases, lines and sentences from the various collections of letters and poetry. I have, however, avoided including too much extraneous detail for fear of losing the story in a mass of biographical detail that is available and in the main relied on his major biographers.

But most importantly, I am indebted to the writings of Thomas Hardy, in particular, for the inspiration he provided in first drawing me to Dorset and for unwittingly providing the impetus of this book through the considerable steps he took to protect his privacy and reputation, even posthumously. The collective bonfires of Emma, Thomas and Florence, consisting of letters and notebooks, and the subterfuge employed by Thomas and Florence in writing *The Life* all served to fuel the speculation, the intrigue on which this novel, as with its predecessor, is at least in part, based.